Nigel Watts was born in Winchester is 1957. He spent two years in Japan where he wrote a large part of THE LIFE GAME, his first novel. This was awarded the Betty Trask Award in 1989 and was followed by BILLY BAYSWATER (1990), which was shortlisted for the *Mail on Sunday* – John Llewellyn Rhys Prize, and WE ALL LIVE IN A HOUSE CALLED INNOCENCE (1992). His new novel TWENTY TWENTY is also published by Sceptre. Nigel Watts is married and divides his time between Swanage and Richmond.

SCEPTRE

'Watts has taken plenty of risks . . . but they pay off in this warm-hearted and candid comic novel'
The Sunday Times

'Nigel Watts' vision of humanity may not be edifying, but he articulates it so powerfully that it has a hypnotic effect on the reader'
Daily Telegraph

'Hate becomes love . . . in elegant and complex prose that lays bare the nature of male insecurity and its allied game-playing'
The Glasgow Herald

'Should be required reading for women who can't understand men, and ALL men. Highly recommended'
South Wales Argus

We All Live in a House Called Innocence

NIGEL WATTS

SCEPTRE

Copyright © 1992 by Nigel Watts

First published in Great Britain in 1992 by Hodder and Stoughton Ltd
First published in paperback in 1993 by Hodder and Stoughton Ltd
A Sceptre Paperback

The right of Nigel Watts to be identified as the Author of
the Work has been asserted by him in accordance with the
Copyright, Designs and Patents Act 1988

10 9 8 7 6 5 4 3 2

All rights reserved. No part of this publication may be
reproduced, stored in a retrieval system, or transmitted
in any form or by any means without the prior written
permission of the publisher, nor otherwise circulated
in any form of binding or cover other than that in which
it is published and without similar condition being
imposed on the subsequent purchaser.

All characters in this publication are fictitious
and any resemblance to real persons, living or dead,
is purely coincidental.

British Library C.I.P.
Watts, Nigel
We all live in a house called innocence.
I. Title
823 [F]

ISBN 0-430-57983-8

Printed and bound in Great Britain by
Cox and Wyman Ltd, Reading

Hodder and Stoughton
A Division of Hodder Headline PLC
338 Euston Road
London NW1 3BH

WE ALL LIVE
IN A HOUSE
CALLED INNOCENCE

1

Mother died two years ago, or perhaps it was three. I can't be sure. I squint at the letters as they appear on the computer screen. All right: I know it sounds like Camus, but it happens to be true. Or nearly true – the fact is, I know exactly when she died. Two years and three months ago to the day. February the fourteenth it was. St Valentine's day.

I sit back and stare at the green letters: sometimes I can't believe the pathetic bullshit I write. I hold a finger on the 'x' and watch as first one line then another zips across the screen. I hold the key down until the whole screen is filled and it looks like a knitting pattern. With crossings out, or kisses, I can't say.

The way the doctor announced the presence of delinquent cells in Mother's stomach had been a study in equanimity. Calm and heroic in his white coat, the 'c' word was uttered without a blink; *benign*, the doctor even called it. We can cure cancer, his brave look had said: she'll live to be a hundred. Liar. Even then, I could see it taking her over. The evasiveness, the cheery optimism of the nurses, all pointed in one direction: the yellow woman's time was up. They had cut out her stomach: it had been left too late for anything else, but they were still confident of course: weren't they always confident? And so it was pills and prognoses and not a whisper of her mortality.

I press *delete* and watch the crosses disappear from the screen. Once upon a time cancer was the great Satan of medicine; now it's just one of the foot soldiers in the enemy army. We may be winning the battle with our Exocet missiles and radar tracking, but the war still wages, and we still lose the fight every time. Death, that's the

1

big one, the king and queen of taboo. I type in capitals: DEATH, AIDS, SEX. Why didn't the doctors say it? Why didn't they just say she was on her way out, doomed, soon to be ashes? Why do we have to be so protected from taboo? Death, Aids, sex – the three unmentionables, the three incurables.

A little biographical detail. My name is Morrison. James Morrison. Double-O nothing, licensed to supply books. Six months short of my thirtieth birthday and my current bank balance, so this morning's statement informs me, stands at fifty-six pounds fourteen pence. That is the grand total from five years of wages, which works out at a net saving of just over ten pounds a year, or somewhat less than a pound a month. Or three pence a day. That means that if I reached into my pocket for some change and accidentally dropped a five-pence coin only to watch it roll along the pavement and disappear into a drain, the clink! that indicated its descent into the sewer would represent a day and a half's profit. Down the drain.

All right: I own the flat I live in, and there's a steadily growing sum of unit trusts I inherited from Mother, but that doesn't count. That's just luck, not masculinity.

What do masculinity and money have to do with each other? Only a woman would ask such a question.

I've given almost five years of service to this library. The best years of my life, the years I should have been ravishing the world, plucking a living from the great outdoors, doing *something* for God's sake. Sometimes I think we'd do better to let the trees grow rather than cut them down just to make more books. Engineering, law, literature, accountancy, theology, textbook upon textbook, shelf upon shelf of the bloody things. It's not just the waste of paper that appals me, it's the waste of lives. I can't help but find myself being sucked under by a rip-tide of depression whenever I look at students with their heads down in their partitioned desks, ticking their lives away with second-hand knowledge. Why do they do it? For other pieces of paper: degrees or certificates or diplomas to enable them to get yet more bits of paper

2

with which they can buy more books. I know it's a crass generalisation, but I'm in that sort of mood. I've been reasonable for too long: I want to release my spirit, and my spirit is Crass.

Some days are worse than others: today I have it bad. It's on days like this that I wonder if I wouldn't be happier working in a gym or on a building site. Somewhere that I could get on with the real business of life: making things. Muscles or buildings, it wouldn't matter much, at least I would have left my mark on the world.

We're animals, obviously. Flesh and blood and hormones and two million years of chthonic lust all buttoned into our shirts and skirts. And all just busting to break out. You can see all the repressed adrenalin in their tight faces, the stiff bodies, see it crystallising in joints, ossifying cartilage, petrifying bones and leaving us rusting at premature middle age. What are we doing with our lives? We smoke, we drink coffee, we read the paper, we talk and talk and talk; and all the time our fuse is burning away. Just look over there, at the fellow with his nose in Bertrand Russell; look at his foot tapping out a nervous tattoo on the floor. He's a philosophy student, one of our regulars; but ask him about life and what would he say? First define your terms? But give him a spear and a gazelle and enough space and he'd laugh at you. And quite rightly too.

My life seems to have finished before it has started. Here I am, stuck in this bloody library, dealing out novels, other people's lives, as pressed flat as a dried flower between the pages of a Victorian novel, every day another name added to my mental hit list of writers. You see, I love books, I love literature, but more than admiration, it's resentment that gets the upper hand. I find myself hating writers I should be admiring, and junk fiction makes me murderous. Why? Even the worst author has some sort of progeny, leaves some sort of mark on the world, *something* to show that a life has been lived. But if I died tomorrow, what would I leave behind? The will, if there had been one, would read like the free ads in the local paper: four-speed bicycle, good condition; hi-fi system and collection of

3

used records; five hundred paperback books; assortment of kitchen-ware. Fifty quid the lot. It would have to be sold. Who would want the miscellanea of a barely lived thirty years? Not Ruth. It would have to be sold, or given away to Oxfam.

Of course, there's the flat, but I keep forgetting that.

I nearly had progeny of my own: a real live baby. Or rather, Ruth did. It would have been coming up to its third birthday about now. An Easter baby.

Working on the desk in a city library is the front line of the book-borrowing world, especially in the more desperate London boroughs. Libraries, in common with bus stations, launderettes, parks and shopping malls, are as sticky as honeycomb to the misfit bees of city life.

They come and go: this is bed-sit land. A retreating army of transients: Irish labourers, the unemployed, the unemployable, battered wives, whole families living in cheap DSS bed and breakfasts. Hammersmith is the delinquent neighbour of comfortable Kensington: the home of the downwardly mobile: slippy sliding into prison, hospital, the mortuary. And the library has more than its fair share who come only to get warm and talk to themselves, or doze in the comfy chairs reserved for newspaper readers. The worst times are on a wet day, after the pubs close in the afternoon. The abuse is mostly verbal, but the odd bout of fisticuffs is not unheard of, fortunately usually confined to the punters.

There are a handful of regulars, each with their story, some of whom insist on telling it, but it's the old folk who fascinate me the most: the men who can't seem to shave without lacerating themselves, the old geezer who brings his magnifying glass every day to read the *Telegraph*, and then ends up falling asleep over it, the seventy-year-old woman with pencilled-in eyebrows and shocking black hair who we found hiding new Mills and Boon's behind the radiator so nobody else could take them out. And there's Madge of course. She's an *Evening Standard* reader; won't even glance at another paper. Completely batty, though not without a certain manic style, her hair is piled up in matted

4

dreadlocks, crowned with a tiara of ivy. Dandelions poke from her jacket pockets as though she's the King Lear of Hammersmith. It's hard to put an age to her, but she must be over sixty. There had been an equally eccentric husband, but I suppose he died, because I haven't seen him for some years. Madge is getting worse, her personal hygiene slipping with the years. Her black overcoat is fading to a sort of shiny green, and she has a constant aroma of pee about her. The staff sometimes gets complaints about her smell, but what can we do? Suggest she washes more often? Ban her from the library? Not me buster, not until they pay me for it. Things could be worse: at least she's quiet and polite, just sitting there with her *Standard*. She reads her paper cover to cover. Literally – I've watched her. Starting upper left of page one, she works her way, page by page, to the bottom right of the last page. Even the stocks and shares. It takes her all day, and has generated so many complaints that we now order two copies – one for Madge and one for the rest of the world. Only twenty pence to keep the peace.

Oh, that it were always that easy and cheap.

There used to be Jim too. I liked him: fifty years of alcohol abuse and nicotine had set up home under his roof, though even those ragged tenants looked constantly on the verge of eviction if the 'for sale' sign of his nose was anything to go by. I learned an important lesson from him: he looked like a derelict, and I assumed he was in the library just to stay off the streets, but the quality of the books he tried to nick never ceased to impress me: Beckett, John Barth, Kundera. We tried to explain that he could legitimately borrow as many as he liked if he joined the library, but he always refused. God knows why. Me and Jim developed a sort of grudging respect for each other, and to give him his due, he always handed over the books when I asked for them. He used to disappear every winter, locked up for three months for chucking bricks through shop windows. Prison, he said to me one day, wasn't so bad: it was warm, and the food was good, but the quality of the clientele left something to be desired. He disappeared for good one day, and then a small item in the local paper said that he'd been

5

found in the river. I hope it was a drunken accident and nothing more.

Ruth works in one of the posh art galleries in Bond Street. A world apart from smelly old Madge and poor drowned Jim.

It was out of the question to have the baby, she said. And I had to admit, it was hard to see how we could afford to live on one person's wages in such a small flat. Ruth wasn't ready for children, and me . . . ? I hadn't given it much thought, even less since the termination. Termination? It was the end of a life, not a railway journey. I wasn't asked what I thought, what I wanted to do. Okay, the Church is out of date, it was her body, but this bundle of cells was half me: there was a baby Morrison tucked into her uterus lining. My son or daughter nestling there, merrily growing away. Eight weeks old. I recently sneaked a look in a medical textbook. Eight weeks: hands, fingers, a little nose. And all nipped in the bud. Ruth took three days off work, and a month off sex and it was never mentioned again.

Women don't realise how lucky they are. All they need for a baby is a teaspoon of sperm. A man, however, has to come up with that *plus* convince another person, a woman at that, to give nine months of her body away.

Be careful what you ask for – you may just get it. Standing there behind my librarian's desk, mechanically stamping books, cursing my luck, I'm not aware that my soul is beaming distress calls to the universe. The SOS signal has been broadcast for so long that I've grown deaf to its ceaseless dit-dit-dit dah-dah-dah dit-dit-dit. If I'd been pressed, I may have eventually recognised the call, admitted my distress to myself. But nobody pressed me, and as far as I'm aware, this floundering motion is as close to swimming as I can get. It's just another day.

So, what's the message?

Get me out of here. Quick!

If I knew who was about to walk into my life, I would have approached my Fate with a little more dignity, but as far as I know, it's just another day. And so I walk, smack! into the face of my kismet with the confidence of a blind man striding into a wall.

I see them come in, but there's no drum roll, no striking major chords, so I only glance at the two people and then return to the pencils I'm sharpening. How am I to know that my life is about to be exploded into? I'm an unsuspecting nearly thirty year old who has not the faintest inkling.

I had asked for rescue, and sure enough, my request is about to be heeded. A pity that I omitted to ask for a safe passage.

I've just snapped the lead of the pencil for the third time when I hear the clarion call for the dismemberment of the summer of my discontent. *Wild Thing*, the Troggs number, first verse teetering between tenor and falsetto. And loud.

The racket stops by the time I locate its source, so I can only frown at the grinning face in the wheelchair.

'Let me introduce myself,' the cripple beams up at me like a scrunched-up Peter Pan. 'Tad Czapski. Here's my ID.'

I have to lean over the counter to reach the official-looking pass he holds out. I glance at the photograph of an attractive young man beaming out at the world.

'I'd like to join your library please. My form has already been filled out.'

I take the paper and check the details quickly: it has been completed in a painstaking hand, the signature though is nearly illegible.

'Czapska?'

'Czap*ski*,' he corrects. 'And the "c" is silent. As in "Tad".'

'Tad?'

'There – see? Absolutely silent. Not a whisper.'

I catch the assistant's smirk while I copy the name on to a plastic card and type the number into the computer.

'Here.' I take the book from him. He's tiny: though he has the face of a twenty year old, his body is that of a child. His arms seem to work well enough, but the legs

7

that dangle from the seat of the wheelchair are withered and clearly useless. I stamp the book – the new Oscar Wilde biography – and slide it over the counter with the new card.

The cripple thanks me, and then jerks the battery-powered chair backwards and turns to face the exit. He starts singing again, his voice high and croaky like a cartoon character's, fading with the distance as his wheelchair buzzes out of sight.

I stare at the empty space in front of the desk. What a body: his chest had buckled as though it had been squashed by an enormous vertical force, his legs tacked on to his trunk as though as an afterthought. I sigh and return to my pencils, and that's that. The life-changing event. Big deal.

Oh, *Wilde* thing.

He comes in again a few days later. Something about his air puts me immediately on guard. Five years behind this counter, and I recognise the whiff of trouble a mile off.

He wheels over to the desk and parks in front of it. Tilting his head on his thin neck, he smiles up at me. His body reminds me of a car that has been in a smash: all crumpled bodywork and buckled wings. 'Do you keep back copies of *Time Out*?' The same high, croaky voice.

'Yes.'

'November 1986?'

'It'll be upstairs in the reference section.' We both look towards the stairs. 'I'll get you it.'

'So kind.'

I can feel him watching me as I leave the desk and hurry up the stairs. Back issues of *Time Out* are bound in book form, and quite heavy. When I hand it to him, I wonder if he has the strength to hold it, but he takes it easily in one hand. His arms are disproportionately long, as though they had decided to grow normally while the rest of his body mutated along its own eccentric lines. I notice his fingernails, long and glossy and perfectly manicured.

8

'All right?'

'Could you photocopy some pages for me, please? I can never understand how to use these machines.' He leafs over the pages to the one he wants. 'This article. Thank you so much.'

I take the book from him and start towards the photocopier. He follows in his buzzing wheelchair.

It's a two-page article. Twenty pence. 'What's your name?' he asks as he tugs out a red velvet purse.

'James,' I say, surprised at his question.

'Do you live alone James?'

I'm a bit hard of hearing, and at first I think I've misheard him, but then I realise I haven't. 'No.' A bit bloody personal, I think, spreading the book face down on the photocopier. The photocopied page buzzes into the tray and I check its tone. It's an article about some woman: the headline, 'Unspeakable Acts', in heavy print.

'Married?'

What the hell's going on? I position the book for the second page.

'You don't mind me asking?'

'No, not at all.' I poke a finger at the print button, minding like hell.

'Well?'

'No, we're not married – we're living in sin.' I frown at the old-fashioned phrase, aware of how nervous he's making me.

'I live in Innocence.'

Aye, aye. A religious nutter.

He must have seen my look. 'It's a home for handicapped people. "Innocence". You must come and visit some time.'

'Thank you, I'd like that.' I snap the book shut and give him the photocopied pages.

'Why don't you come tonight? After work?'

'Oh.' I want to kick myself. 'Sorry, I'm busy tonight.'

'Tomorrow?'

'We-ell . . .'

He smiles up at me. 'You do want to come?'

'Yes, it's just I'm rather busy.' Liar.

9

'So *you* choose a time then.'

'Friday?'

'What time?'

'Six thirty?' I can feel the discomfort in my face as I lie to him. I determine to forget it by Friday.

'Great.' He waggles the sheets of paper. 'Thanks for your help.' He looks at the photocopied sheets. 'Karen Finley – now, *that's* a woman I'd like to meet.'

I've never heard of Karen Finley. I only have time to read half the article before I'm called to the phone, but I learn enough to discover that she's an American performance artist who is enduring what is presumably brief notoriety for a stage show which includes pouring canned yams between the cheeks of her naked buttocks whilst singing 'Yams up my Granny's ass', a tune whose lyrics go:

> *Ooh she's such a nice Granny,*
> *just love to stick those yams up my Granny's ass,*
> *but I never touch her snatch, baby . . .*

Snatch, I know, is American slang for the female pudendum.

2

'Hello James.'

It's Friday, and here, grinning up me, is my nemesis.

'Hello James,' he says a second time. 'You haven't forgotten our date, have you?'

'Ah!'

It's hardly any distance to his place, but long enough for me to die several times. He asks how quickly I like to walk, and sets the speed on his machine, but it's going a little fast and I have to skip occasionally to keep up.

10

I hope to God I'm not going to come across anyone I know.

It's a modern building, wide swing doors, newly carpeted corridors, the smell of cooking. Home-made paintings on the walls, potted plants, fire-drill instructions. It's pleasant enough, but it's still an institution. I'm reminded of boarding school. We pass a few people in the corridor, most of them in wheelchairs, but my escort ignores them, heading straight to his room.

'It's a strange name – "Innocence". How did that come about?' It's nerves rather than genuine interest that prompts the question.

'When Branleigh House was closed down, and we were moved out here, the staff held a competition to find a new name for this place. They made the mistake of deciding by vote, and as there was pitifully little competition, I won. They weren't pleased with the result, but I'm singularly stubborn, so "Innocence" it was. I expect they'll change it when I've gone.'

'But why "Innocence"?'

'Have you ever read *Lady Chatterley's Lover*?'

'Yes.'

'Then you must know that the working title for the book was *Innocence*?'

'Really?' We reach his door; a hand-drawn sticker on it: *This is a guilt-free zone*. Tad unlocks it with a key from his pocket. 'No – but it should have been. Lawrence called it *Tenderness*, but I think *Innocence* would have been better.' He nods at an armchair. 'Make yourself comfortable.'

I sit down, for the first time almost on a level with the wheelchair. I look into the cripple's face: dark hair and eyes, long eyelashes, a Roman nose. Actually, quite handsome, the sort of look I've often wished I had. 'And Tad?' I ask. 'That's an unusual name.'

'An assumed name. People, of a more acute sense of humour than my own, assure me that, in a certain light, I resemble a tadpole. You know – all head and no legs. My original name, though long unused, is Piotr. Piotr Jesu Czapski. Polish Jew and Italian Catholic, one tucked into the other like a slice of salami inside a bagel.'

11

He has clearly inherited more of his looks from Italy than Poland. His face is an unusual shape, narrow at the chin and broad at the crown, but there is something of the Latin sensuality about the lips and eyes. His eyes are nearly as dark and silky as his hair. Straighten him out, erase the damage caused by a lifetime of pain, and he could be another Al Pacino.

I notice the photocopied sheets of Karen Finley taped to the wall and stand up to finish reading the article. It's a report of a performance in Amsterdam, an interview tagged on to the review. What sort of woman is this? *Wrestling with a chair covered in cooking oil, wiping her arse and throwing the paper on the stage.* Such behaviour lurks only in the corners of my imagination: to know that there are people actually doing such things . . .

Tad wheels himself up behind me, but I can't take my eyes off the photograph of the woman: this is presumably the 'Yams up my Granny's ass' number, for there she is, bent over, naked buttocked, some unidentifiable wet matter cascading on to the stage. No wonder she caught the public's imagination. It's quite a sight, those long legs, the slippery vegetable.

'I wouldn't mind being a fly on *her* dressing-room wall,' comes from behind me.

I shudder slightly. I wouldn't mind being a piece of that yam, I think to myself.

'I'm thinking of using her in a story of mine.'

'You write stories?'

'It's better than basketwork, though I'm a long way from earning a living at it.'

'You sell stories?' I'm jealous of him already.

I try not to stare while Tad zips about in his wheelchair making coffee. His hands seem to work well enough, but still I want to volunteer help, though I know enough to hold back. This little cripple's system is clearly under control: a low sink, special bars on the wall for him to lift himself into bed. I take my cup from him and watch him over the rim as I drink it. 'It's a nice room.' It's not really, but it's something to say.

'Do you like it?' He's pleased. 'I've always slept in

12

dormitories until recently. It *is* a bit of a luxury, I must admit.' He pats the bed as though it's a dog.

'Have you lived here long?'

'Nearly two years now. I've always lived in homes.'

I want to ask about his family, but I'm still trying to phrase the question discreetly when he answers it himself.

'I've got a brother and a sister in Australia,' he says in his quacky voice, 'but nobody in this country. My family were so horrified at my parents they wouldn't have anything to do with them. You see, there was a forty-four-year age difference between my mother and father. She was seventeen years old, Italian, and he was sixty-one. Can you believe it? A Polish refugee, who hardly spoke a word of English. A Jew as well.

'My grandmother – my mother's mother – was the only link with my family here, but she never did anything except send me a card at Christmas and Easter. I think she must have bought in bulk because the same ones kept coming every year. I still remember them: Christmas was a photograph of a tree with lights and bunting and stuff. Easter was a badly printed painting of an agonised Christ. That picture used to give me the willies when I was young. Some years, she'd get them mixed up, and I'd get the agonised Christ for Christmas.'

I let him talk on, nodding occasionally. His grandmother hadn't approved of the marriage, and who can blame her? A sweet seventeen-year-old *chiquita* giving her virginity away to a crusty old Polish bagel. A more unlikely pair is hard to imagine. And this, their offspring, chattering away while his legs dangled below him without touching the floor.

'She never sent me birthday cards, so I wrote her a letter, telling her that my eighteenth was on its way. She sent her first birthday card ever – a picture of a young man on a motorbike – a particularly tactless touch that, I thought. And a letter – in *Italiano* – outlining her beliefs about my being God's punishment on the family because her daughter had dared to beget a child of a Jew. I remember the words she used to describe me – *'un bastardo e deformato'* – even though the *bastardo*

13

bit was untrue. Apparently it was miscegenation of the highest order, the conjugation of Polish Jew and Italian Catholic, and the age gap just compounded the sin. I wrote back telling her to fuck off.' He smiles bitterly. *'Va fa'n culo*. Up your arse, you old bag. Strangely enough, that's the last I heard from her.'

I enjoy the visit more than I thought I would. Is it always the way when we extend ourselves and live to tell the tale? There was something scintillating about this lively little cripple. Tad. I can't stop talking about him to Ruth.

'Can you believe it? He showed me a photograph – the only one he has – of his family. Mother, uncle, aunt, cousins – a real family gathering. I asked him which one he was. "I'm not in it," he said. "My mother refused to allow anyone to photograph me." What a bitch! And his grandmother . . . phew!'

'Where's his family now?'

I relate the story I'd been told. He was an unusually happy baby, he said, which was more than could be said for his parents: his father died from undisclosed causes soon after his birth, and his mother left him and his brother and sister at his aunt's, took a bus to Blackpool and threw herself off the pier. She died, not from drowning, but from her neck snapping on an underwater concrete support of the pier. Nobody knew why she decided, at what was presumably a youngish age, to kill herself.

The aunt, with two children of her own, agreed to adopt the elder brother and sister, but Tad, six months short of his second birthday, and clearly destined for a life of dependency, was placed in council care. The aunt apparently visited him once or twice, but when they moved to Australia a few years later, omitting to leave a forwarding address, the final thread between him and his hapless family was cut.

Such injustice. I couldn't believe the calm way he had recounted this horror story to me. He wanted to tell it, that was for sure, but he was clearly not seeking sympathy. He just liked to talk.

14

When I had finally torn myself away after a couple of hours, I had felt small and humble, and very, very English.

Tad's not the only one who writes short stories, though unlike him, I've yet to sell any. I got close with my last one, but close isn't close enough. *A beautifully written and touching piece,* the rejection slip had said, *but unfortunately rather too similar to one of our recent stories.* I wrote back and told them they could keep it until a decent time had elapsed, but they didn't even bother to answer. *Bastardos.* It may not have been Shakespeare, but it was no worse than the rest of the stuff they print. It's a long time since I've believed in God, but I still prayed. Please God, my orison went, send me a break. Just get me away from this bloody library.

Second only to bed as my favourite place of refuge is the bath, and in the evening, water up to my chin, I toy with a new story line. A young crippled boy – Rad, no – Cam – his arms and legs blown off by a bomb in the war. Which war? European? Contemporary. Beirut? No – Northern Ireland. His mother, a Catholic beauty, young and fiery; his father Protestant, old. His maternal grandmother, cursing the marriage to a Proddy, spurns the boy . . . That's it! (Oh, the warm feeling as a plot slips into place; this is the stuff of writing.) The boy, Cal, not Cam, is born normally, loved by the parents, but spurned by society (in the form of the grandmother). No matter what the child does, his grandmother (mother, too?) will not accept him, but then a bomb cripples him. His grandmother sees the error of her ways, and accepts him into the fold. Which side plants the bomb though: Montague or Capulet? Perhaps the British Army? No – they don't plant bombs, idiot. How about an accident – neither side claiming responsibility? Cal, a victim of the senselessness of sectarianism.

Not bad, not bad at all, I decide. There should be some motif the story hangs on: a rose in the rubble, a broken cricket bat. How about a pair of shoes that the boy will never wear again? The title: *A pair of shoes.*

15

I turn the hot tap with my toe and let it run for a moment, the warm water snaking up my body. I close my eyes and see James Morrison, writer *extraordinaire*, receiving the Booker Prize for my first novel. Being interviewed on *Wogan*. (I can wear my black silk suit for that with my polo neck; maybe have my ear pierced with a heavy silver earring.) Choosing my eight records and being castaway on a desert island for an afternoon. I see the money. The fame. People asking my opinion about things I know nothing about. Receiving lewd and bizarre sexual propositions through the post from frustrated housewives. Being sent unsolicited photographs of attractive young women in compromising positions of undress. I see the sex. At the breakfast table, tearing open another imploring letter, disdainfully pushing the candid snapshots across to my current live-in girlfriend.

There's a stirring in my groin, the tip of the child tyrant peeping at me through the bubbles of the bathwater. It nods encouragingly at my blank stare. Hello there – remember me?

'Yams? Up her backside?' Ruth says, switching the light off. 'Don't be ridiculous – do you know how big a yam is?'

There's a pause while I think about it. 'Presumably she slices them first.'

'My only memory of home is of lying on my back on a sheepskin rug whilst two other children – presumably my brother and sister – played with me. Though I haven't seen them for nearly fifteen years, I often think about them. They would be about thirty-two and thirty-four now.'

This is clearly turning into the second instalment of Tad's life story. I'd been pleased to see him when he turned up at the library this morning. On Mondays I work half-day, and so when he invited me back to Innocence, I accepted. I didn't know why I was so keen to spend the afternoon with him. It just seemed like a good idea.

'Though my condition was clear right from the start, I lived the first eighteen months of my life within the bosom of a normal family. Stressed out, perhaps, but not

16

too bizarre. Apparently I was a baby much like other babies, but it didn't take them long to label me as defective. I kept breaking bones, you see.

'My earliest coherent memories are of St Charles's hospital where I spent the first six years after my mother's death. This was home to me, albeit one in which I was drugged and operated on twice a year for the duration. I know most people are afraid of hospitals – the starched uniforms, and machines and shiny floors – but it was familiar to me. It was the outside world that scared me. But even though it was an uncomfortable childhood, I was happy enough. By the time I was eight the surgeons decided to put their scalpels away and I was moved to a children's home near here. I'd clearly never walk, they told me, but I was continent and compos mentis.' He smiles at me sweetly. 'And that counts for a lot where I come from. Anyway, enough about me. Tell me about you and – what's your girlfriend's name?'

'Ruth.'

The tables are turned this time. It's his turn to ask the questions, my turn to answer. And like him, I'm glad of an audience to hear me. He sits in his chrome wheelchair with his long eyelashes and silky black hair while I tell him the uneventful story of my life with Ruth. The continuum of James Morrison only starts at the age of twenty-five. I don't know who it was that inhabited my body before then, but it wasn't me. And so Tad gets nothing of boarding school, no mention of Mother.

Ruth: together now for nearly four years. Four years. Something inside me withers at the thought. I was still a comparatively fresh-faced graduate at twenty-five. I'd been working in various libraries for a year or so, just come back to London after a seven-year gap. Ruth was twenty-four and already as sophisticated and bitter as dark chocolate. I can hear the resentment and sadness creeping into my voice the more I tell of my story, but the relief of an attentive listener is too great to check myself. I remember just how brilliant I was when I first knew her. When there was the excitement of a new game to play, I could be as witty and wise as you could hope for. It never lasted long, of course, not past the courtship, and Ruth was no exception. It seems

17

so long ago: not the years, but the gap between the James of then and the present specimen. Was I truly that naïve and excited at twenty-five? It was the last year of my youth. Somehow it had been all downhill since then.

Ruth and me only began living together because it seemed the obvious thing to do. We had a damp basement flat in Earls Court and then Mother died and I bought Ellsbirch Avenue. Resignation now.

'I suppose any relationship gets stale in time, and maybe that's what's happening to us. We're going off.'

'You sound like a loaf of bread.'

I shrug. My granary loaf to Ruth's baguette.

'And how's your love life?'

'Sex? Kind of boring, I suppose.' I tweak the frill of the counterpane. Tad's eyes are on me, but I want to take my time in answering. 'I wonder if we're not just sexually incompatible,' I finally say. 'She's beautiful enough, a nice face, long silky hair, a great figure – she's even enthusiastic enough in bed, but it's just that . . . ' And so on.

Why is it so easy to talk like this to this weird little guy? Scrunched up in his wheelchair, encouraging me with nods of his wobbly head, he's a leprechaun Confessor. Forgive me, Father, for I have sinned. What a relief to let whole slabs of secrets unbuckle and fall into view. Sex, I finally admit, has become a cannibalistic rite. A ritual feeding off each other. It's hard to tell who comes off best, who eats the most, who manages to save as much of themselves as they can.

'But in my opinion, Ruth generally wins – she wants as much as she can get, and truth be told, sex exhausts me.'

'Swift and simple, is that how you want it? Like scratching an itch?'

He's got it in one. Lust is an itch to be scratched: up a bit, up a bit . . . there! Aaah! 'I'm just her walking, talking dildo, and she's my living Barbie doll.' I surprise myself at my forthrightness.

'There's a simpler way of putting it than that.'

'How would you put it?' I ask. I think my metaphor is daring and witty.

18

'You're a pair of wankers.'

I laugh uncertainly. There's something about that word that makes me wince. I focus on the zig-zag pattern of the rug, wanting to protest: it's one thing to deride yourself, but coming from another person, especially a newcomer . . .

But he's right. I said it myself: it's mutual masturbation, nothing more or less than that.

'Oh, by the way,' Tad says as I'm leaving. 'Would you do me a favour? Get me a copy of *Hot Tips*?'

'Okay.' It's nearly six o'clock. I've been there five hours.

'Take a tenner out of my purse.' I do as he says. 'You'll need to go to Notting Hill Gate to get me one. Do you know Pembridge Books?'

I don't, so Tad draws me a clumsy map, and writes the title of the magazine he wants.

'I'll see you in a couple of days,' he says, wheeling himself to the door. 'I'll pop by the library to pick up the magazine.'

3

I'm not starting work till late the next day, so I catch the bus to Notting Hill Gate in the morning and dawdle along Pembridge Villas, looking in the shop windows. One of my favourite shops there sells second-hand men's evening wear: cummerbunds and white silk scarves and mouldy top-hats. Though I hate the thought of wearing second-hand clothes, I occasionally go in just to enjoy the musty smells and the attention of the aged and effete shop assistants. There's something reassuring in the shop's atmosphere of antique gentility: undeniably masculine, yet flamboyant too, these clothes are reminders that there once was a time when the world was a more dignified and simple place to be. A time when the easy consciences of men and

19

women were unassailed by the complications of too much information.

According to the hand-drawn map, the bookshop is on the corner of Portobello Road, next to an antique shop, but when I get there, I find just a private house with drawn blinds. I check the shops on either side: a clothes boutique and a pub. Confused, I'm about to give up when I see the sign hanging above the doorway of the house. 'Books', it says. I click the latch of the shop door and push it open.

I'm two steps into the shop before I realise I've been here before. Not this shop, but one a lot like it. It's the ambience I recognise: the cheap carpet, the hushed privacy. This can be only one of three places: a men's club, a posh cloakroom, or a sex shop. One glance at the racks of magazines confirms my guess. A porno emporium. The shop is empty apart from the man at the counter who is watching a black and white television in the corner and who hadn't even glanced up when I came in. Should I stay? I have the place to myself, so I advance on the magazine racks, my blood hammering in my ears.

There's a second's confusion before I realise the naked body on the cover of the first magazine is a man's. I look at the next magazine: a group of cowboys, naked to the waist, stare out at the camera. Uh-oh. I turn to the second rack, scanning the contents; the third rack. It's all the same: homos, as we used to call them at school.

The door opens and somebody comes in. I duck down behind the rack as though my legs have been kicked from under me. Caught *in flagrante delicto* in a homosexual sex shop, it's a reflex action to take cover. Nobody's going to accuse me of being here for myself. I crouch behind the rack, willing the new customer to walk to the other end of the shop. What if somebody here gets the wrong idea, starts chatting me up?

Here I am: a grown man, nearly thirty, quivering with suppressed lust and fear, hiding amongst expensive pornographic magazines like my very worst image of a masturbator. Why the crippling guilt? I don't know: it's just a blank wall of panic, no handholds, no possibility of scaling

20

it. I'm squared up to the north face of Original Sin, and it's a mile-high ice-cube.

My attention is caught by the title of one of the American imports on the bottom shelf: *All boys together*. And so we are. If I can't be at home surrounded by ten thousand penises, where can I?

I consider my choices: to remain crouched on the floor until the shop is empty again, to make a dash for the door, or to stand up. It's only sex, Jimmy boy, I tell myself. Nothing to be ashamed of. I start scanning the nearest magazines. The titles are no more imaginative than the sort of pornography my local newsagent stocks: *Black and Horny, Leather Bikers cum to Play, Studz. Hot Tips* makes a lot more sense now. I'll get you for this, Tad, you bastard, I hiss, standing up.

As if choreographed, the other man in the shop decides to turn to the same rack at that moment and our glances click together. A smile lights up his face, but I scowl back and turn away. James Morrison has disappeared: I'm on the run now, fuelled by adrenalin and paranoia, and no more in charge of myself than a wind-up toy. I find myself walking towards a glass cabinet at the end of the room. I can feel the man's eyes on me, or am I imagining it? I try and make out his reflection in the glass, but I can't see him. I glance at the contents displayed on the glass shelves of the cabinet. At first, they appear to be medical appliances, function unknown, but then I realise they're cockrings and a range of cling-film-wrapped dildos, graded in size from pink tiddlers to a black two-foot monster that resembles nothing so much as a rhinoceros horn. I stare at them, forgetting for the moment where I am. These are for fancy dress, surely? Half of the dildos are far too big for any human orifice: those at the top of the range could split an arsehole apart. There's one, the size and proportions of a fist, that is clearly intended to injure somebody. I'm horrified, but even as my eyes widen in disbelief, so something inside me responds to their fantastic size. In the masculine world big is beautiful; unchecked and fed man-to-man, this is what it results in, these giant totems to the male psyche.

21

I shudder and turn back to the rack, my eyes alighting immediately on a copy of *Hot Tips*. I pay fifteen pounds for it, and leave with it wrapped in a brown paper bag.

I've read about so-called 'fist fucking', a male homosexual practice which involves inserting the fist and a quantity of forearm via another person's rectum into their sigmoid colon. Assuming it was hyperbole, I chose to believe that the larger of the dildos I had seen were for display only. I was wrong.

I'm haunted by those black phalluses all afternoon. That is me, in that glass cabinet. The mentality that had designed and created those grotesqueries is mine. I can't shake the images from my mind: memories of rampant satyrs I'd once seen on Greek pots, three-foot penises stuck in front of them like an abdominal unicorn's horn. The Cerne Abbas giant with his fifty-foot cock. The maypole, Siva's lingam, the column of Heliogabalus. There is a ten-thousand-year cultural inheritance surrounding this strip of flesh hanging between my legs. Penis-power: born as a man, I'm fated to be led through this life by my cock, like a dog by a tugging lead.

The magazine, safely zipped into my briefcase, sits by my desk all day. I have fantasies of Judith Brown, our spinsterish head librarian finding it and disbelievingly turning the pages, a lifetime's beliefs crumbling with every page. What would she make of it? She's probably read Burroughs, Henry Miller, I know for certain she's read de Sade's *Justine*, but this – these pictures that I haven't dared look at yet – is nothing other than sex. Art it certainly isn't.

Cycling home that evening, my briefcase in one hand, I feel like the man with the key to the Bomb in the locked briefcase who is supposed to follow the US president wherever he goes. I attempt to measure my pace, but deny it though I try, I'm in a hurry to get home and examine my dangerous treasure.

Ruth is watching television when I get in, so I go into the kitchen to see if she's made anything to eat. She hasn't, so I

22

make a ham and cucumber sandwich and eat it over the sink. She's watching a soap opera, *Dynasty* or *Dallas*, I can never tell them apart: her weekly cultural slumming. I glance at the clock over the sink. It won't finish for another fifteen minutes: the time between now and then is inviolable; I have a clear corridor of time to myself. I carefully wipe the margarine off my fingers, unzip the briefcase and take out the magazine. Fifteen quid for thirty pages: someone somewhere is making a lot of money.

The cover is innocuous enough: a Black man naked to the waist, heavy gold chains round his neck, winking lasciviously out at me. I turn to the first page expecting a table of contents, some sort of written introduction, but there's nothing. I smile at the editorial honesty: there's no pretence here, no foreplay, this is onanistic printed matter and it's straight to business. Page one: two Scandinavians with erect and abnormally long penises cavorting in what looks like a recording studio; the expression of ecstasy on their faces belied by the fact that throughout the sequence they make no physical contact with each other. Obscenity laws apparently forbid the photographing of any direct contact between genitals, and so the two models have to dance around, thrusting their dicks into the air between each other, like two satyrs fucking an invisible nymph. Homosexual pornography is a new experience for me, and I struggle with the rules of the game: two erect penises facing each other like mirror images, but the question is: where to put them? I stare at the waving phalluses and then turn the page. There's a two-page story, 'Hard to please' by Brett Fullwood. The next sequence of pictures is the hero of the publication, Mr Hot Tips himself. A young black man disrobes from a black leather number, revealing more and more of himself until he produces what looks like a coiled snake from within a satin pouch between his legs. The paying customer is then treated to a display of self-stimulation until by the centre spread of the magazine, he has achieved full stature and his nine-inch oiled cock is at its proudest. Mr Tips stands above the cameraman, a staple in his navel, and looks down at me, a chillingly blank stare in his eyes.

The final sequence is a group orgy of sorts, involving

a further four men, two white and two Black. One of the young men is presumably the female of the group. Pretty in an offensive way, I recognise some of his posturing from girly magazines. Legs raised to expose the dark cleft of the bum, knickers pulled down, the coy look over the shoulder. He looks like a woman with a prick and balls.

It's hard to tell who's doing what to whom: somebody's flaccid penis is being held like a truncheon to a hairy anus. A pair of black hands is forcing apart a pair of white buttocks. A head is dipping towards somebody's groin. The pictures are spotted with bright orange blobs, obliterating any point of genital contact: glans to tongue, cock to cock; presumably this is as far as the law allows. I can see why the magazine is so expensive: money, as the sex industrialists well know, loses a lot of its power when a punter gets a hard-on. Talking of which . . . I glance up and stare blankly out of the window. The Prince of Parturition has stirred and woken. Surely I'm not getting turned on by this stuff? I slip the magazine back into the bag and then wash my hands under the tap. How could I? I'm a no-nonsense heterosexual, as clean and straight as John Boy Walton. I splash my face and let the water run down on to my collar. Not once have I entertained men in my fantasies; I won't even consider the possibility that I'm going to start now.

I wander into the sitting-room and watch the telly for a minute. I try to say something to Ruth, but she waves at me to be quiet so I go back into the kitchen. The paper bag is open in a second and I'm flicking through the pages again. Is this what women see when they look at girly magazines? The same baffling wonder that anybody should do such things, should be excited by such pictures? It's just meat after all; meat and imagination. I turn back to the beginning, unconsciously flicking through for my favourite pictures.

I'm halfway through Brett Fullwood's story when I recognise the theme tune to Ruth's programme. Too late: Ruth comes in just as I'm pushing the thing back into its paper bag. Ruth, as I knew she would, wants to know what it is. She hates not knowing everything that goes on in the flat.

'Oh,' I say, the quiver in my voice belying my non-chalance, 'something Tad asked me to get.' I slide it back out of the bag and pass it to Ruth. I watch her expression expectantly.

'You didn't tell me he's gay.'

'I didn't know.' I hadn't really thought about it, con-cerned as I was with my contraband, but yes, I suppose: Tad is a gay. One more burden to a Jewish-Catholic cripple. I edge round Ruth to watch over her shoulder. She opens it to the centre page and we're confronted by that giant prick, those relentless eyes.

She glances at the cover and then puts it under her arm. 'Are you making coffee?' I'm not, but I fill the kettle anyway.

Ruth goes back to the settee, tucks her legs under her and settles down with the magazine. I watch her from the kitchen while the kettle boils. I'm surprised at her equanimity. She's leafing through it as though it's *Harpers & Queen*. What do I expect? Disgust and outrage, judging from my relief. When I bring the coffee through with a plate of biscuits, she chucks the magazine on the table.

'Do men really get turned on by this sort of stuff?'

'Some men, I suppose.'

She leans forward and opens it at random. It falls open to a page of the Caucasian cocks. They're oddly similar, like twins, both long and curved like bananas. 'It's a bit ridiculous, really.'

I frown noncommittally. Ridiculous perhaps, but do you think we can keep our hands off the thing? She picks it up again. 'They look so weird, these disembodied penises.'

I glance at the magazine and nod. It's true: the picture she has turned to is of an enormous erect penis, filling the page. If this is standard male equipment, I'm clearly lacking something. Like two or three inches.

'Like little animals or something,' she persists.

I say nothing, but the image of a giraffe came unbidden to my mind.

'I mean, look at them.' She proffers the magazine, but I make no move to take it from her. If Ruth knows anything about men, she should know our sensitivity about our

25

genital organs. Penises are not things to be laughed at. I bristle with male solidarity: mock my brother, you mock me.

Ruth senses that she's upset me, but she's not going to ask me about it. She drops the magazine on the coffee-table, and there it remains for the rest of the evening, both of us affecting disinterest in it.

Ruth is not as untouched by Mr Hot Tips as she pretends to be. She makes no further comment on the subject, but from the way she immediately turns to me once we're in bed, I know she's aroused and that she means business.

We say nothing as we start the engine of our copulation. Pornography is fine, we are as permissive and modern as is required; but those horse penises, those threatening, ball-bursting erections are a little too close to the truth for comfort.

So it is in silence that we do our manoeuvring and pumping. And save for the squeak of bedsprings, the quiet of the room is undisturbed until Ruth comes, barking into the pillow like a sea lion.

4

'I want to have a word with you.'

'Hello James.'

'Why didn't you tell me what sort of magazine that was?'

'Did you get it?'

'Keep your voice down.' I can see Hilary, one of the other librarians, cocking an ear to the conversation, and so I lean over the counter, bringing my head down to Tad's level. 'That was a dirty trick you played on me. You knew I didn't know.'

'I couldn't resist it.' The little bastard grins back at me. 'Did you get it?'

'Yes, I got it, but I'm not giving it to you here. I'll bring it round tonight after work.'

'Why the secrecy?'

'Shhh!' I glance sideways at Hilary. She's frowning at a catalogue card, obviously straining to hear what we're talking about. 'Are you deliberately trying to embarrass me?' I hiss back at Tad.

'I'm sorry.'

I stride round the counter. 'And by the way, you owe me a fiver.' I try shoving the chair forward but it only drags on the carpet for a few inches.

'Come over tonight and I'll apologise properly,' he says over his shoulder as the chair buzzes towards the door. 'You drink, don't you?'

'Hmm,' I say.

My eyes narrow to slits as I look at Tad through the sharpness of the lemon. What the hell am I doing, getting drunk on tequila, subjecting myself to a reading of one of Tad's dirty stories from a magazine? Yes – *his* stories, for I discover now that my three-foot tormentor is none other than Brett Fullwood, author of 'Hard to please' and twenty or so other pornographic stories. My unwitting foray into the world of the homosexual sex shop was to fetch him his latest masterpiece.

At first I'm shocked at the story, but even as I cringe at the clichéd orgy fantasy, one part of me admires Tad for his shamelessness: if nothing else, the little guy is honest. No literary pretence here, no characterisation, no plot to speak of: the story is aggressive and lustful and nothing else. I squirm as the language becomes more graphic, but after the third reference to gushing spunk, there's no further that the story can go, and I relax. It's just men with rampant cocks visiting acts of thinly disguised violence upon each other, not really erotic at all: only tangentially related to sex. Their penises and arseholes could be pistons and valves for all the sense it makes.

Mid-sentence, Tad lets the magazine drop on to the floor and wipes his fingers on the lapel of his jacket. 'I've tried writing love stories for them, but this is all they want –

27

huge cocks and bucketfuls of semen.' My distaste must be visible on my face. 'Are you shocked?'

'No,' I lie. 'Just surprised.'

'Why?'

I can't tell him that I'd assumed a cripple would know as much about sex as he would about running a hundred-yard dash. 'I always wondered who wrote those sort of stories. I always thought they'd be some sort of – ' I hesitate.

'Pervert?'

He's taken the word out of my mouth, and he gives a high-pitched giggle. 'Fill me up could you?' he says, holding his glass out to me.

I splosh some tequila into his glass and pass the salt. Tad puts a pinch on the back of his hand and then licks it off before gulping back the tequila in one. His face contorts as though he's in pain, and then he bites into the lemon. 'If you're looking for some easy money, I could put you on to a publisher.'

'I wouldn't know where to begin. I don't think my imagination is quite as active as yours.' I glance at the bookshelf. He's got quite a stack of glossy magazines there. I wonder if the arrangement is intentionally alphabetical: porno, I see, is between *Peanuts* and Proust. Something for everyone.

'You think I have an overactive imagination? These stories are nothing. I'm planning a science-fiction story about a genus of animal who reproduce themselves by the male placing a blood-engorged sperm-conduit inside an abdominal cavity of the female, agitating until single-cell carriers of DNA are released into the female, which upon finding the DNA-carrying cells of the female, fuse nuclei, reproducing themselves until an autonomous organism with its own will and intelligence is formed, whereupon, it is ejected back into the external environment.' He's pleased with himself, and lets me know it by giving a long, loud belch.

I try to smile, but I seem to have lost control of my facial muscles.

'You should hear me on asexual reproduction.' He looks at me, one eyebrow raised. 'We all have fantasies. You've

28

just got to write them down – what could be easier? You *do* have sexual fantasies?' he asks doubtfully.

I pour myself another drink. 'Of course.' I shudder as the tequila burns its way down my gullet to my stomach before biting into the lemon. This is getting too close to the knuckle for comfort.

'So?' Tad says. He's getting drunk, too. 'Let's hear one of them. Give me an idea for a story.'

'I don't know.' I'm embarrassed now.

'What don't you know?'

I shrug. We look at each other in silence for a moment. What don't I know? I slip the memory out of storage and flip through it as though it's a dirty book I've snuck from the top shelf of a newsagent. I glance again at its cover. No – I can't tell Tad. It's disgusting.

'Come on, James, they're only words.'

'But they're not. They're ideas, thoughts.'

'Okay. They're only ideas, thoughts.' He sees the doubt on my face. 'Come on – you show me yours and I'll show you mine.'

'I don't know which one to tell you,' I grin, hating myself.

'Yes you do – *that* one.'

'Well – ' I swirl the liquid in my glass, take a deep breath and spill the beans. It's an idea that has grown from a passing remark I heard about the sexual circus that the Indian guru Bhagwan Shree Rajneesh had created for his followers. It went something like this: the female disciples would lie on their backs, naked, a ripe mango held between the lips of their vagina, and then their male partners would proceed to eat the fruit.

This seed of thought had germinated into a three-course food fantasy. I've always wanted to get messy with sex; nicely messy. Fruit and cream and sweet sticky sauces, yoghurts. Yams.

It's not enough just to precis: Tad wants details, specific and exact details. I stall once or twice, like a horse refusing a jump, but Tad is a persistent rider. 'And then what would you do?' he keeps asking.

'*You* know!'

'I don't, James.'

I'm enjoying this; the warm fuzz of alcohol, the illicit thrill of airing naughty thoughts. I stop when I notice an ache in my groin. I'm getting an erection.

'Another drink?' We repeat the tequila, salt and lemon business. I have trouble looking Tad in the eye as he hands me the plate of sliced lemon. In a matter of a few days, the little bugger has got more dirt on me than anyone else I can think of. It's my turn now: if Tad doesn't pay his dues with a shared secret, the whole relationship would be under review.

'Have you ever had sex with a man?' he asks.

'What? No.' I field the question and toss it back at Tad as though it's a live grenade.

'Never even thought of it?'

'Not even at boarding school.'

'You went to boarding school?' he squeals. 'Lucky you.'

I stiffen with a flash of anger. 'Lucky to be sent away at the age of seven to be tyrannised by Catholic monks?'

'Perhaps not. Just a silly fantasy of mine.'

Seven years old? The older I get, the harder it is to believe. I know there wasn't much of an option in my case, but how many parents still send their children away under the delusion that it will do them some good? I glance at Tad. How old was he when he was wrenched from his family?

It's getting dark, so Tad turns the bedside lamp on, and asks me to shut the curtains. I stare into the quadrangle of scruffy grass for a moment before I pull them shut. I haven't thought about St Jude's for years, but these visits to Innocence have rekindled memories of school I thought were long extinguished. I suddenly realised how pissed I am. 'Your turn.'

I turn round to look at Tad. Your turn? Here's a cripple; a folded, crushed paraplegic. What's sex to him? I wish we'd never got on to the subject.

'Sit you down,' Tad says, nodding at the chair. 'My fantasy?' He waits until I'm sitting comfortably. 'Close your eyes if you will and imagine yourself a world away in a steamy, soft landscape. There's no sun in the sky: the dim amber light seems to come from everywhere. The

30

ground is made of some sort of rubber, soft but firm to the touch.'

His fingers waggle as if he's feeling the ground for himself. 'Come on, James, shut your eyes.' I do as he says.

'It's a sci-fi world, a world where everyone is free, and well-fed and healthy. It's warm and windless, and people are walking by, floating almost, there's so little gravity. The only clothes worn are silky, loose flowing robes. It's hard to tell the difference between the men and the women: they're dressed in the same way: short Roman skirts, leather greaves. Some people are wearing togas, left arm bared, the occasional breast showing. Most people are bare-chested though. Nobody is ashamed of their body, because everyone is beautiful: bronzed and youthful. Young men walk past, bare-chested and muscular, their silky skin glowing in the half-light. Everyone has golden hair, shining and curling. I'm standing tall and perfectly formed, I look down at my legs: they're strong and firm. I feel my arms, hold them in front of me and flex the supple muscles. I'm tall, over six feet. I look up and in the sky I can see a speck. It looks like a bird at first, something flapping its way down to the ground. Then I can see that it's an angel: a beautiful bronzed man with enormous powerful wings attached to his back. I can feel the air brush against my cheek as he lands in front of me. He stands there, in a clearing, looking around, proud and majestic. He's like a god, perfect. Our eyes meet and then he strides towards me. He only wears a loin-cloth, and his body is glistening with sweat. Silently, we reach out and clasp each other's hands. And then he's looking over my perfect body while I gaze at him. His chest is firm, almost sculpted; his belly muscles, ribbed and manly. His collar-bone is well-defined, his neck rising thick and strong from his trunk. His chest is perfectly hairless, and as I pull his loin-cloth from him, I see his groin and legs are without hair too. His penis hangs loosely, and I kneel and press my head into his thighs, running my tongue over his belly, down to the base of his cock. His penis quickens and stirs, a smooth golden rod. The foreskin slowly creeps back from the glans as the shaft

31

thickens and rises, nodding to my mouth. I slip the tip of his cock into my mouth and delicately hold it there, tasting the salty dribble of semen that slips like a pearl on to my tongue. Then I can feel his hands on my head, lifting me until I'm standing face to face with him. His hands slide down my back, exploring the ripples of muscles, smoothing down to the tops of my buttocks, gently rounding the curve of my bum, slowly prizing the cheeks of my arse open, his hand slides into the cleft of my bum, his finger searching out my arsehole—'

'Tad! Stop it!'

He opens his eyes, surprised. I'm standing, red-faced. We stare at each other.

'What is it?'

'My God,' is all I can say. What *is* it? What the hell *is* it? It's disgusting, that's what it is. I wipe my forehead with the back of my palm. I'm sweating. I turn away from Tad, scanning the wall for something to fix my eyes on. 'Unspeakable Acts', the Karen Finley article catches my eye, and for a second I stare at the photograph of the naked woman without realising what it is.

'James?'

I take a deep breath and sit down, still not meeting Tad's enquiring look. I try a cynical snort of laughter, but there's a catch in my throat and a falsetto peep! comes out.

'James, I can't read your mind. You're going to have to use words, I'm afraid.'

'How can you be so . . . ?' I trail off. Tad frowns back at me, waiting. '*Blatant*,' I say at last.

'Why hide it?' Tad says simply. 'We all get hard ons. We've all got imaginations. Why pretend otherwise?'

Why indeed? I pour myself another drink and glance at Tad. What am I doing here? I hardly know this guy and here we are pulling our trousers down and comparing our willies. It's time for me to go.

Tad is thinking, staring at the floor with unfocused eyes. It's at moments like this that I wish I hadn't given up smoking.

I don't know what Tad is thinking at that moment, but

a quote from the very same Karen Finley article would be appropriate:

I think people get really upset about what other people do or do not put in their orifices, especially the asshole. I don't know why we're all so anally obsessive.

'Why don't you do it?' he says eventually.

'Do what?' I'm aware of the coldness in my voice: a wall is suddenly between us.

'Your food fantasy.'

I frown, surprised. He's serious. 'It was just . . .' I inhale on an imaginary cigarette. An idle thought? 'I couldn't possibly,' I say.

'*I* couldn't possibly. The only thing stopping you is lack of guts.'

'Ruth wouldn't be part of something like that.'

'Have you asked her?'

I've had enough of this. I'm surfeiting on sex. I take a gulp of tequila. 'I don't want to.'

'You could have fooled me. You were getting quite rosy cheeked when you described what you want to do to Ruth.'

I get up to go. Tad has pushed too far, too soon.

I sway home with furrowed brow, a clamour of protest inside my head. I'm disgusted with myself; horny and embarrassed and guilty. And, goddammit, drunk too. I need to shed this burden into the lap of someone. And that someone is Ruth. I hurry through the dirty lamp-lit streets as if it's a toilet I'm seeking.

Ruth's out. I crane my neck to look up at the windows, nearly losing my balance and falling backwards into the street. No welcoming lights visible from down here. Damn! Sometimes, just sometimes at the end of a long day, I want to come home to a lighted, warm, occupied flat. Just to slide the key in the door, be greeted by the aroma of dinner cooking, call out 'I'm home,' slip out of my coat and pick up the evening paper. Once a month, maybe. Today is my day, and here she is – gone. I drop the keys on the doorstep twice before I manage to open the front door. The stairs to the second-floor flat are steeper than I remember them being. I'm drunker than I realised.

I squint suspiciously into the darkened living-room. So, where the hell is she? I listen as if I might hear the answer on the air; but nothing. Two steps into the room, I bark my shin on the edge of a chair and half fall into the arms of the sofa.

'Bollocks,' I say loudly. I say it again, louder, enjoying the sound. Nobody to tell me off for my language. 'Fucking bi— ' I stop. What was I going to say? Biff? Binge? Bitter, big shits.

I remember. 'Bitch.'

I suddenly remember where Ruth is: she's gone to some stately home in Worcester or Winchester or somewhere to oversee the cataloguing of some pieces of china. 'When did she say she'd be back?' I ask the lamp-stand. Not till Wednesday evening? Bollocks. Bloody bollocks.

I sit in the dark, studying the walls as they expand and contract until I start to feel sick. Whoops! I go to the kitchen for a glass of water, steadying myself against the furniture. I can't believe that I've just walked all the way back from Tad's: it seems like a dream now. I make a cheese and pickle sandwich, nearly slicing the top off my thumb with the bread-knife.

I take the stairs up to the bathroom on my hands and knees and sit on the loo and pee while I eat my sandwich. It's too early to go to bed, so I decide to have a bath. Without standing up, I turn the taps on and morosely watch the bath fill.

I love bathing. But I hate our bathroom. Somehow Ruth managed to take over its design: no matter how much I protested, she still managed to get what she wanted. And it was me who bloody paid for it. Painted in an unobtrusive peach-cream with splashes of puke-green, the colour scheme isn't too objectionable; it's the mirrors that cause offence. I don't know where she got the idea from: some classy magazine probably, but it shows amazingly poor taste if you ask me. To the height of six feet on three of the four walls have been affixed an acre of mirror tiles: Narcissus couldn't have designed it more to his liking. Smoky brown, they're presumably designed to enhance even the ugliest mug, and in moderation perhaps it might have been successful. But even a first-year design student wouldn't have put three mirrors in such a confined space. A moron could have told her it would be like living in an unending tunnel of echoed images. It's the sort of effect that reminds me of an early *Dr Who* programme. If someone was locked in our bathroom and started trying to count their reflections, they'd have to be carried out in a strait-jacket.

I hiccup and burp simultaneously, the taste of bile filling my mouth: I hate what she's done to my bathroom. And it is my bloody bathroom: me who paid for the flat, even paid for the bloody mirrors. Christ knows how she managed to persuade me to have this done. There's no corner of the bathroom that can't be spied into, no bodily part that can't be viewed from 360 degrees. No matter what activity you engage in, these staring walls amplify it ten, twenty, fifty times. Male guests often comment wryly on the effect when using the toilet. Standing to piss, the hapless male witnesses a thousand penises issuing a veritable waterfall of urine. If he dares look. This optical tyranny has forced me to gaze at the ceiling whenever I piss, a clumsy operation when you're drunk. Hence the sitting down.

But – and this is the turn of the blade – even in this hall of mirrors, I still have to duck slightly if I should be so rash as to want to see the whole of myself. The mirrors, God damn Ruth, are six feet high: precisely two inches shorter than I am. I don't know if it was an intentional snub, or just an oversight, but every time I stoop to brush my hair I curse her.

I frown at the sitting image. I don't like my body. I never have. I remember when I was eight or nine years old listing the things that were wrong with my body. Not the things I didn't like, but were *wrong* with me. I can still remember how it went, in ascending order of despicableness:

1. Sticking-up hair
2. Bald patch on the back of my head (scar from falling off a swing)
3. Freckles in summer

35

4. Birthmark on thigh
5. Big front teeth

How we arrive as adults, crippled with self-consciousness is no mystery. Enough lists like this at a tender age will ensure a lifetime of worried consultations in the mirror. The 'why' is more difficult to uncover. Why would a child compose a litany of self-hatred? What was it that caused my childhood to end and this self-flagellation to begin?

I recite my one Baudelaire quote into the mirror:

O Seigneur! donnez-moi la force et le courage
De contempler mon coeur et mon corps sans dégoût.

Nothing has changed since then. I've grown up and out of these stigmata, but I still have a list. It has changed of course, but in essence it's no more sophisticated than the original one. My deafness has become an addition: it didn't become noticeable until I was fifteen or so. I couldn't believe my bad luck when it was diagnosed: as though I didn't have enough to worry about, here was another straw designed to break my back. I was probably always hard of hearing, but it seemed to take a turn for the worse in my adolescence. Thankfully, it hasn't deteriorated for ten years and I've managed to escape the humiliation of wearing a hearing aid. I disguise my hearing loss fairly well; most people who know me aren't even aware of it. There are some advantages, I suppose, in having an invisible disability. But there again, there must be some relief in having a handicap so obvious that it's undeniable. Tad for instance.

I'm not the only one who doesn't like the way I look: Ruth doesn't like my body either. I know this because she has told me. God in his wisdom made me a tall, skinny ectomorph, while Ruth, or so I accuse her, goes for the Neanderthal type: hair and biceps and a barrel-like chest. I can look presentable, even stylish when clothed, but when I'm naked I resemble one of the 'before' pictures in the Charles Atlas adverts. I was the kid who got sand kicked in my face. I still am.

Me and mirrors don't see eye to eye. Mirrors would have no place in a redesigned world. Certainly, bathrooms would be empty of them. Watching a thousand Jameses disrobe is not the agony it once was, but it's still uncomfortable. Once upon a time, I wasn't able to consider my body without aching with disappointment and humiliation. Now, I've learned not to look, or just to look selectively. But the tequila forces me to look tonight. I'm in the mood for humiliation.

My clothes fall off me like over-cooked meat off a chicken bone and there I stand, queuing up in the mirror: a skin and bone army: prisoners of war, famine victims, weeds, wimps. Standing at one spot in the bathroom – just beside the wash-basin – affords an interrupted toe to middle of forehead reflection; and there, in that hot spot, stand I.

It's not me: I'm very clear about that. There has been a conspiracy to put me in somebody else's body. Perhaps a brain transplant, who knows?.I could deal with the injustice if it wasn't so permanent, but I've been abandoned here, stuck with this body for the whole of this lifetime. This is it, this is what I've got. I'm not the sort of person that has these legs, but here they are: thin, flaccid, stringy. The too-wide hips, the canyon of that belly, the frying-pan chest: whose are they? Not mine.

Do you do it? Play the if-I-were-a-welder-and-my-body-were-steel game? I can't be the only one to imagine snipping bits off, hammering other bits out, moulding my body to suit my taste. I know exactly how I could improve myself: I would lose an inch from the lumbar, half an inch from the neck, add six inches to the chest, fill out the limbs. The feet would be reshaped, the elbows and knees rounded off. Biceps, quads, calf muscles would be welded on. The nose reshaped, the jaw squared, the teeth pushed back a fraction, the birthmark erased.

Standing in front of these smoky mirrors, I'm Saint Sebastian firing arrows of spite at my reflection, wounding every part of myself.

I grip the edges of the wash-basin and lean towards my reflection. Then to my surprise I buckle at the waist and vomit into the sink.

5

I'm working with Hilary again. She's the type who regards librarianship as a sort of social work, and consequently has a perpetually helpful look about her. *Use me*, it says; nothing is too much trouble. I don't know, but I suspect she never issues fines for overdue books. Not me: Jeffrey Archer's *Not a Penny More, Not a Penny Less*, thirteen weeks overdue Mrs Bloggs, that'll be half your week's pension.

I'd like to see a study done on the most commonly overdue authors. It seems to me that the same names keep cropping up: usually thrillers or romances at the pulpier end of the market. I wonder if there's something significant about the moral standards of such a readership. Or perhaps they're just the sort of book that people forget they've borrowed until they discover them a month later jammed down the back of the settee with a handful of change and an unclaimed black nylon comb.

The smell of cigarette smoke makes me look up, and I'm just in time to see the culprit grind the butt out under his heel. Goddammit – smoking in a library! Ignorant bastard. I watch the young man walk over to the newspaper section and leaf through the papers on the table. He's wearing motorbike leathers, heavy black boots, and a white scarf tied round his throat. I immediately hate him: cocky and self-assured, he's a young stud: Marlon Brando playing *The Wild One*. I'd sell my soul to the first bidder if I could look like that.

I'm bored. I can't talk to Hilary; she's busy with a regular of ours: an old man who's researching an apparently unending book about the war. Which war, I can't say. He usually buttonholes one of the female staff to help him, a bit of a dirty old man I expect. I look over at the biker. What a difference between him and old man War: a hundred and fifty years at least.

I ignore them and take out my manuscript of 'Pregnant Pause', the short story I'm working on at the moment. It's about a young couple coming to terms with a miscarriage; the man this time being the sensitive and hurt one. Something for one of the women's magazines. I scan through it, my enthusiasm for the story dissolving with every page I read. Anyone who knows anything about me would recognise it as thinly veiled autobiography. It is pale and sentimental and clumsy. 'Crap!' I say rather too loudly. I glance round. Nobody has heard.

Sex is where the power is, not this sentimental garbage. Sensitivity is only for wimps. The only respected commodity in this world is power, and that means money and sex. I consider myself: I'm a *librarian*. One who knows but doesn't do. Become a man: toughen up, get a *real* job, get that testosterone flowing. I don't even drive a car, *for God's sake*.

I disengage from the world, unfocus to middle distance, and dream. The new Hemingway, that's it. No cave man, I'd have a brain in my head as well as a bulge in my pants. I'd be a sort of literary Marlboro man, an attractive scar on my left cheekbone from a switchblade fight with a pimp, a jaw line lean and mean from years of hard drinking. I'd be a thinking-man's man; but no armchair intellectual: I'd write standing up. Go to bullfights. Learn to drink and brawl and never throw up or cry.

So, what shall I call myself? Jim Morrison? That has already been taken. But what's wrong with *James* Morrison? That gives a touch of class. I could marry a Bond girl and become James Morrison-hyphen-Bond. Not too much? A trifle gauche? How about James Marlborough-Morrison? The Americans would love that. The British aristocracy gone slightly bad.

She's standing, her back to me, flicking through the pages of an encyclopaedia. Silky brown hair halfway down her back, tight blue jeans, a cute arse, suede cowboy boots. How old – about twenty? Her hair keeps falling over the page she's reading and she has to flick it back, every time she does so, the silver bangles on her wrist jangling. She turns sideways to rest the book on the top of the shelf, leaning with her elbows either side of the book. From where I'm sitting, I can clearly see the line of her bra, straining under the pressure of those lovely youthful breasts.

I vault the table between us and in a second, I'm standing behind her, my hands on her hips. She doesn't want to turn round at first, but I pull her until she stops resisting and turns to face me. My hands are in her hair, tugging gently backwards, tilting her face to meet mine. We kiss, tongues searching each other out. I can taste bubble-gum on her breath, feel the firm tits pressing against my chest. And then my hands slip inside her blouse, pushing the material down, popping the buttons off, exposing the pert white breasts, the young belly. I tweak her nipples, first the left, then the right. They harden under my fingers and she moans. I allow my hands to slide down her body, slipping one inside her tight jeans, pressing past the knicker elastic, the fuzzy pubic hair, until I find the moist warm slit. With the other hand I unzip the jeans, pushing them down, past her knees. The pants are pressed down and she steps out, naked. I lift her on to the bookshelf, her bottom pressing the open pages of the encyclopaedia. I only have to stoop slightly and I can inhale her musty sex smell, nestling my head in her crotch. My hands work their way under her buttocks as I prise open the legs, exposing her sweet swollen carnelian lips.

Oh my God – she's coming over! My heart is thumping so violently that my vision twitches with every beat. I haven't taken a breath for thirty seconds, and I choke a little as I inhale.

'Do you have an American biographical dictionary here?' she asks.

'Umm,' I say shakily. I stare blankly back at her: my body has ceased to exist from the head downwards. She's not as pretty as I thought: just a girl, really. A teeny-bopper, too innocent to be sexy. Biographical dictionary. American. I know we have a couple on the shelves, but I can't remember their titles. 'Let me show you,' I venture. I wonder if I'm blushing or if it's just high blood pressure that's making my cheeks burn. I lead her back to the bookcase she'd been standing against.

Ignoring the still-open encyclopaedia on the top shelf, I squat in front of the books, scanning the titles. Amazing what a fright can do to an erection. There's nothing there now: no sensation, no awareness at all.

'Here,' I say, sliding both volumes out half an inch.

She smiles into my face. 'Thank you.'

I give her a sickly grin and walk back to my desk, my legs shaking.

Damn! Where is the confidence I yearn for? Where the action behind the fantasy? Why can't I be like the motorcycle kid: cool and hip and full of snappy one-liners? What chances of a cute young girl like that being interested in a hung-up nearly thirty year old? I watch her copying something into a notebook, one hand holding back the lock of hair from falling over her face.

What maketh man? Manners? Muscle? Meanness? A moustache? Perhaps I should grow a moustache, learn to drive a motorbike. It could help.

I'm downstairs in the lending section when my thoughts are interrupted by a huge West Indian woman plonking her shopping basket on the table in front of me. She pushes two books across for me to stamp. I glance at their covers: paperbacks from our romance list: a new populist line for the less demanding punter. *Silver Moon,* a seascape at night, our hero clasping his adoring quarry in his strong, bronzed arms. *He held her tightly, the warm sea-breeze ruffling her auburn hair. 'Don't let me go, darling,' she murmured, 'don't ever let me go.'* I'm aware of wrinkling my nose as though the books are emitting an offensive odour. The same stance in mirror-image, is on the cover of the other book, *Harvest of the Wind,* the dominant man, the passive woman, her hair thrown back, a fruit ripe for the picking. I stamp the books.

The woman thanks me with an enormous smile and I nod politely. Why is everyone suddenly smiling at me? I watch her stuff the paperbacks into her bag with the

41

vegetables and breakfast cereal. Two mangoes peep out of the top. Ripe mangoes.

If I don't do it now, when will I? I idly watch the woman as she squeezes through the swing-gate. What was it Tad said to me? *The only thing stopping you is guts.* Twenty-nine, nearly thirty. *Could* I do it? Act out my fantasy with Ruth? Do it, a voice urges, cloven-hooved, blood-red. *Do it.*

Skippity hop goes my heart. My dreamiest dream, my hottest fantasy, my food orgy. Objections rattle out like bullets from a Gatling-gun, but it's too late: it has been decided. I'm scared, yes. We've never done anything like this before, I know. Never even talked about it. But the one-eyed beast has spoken. I'm going to do it.

I can see it now, the ripe mango poking from between her vagina lips, the juices trickling down her thighs, into my mouth, down my neck.

I take a scrap of paper and with trembling hand, write the shopping list.

One mango (ripe)
1 lb bananas
½ pt single cream
½ pt clotted cream
strawberry yoghurt
jelly
custard

My vision is blurring with images of stuffing, ramming, sucking, licking, prising, pouring. Curaçao, glacé cherries, fancy red candles, golden syrup: the ache in my groin is growing with every added item on the list.

Liberation, that's what it's all about: setting ourselves free. And sexual liberation is just part of that. The freedom to enjoy our bodies free from guilt. Those faces in Tad's magazine: blatant, unashamed, exposing all they had got, and why the hell not? We've all got bodies; bodies that feel, have wants, needs. Why not enjoy them? We're all consenting adults; we've got nothing to be ashamed of. Catholic guilt is a thing of the past. I'm free to do as I please.

42

I can feel my face set into that soured, concentrated look of a sexually aroused man. I have only one end in mind for the rest of the afternoon: the depositing of my semen in or on or around Ruth. Nothing else matters.

I go shopping after work. I can't find mangoes in the market, so I buy the largest and ripest plums I can find. A pity, but my disappointment is cut short by my discovery in the local pâtisserie: chocolate éclairs, fat and sticky and just oozing with cream. The shop assistant selects two from the shelf and lays them side by side in a little cardboard box as though they're a brace of duelling pistols, primed and cocked and ready to shoot.

I'd once seen a jelly mould in the shape of a female breast in a joke shop, but the local supermarket only has lozenge shapes or rabbits, and after a moment's deliberation, I settle for a rabbit. I cycle home that evening as quickly as my legs can pedal me, my groceries under my arm.

I follow the instructions on the packet of jelly and put the rabbit mould in the freezer to set. Only two hours till Ruth is due home. Let's see: on the dining-room table, or the low coffee-table by the sofa?

He forced her forward, her face pressed against the table-top, her ample bottom presented to him like an exotic sweetmeat.

Yes. I throw a clean table-cloth over the table. It's just about the right height. I rest my groin against the table edge for a moment, eyes closed.

Her fingers clutched at the table-cloth as he humped her from behind, her face contorted in ecstasy.

Hump? When did I last hear *that* word? Probably not since school. I catch sight of myself in the mirror above the telephone and hold my gaze for a second. I hope I'm not going to regret this. I take a couple of deep breaths and go into the kitchen.

I make a pint of custard. Somehow lumps form in it, but it's palatable, so I pour it into a gravy-boat and put it on the table. Single cream for pouring, clotted cream for moulding, each in its own pot; my hands are shaking

43

as I pour them out. I peel the plums and put them in a glass dish with the bananas. I arrange them so they nestle at the base of the bananas: purple testicles to giant yellow penises. I'm thrilled and terrified.

I survey the table. What else? Strawberry yoghurt. I only have a vague idea how we can use this. I daren't give it too much thought.

'Oooh,' I groan. 'Hurry up, Ruth, or I'll start without you.' I spoon out the yoghurt, scraping out the last of it with my finger. I study the pink blob of yoghurt on the tip of my finger for a moment before putting it in my mouth. Could I? Would I? If that was a prick, would I suck it?

I wash my hands in the sink, splashing water over my face. I open the fridge, looking for something I can press into my crotch to cool myself down. I thought there would be a can of beer, but there's only a bottle of tomato ketchup. I hesitate and then shove the bottle inside my jeans, wincing at its coldness. Now what? Ah – the chocolate éclairs. I put them side by side on a plate on the table: chocolate-covered dildos.

I find some candles in the kitchen drawer and take them out. What to do with these? They're long and tapered to a point like wax missiles. I have a dim memory of something like this before. Where was it? Ah – I remember: a porno film I'd seen about ten years ago. A lighted candle stuck up somebody's arsehole like a featureless face smoking a cigar. I jam a couple of candles in holders and put them on the table and then step back to view my work so far. I'm getting there. I go back into the kitchen to look through the cupboards for anything else we can use.

I'm not sure about arseholes, never having given them much thought.

He forced apart her ample cheeks, laying his throbbing knob along the crease of her . . . her

Perineum, anatomically speaking. What was it William Burroughs called it – *perennial divide*? I sort through the contents of the cupboard. Butter, jam, okay. Liver pâté? No. I check the second cupboard.

. . . along the virgin crack of her arse. He drew back, dipping his penile head into . . .

44

Mustard? No, I put it back. Ah! Honey.

the bowl of honey. He nuzzled it against the peeping eye of her . . . her

Dammit! Where is all the vocabulary of anal sex? Arse, bum, butt, rectum, anus, back passage. Mayonnaise? I consider it for a moment before putting it back in the fridge. The theme is sweet: let's not get confused here.

I check the jelly in the freezer: the steam has melted the ice which has now frozen into a mini-glacier and I have to dig the mould out with a spatula. The jelly has set, but no matter how much I shake it, it refuses to leave the safety of its bunny mould. I try scooping it out with a knife but there's clearly something about the nature of gelatin I'm failing to understand, so I give up and put it on the table as it is. 'I'll handle you later,' I tell the tin rabbit. If all else fails, I can just scoop it out in pieces.

I jump as the front door slams. Ruth's back. I take a deep breath. 'Hello darling?' I call out.

'Hi.'

Please God she's in a good mood. I take a last glance at the table and then stride out to the hall to greet her. We hug briefly, a peck on the cheek. 'How was Winchester?' My voice wobbles a little, but she doesn't notice.

'Worcester,' she corrects. She looks down at my trousers. 'Is that a bottle of ketchup down your trousers?'

Oh God — I've forgotten! She tugs at the end of the bottle, pulling it out of my trousers.

I laugh weakly. 'Or am I just pleased to see you?'

She frowns at me, handing me the bottle, and then goes through to the dining-room. 'What's going on?'

I stand behind her, my hands on her hips, looking over her shoulders at the laid table. It looks as though it has been set for a children's tea-party. I nuzzle her neck, slipping my hands round to her groin.

'Don't James. I need to go to the loo.' She pulls away from me and walks up to the table. 'Cream? Cake?' She sees the tin rabbit. 'Jelly?'

'I want to trifle with you, baby,' I say in my best Humphrey Bogart voice. She's not amused. 'Here,' I say, handing her the rabbit mould. 'How do I get this out?'

She takes it from me and pours hot water over it in the sink. I should have thought of that. 'Where did the jelly mould come from?'

I want to fill you with jelly, he said. I want you to have my jelly babies.

'What are you laughing at?' she says.

'Nothing.'

The green jelly slurps out of the mould on to the plate. She hands me the plate and then looks at the full table. 'What's going on?'

'Let's have a drink. Martini?' I go over to the drinks cabinet, turning my back on her so she can't see my face. It's going to go wrong; I can feel it.

'James. I'm tired. I don't want to play games.'

'I just thought we could have a little meal together, and, you know – ' I hand her a king-size Martini and then busy myself with the ice-bucket. 'Fool around,' I mumble. I'm a gerbil on a treadmill: exhausted, but too afraid to stop.

'I'm going out tonight – you know that.'

'What?'

'It's Friday. Ballet classes?'

Oh shit!

'I've got – ' She glances at her watch, 'ten minutes before I have to go out. Is this for me?'

I wince as she picks up a chocolate éclair and bites into it as if it's just a cake, and not a chocolate-coated phallus that she wants to thrust again and again into . . . oh well.

And so I'm left alone with a table of jelly and custard and peeled plums. Goddammit, why are we so crazy about sex? Why do we debase ourselves so regularly and so profoundly? An adult – I'm a mature man, and I was prepared to have sex with a cream cake. Can you believe it? I want to blame Tad, but I know the charge won't stick.

Ruth doesn't come back till ten, and then she's too tired to do anything except fall into a hot bath. I sit and watch her from the toilet seat; something I used to do a lot when we first lived together. The table has been cleared, the custard poured down the sink, the untouched jelly in the

46

fridge. I've had a miserable evening waiting for her to come home, immediately sulky when I hear the key in the door.

I grudgingly quiz her about Worcester, and she tells me about the work, how she'd spent the evenings. She seems to have enjoyed the luxury of having had time on her own. Another biff for my ego.

'And how about you? Did you see what's his name?'

'Tad? I got quite drunk with him on Wednesday.'

'And?' she prompts after I've said nothing else for nearly a minute.

I scowl at my smoky reflection in the mirror. 'Nothing.' I'm going to play my foul mood right to the hilt.

Another minute's silence. 'What's wrong?' she asks at last.

'Nothing.'

'James?' A note of annoyance has entered her voice. I sit up on the toilet-seat; if I drag my feet any more, she'll give up on this conversation and go to bed.

'I want you to meet Tad. Can we invite him over for dinner?' I'm surprised at myself: I hadn't considered it until this moment.

'Can he go out at night?'

'You mean, will his mummy let him?' I say sarcastically.

'I mean he's crippled, isn't he?'

'So?'

'Doesn't he have to be accompanied by someone?'

'He can manage well enough on his own,' I say, though I don't know if it's true.

She thinks about it while her fingers fiddle with her groin. I hate it when she does that. 'If you really want to invite him.'

'I do.'

'Okay then. What does he eat?'

'Baby food, what do you bloody think?'

'What's up with you, James?'

'He's a human being, Ruth. He's disabled, that's all. He's not a freak.'

'Did I call him a freak? I've never seen him.'

I pull a face at myself in the mirror. I want a fight. I want to punish Ruth for my disappointment. But I know I'm wrong. 'Sorry,' I mutter. I consider telling her that I'd missed her, but I decide against it.

She's shaving her legs, the slim calves held out of the water, toes pointed like a ballet dancer. I watch her in silence. She has nice legs. 'Did you eat tonight?' she asks.

A sudden intense dislike for Ruth surges over me. She watches me, waiting for an answer, unaware that I'm imagining how she would look drowning in the bath, her arms thrashing the water as she fights to escape my grip.

'Did you eat anything?' she repeats.

'Not really.' I'd had an éclair and a couple of bananas with cream. Three pricks and a cupful of spunk.

'You're too thin, James. You should eat more.'

She's right. Two days on my own and I can already feel how loose my waistband is. Ruth pulls herself out of the bath and I watch as she dries herself. I envy the smooth conventional shape of her body, the ease with which she allows me to watch her. It's a good body, close to perfect. I should fancy her, but I don't. I envy her.

I don't want to make love; I know that, my body knows that, so why am I snuggling up to her damp body in bed, preparing myself for the homecoming ritual? Time was when we were younger and hornier and genuinely hungry for each other, but that's not even a memory now, it's tradition. The manoeuvres are always more or less the same: my upper leg would slide over her thighs, my free hand cupping her breasts, my face in the crook of her neck. I'm doing that now. It's a position that affords maximum physical contact with the minimum of effort. Ruth must sense my reluctance because she pushes my leg away.

And then propping herself up on one elbow so she can have a good look at me, she asks the question I've been dreading all evening. 'What was all that nonsense about the food?'

I've had four hours to prepare myself for the response, but I still haven't been able to come up with anything even remotely plausible. The ready-excuse department of my brain feels as though it's been Novocained. No matter how hard I try, there's no response. 'What food?' I ask lamely.

'You know.' She has her snooping look on her face: something is up, and she wants to know what.

Shall I tell her, shall I tell her, shall I tell her? 'I just thought we could have something different for a change.'

'Jelly? Chocolate éclairs? That's certainly different.'

'Why not?' I can hear the defensiveness in my voice, but try as I might, I can't check it. 'What's wrong with that?'

'You are an odd person sometimes, James. Do you know that?'

'A weirdo, you mean?' I've hit the nail on the head, and we both know it.

'What's all this about, James?'

'You and me. We're so boring. We always have the same things day after day. Steak and chips in front of the telly. Spaghetti. Rice balls. And that fishy thing you do in a cheese sauce.' Why the hell am I talking about food? I know it's ridiculous, but I can't stop. 'We're so boring. We have the same things day in day out. I just wanted a change. Is there anything wrong with that?'

Nothing from Ruth, except a startled expression.

'Is there?'

Cowardice is not a pretty animal to share house space with, and as I reach across her to switch the bedside lamp off, I'm far from being proud of myself.

6

I glower at my reflection as I soap my face. A mistake has been made: I've been woken too soon, not fully reassembled after sleep. I'd ignored Ruth when she asked if I wanted breakfast, and stomped off to the bathroom to shave. I'm in a bad mood, there's no doubt of that, but what sort of bad mood? Am I still annoyed at Ruth? At myself? Am I disgusted or just depressed? Repentant or rampant? Horny or holy? The only thing I can be certain of is that I'm confused. And that I've just nicked my chin with my razor.

I phone Tad as soon as I get to the library. My survival strategy for off-centre days is usually to keep my head low and to speak as little as possible. Calling someone for what amounts to help is a small but significant step away from my past. Tad's impact on my life is beginning to show.

'Tad? Can I come over after work?'

'Of course, Jimmy boy. Is anything wrong?'

'Mmm,' is as noncommittal a noise as I can summon. I can hear Tad's high-pitched laugh down the line.

'Okay – I'll see you later.'

Throughout the day, Hammersmith library is the scene of major hauntings: diurnal succubi sit on my lap and whisper lewd suggestions into my ears; a pair of white-sheeted ghosties strip-tease before my burning eyes; two schoolgirls perform obscene and imaginative acts of lesbian sexual congress among the bookshelves. A phantom blowjob takes place in the Gents', stopping at the very edge of consummation. I'm glad to get out into the fresh air at six o'clock.

It's straight to business at Innocence, and almost immediate relief for me.

'So, Jimbo, how did the love feast go? Tell me all about it.'

'It was awful. The whole thing was a flop.'

'What happened?'

'Nothing. I got everything ready, then – ' It isn't worth finishing the sentence. I suddenly feel very tired. 'Do you really want to hear about it?'

'Of course I do. Isn't that why you came over?'

I feel something dissolve inside me. Bless his little pixie eyes, Tad's turning into my best friend. In less than two weeks he has got to know me better than almost anyone else on the planet. Of course I want to talk about it.

So I tell him the whole story: the preparation, the misunderstanding, my chicken-heartedness.

Tad shrugs when I finish. 'So, you didn't even tell her what you wanted?'

'No,' I admit.

'Why not?'

I shake my head. 'Embarrassment. Shame – I don't know.'

'Is Ruth particularly squeamish?'

'I don't think so. She might have been a bit – ' I wave my hands vaguely ' – put off.'

'Put off?'

'Disgusted,' I admit reluctantly.

'So what?'

So what, indeed. What would be the consequence of Ruth's disgust? She could leave me, she could refuse to sleep with me ever again, but that's not it. It's far more frightening than anything she might do. If another human being is disgusted at me, I would, quite simply, implode and disappear for ever. Pretty scary, eh?

'You're a healthy, straight, white male. You've got it all, James my boy. You're a man designed by a committee – the world is yours to dominate.'

'Yes, and I have enough hang-ups to keep a Jewish shrink like you busy for years.'

'Just leaf the money by the door, m'boy.' He smiles so tenderly at me, I want to cry. 'Tell me, vot vos your first sexual experience?' he says, looking over the steeple of his fingers at me. 'I don't mean that boring psychoanalytic nonsense about sucking on your mother's titty, or crapping in your potty. Real sex. Sexy sex.'

'You mean screwing?'

He shrugs. 'Votever.'

'I first made love when I was sixteen. With Alison.'

'He first made luff ven he vos sixteen. With Alison. Hmm. Alison who?'

I open my mouth to say her name, but I've forgotten. My first real girlfriend and I can't remember her name. I'm showing my age.

'Nefer mind. Please, tell me all about it.'

51

So I do. It's not a particularly interesting story, certainly not at a fourteen-year distance, and memorable only because it was the first time. Tad's insistence to have the details of my sex life is beginning to pall. So why do I tell him? Because I feel sorry for him: if he gets some sort of vicarious pleasure from hearing about other people's experiences, then it's a fairly harmless therapy for someone denied a full expression of their sexuality. Of course, one part of me knows this is crap. Tad's interested because he's a horny bastard.

'And vot's the most outrageous thing you've ever done?' Tad says unexpectedly. 'Sexually, I mean.'

'I'm not going to tell you.'

He pulls a face at my hoity-toity tone. 'And vy not?'

'It's none of your business.' I see his face fall. 'Sorry. I didn't mean to snap.'

'Why won't you tell me?' he says in his normal voice. 'It can't be *that* outrageous – I've got a pretty active imagination, as you well know.'

Ladies and Gentlemen, never before seen in public, the most outrageous, the most disgusting, the most shameful sexual experience of James's life. I cringe every time I remember it. I'm cringing now. 'I just couldn't tell you.'

'And if you can't tell a poor defenceless cripple, who can you tell?'

That's simple. 'No one.'

'How do you feel, carrying around all these guilty secrets?'

'Frozen. Paralysed.'

'Crippled?'

'If you like.' I zip my lip up: I'd walked into that one. I stand up and go to the window. It's going to be a hot summer, already the flowerbeds are looking parched. I can feel Tad watching me, but he's getting no more out of me.

'Why do you act so guilty all the time?'

Why? An image springs to my mind: the black monolith from the film *2001*; the mysterious psychic power source that appears from the depths of space, huge and smooth and irresistible. I have one of these: my own personal

52

megalith of socially transmitted guilt, a giant black slab of sexual angst that aeons ago was implanted into my psyche. Why act so guilty? I can't do otherwise.

'I'd like to meet her,' Tad says.

'Who?'

'Ruth.'

'Oh, yes,' I remember. 'Come to dinner – we'd love to have you.'

Tad's mouth works for a second before he can get a sound out. 'Thank you,' he says at last. 'Thank you. When?'

'Tomorrow night?' A warning voice sounds inside my head, and I check myself. 'Better make it Monday night. Ruth doesn't like surprises.'

My most outrageous sexual experience? Few people would find it particularly shocking. Lacking in good taste perhaps, bizarre even, but hardly criminal. Tad, had he been told, would probably have laughed: even with an imagination as active as his, I'm sure he wouldn't have thought of this.

Entertaining is Ruth's speciality. A quiet dinner party for four; intelligently chosen wines, discreet music, sophisticated conversation: the perfect hostess is one of the set-pieces she learned at finishing school.

It was determined, as Tad was an unknown quantity, to have him *tout seul*, rather than the usual duet or quartet of diners. Ruth doesn't want any embarrassing scenes, and if the experiment of having a physically disabled dinner guest proves too ungainly, the damage can be confined. Aestheticism is everything to Ruth: there are no more distressing blots on her social landscape than *faux pas*.

Is this unfair to Ruth? Yes. The truth is that she and I apparently hail from different planets: Ruth's environment has a far more refined atmosphere than mine. That's not her fault.

Tad had arranged to be brought to the flat by taxi for eight o'clock. And sure enough, at one minute past eight, the intercom buzzes. It's only then that I remember the stairs; all thirty-two of them. I'd forgotten to mention to Tad that we live on the second floor of a converted

53

Edwardian town house. By the time I get down to the front door, he's already in the arms of the taxi driver.

'Sorry, Tad – I forgot about the stairs.'

He's dressed in a grey suit jacket and black trousers, a scarlet silk tie still swinging from the momentum of being lifted from his chair. He looks like a grotesque baby in the man's arms. 'You bring the chair,' he says.

I look at the taxi driver. 'Sorry.'

'It's all right, mister, my little girl's handicapped as well.' He hoicks Tad up, getting a more comfortable grip.

'It's flat two on the second floor,' I say, squatting down by the chair and looking for a lever or catch to collapse it.

'Righto.'

I hear the two chatting as Tad's carried up the broad staircase. Dammit! I rattle the mysterious mechanism of the chair. The bloody thing won't fold. I pick it up and struggle after them, scuffing the wallpaper at the bend in the stairs. It weighs a ton.

In my embarrassment and relief at having Tad back in his chair I tip the driver far too much. 'Thank you very much,' he says, surprised. 'Have a nice evening.'

'Thank you,' I say, but it's Tad the remark is addressed to. I shut the door. Ruth's still in the lounge, giving the cushions a last-minute plump.

'Tidy me up a bit, will you?' Tad asks.

I tug at Tad's suit jacket, straightening it as best I can. His legs need crossing properly, and I watch as he lifts them with his hands. Right over left, the shoe wedged on to the foot-rest; his legs are as floppy as a string of sausages. 'Ready?' He seems no less nervous than I am. Having Tad to dinner was my idea, and Ruth isn't going to let me forget it. She'll happily cook, but there's no doubt on whose shoulders the success of this evening rests. He's your friend, she said simply. I just hope she's not too unpleasant to him.

Ruth has been trained all her life to disguise her feelings, but when she sees Tad her guard is lowered for a second and nothing except blank shock registers on her face. I can see her fumbling with her mental gear-stick, struggling to get it in gear. 'Hello.' She holds her hand out to be shaken, looking over Tad's head at me. She knew he was in a wheelchair, so what's the great surprise? Tad is grinning anxiously, waiting for a path to be cleared so he can push himself into the room. 'What a lovely place you have,' he says.

I snap into action and wheel him around Ruth and into the living-room. Ruth says nothing, just turns to watch. It's up to me, grinning like a baboon, to offer him a glass of wine. I check Tad's expression. He's wide-eyed with fright.

'Why don't you show Tad the flat while I finish off in the kitchen.' It's an order not a request; Ruth has already disappeared into the kitchen. I wheel him round the living-room and into the dining-room, showing him our bits and pieces. The upstairs bedroom and bathroom would have to be taken on faith: I'm not going to carry him upstairs. The tour of downstairs lasts about four minutes. Tad's interested, but with Ruth out of the room, we're both wondering what she's up to. She has finished the preparation; she's probably swigging cooking-wine from the bottle to bring herself back to her senses.

She comes in after a couple of minutes, a bright smile on her face, back into her hostess mode. 'Help me with the table, will you, James?' I'm right: she's been at the wine, I can smell it on her breath.

'I hope you like game,' she asks Tad.

'What game?' he asks. Ruth and I exchange glances.

'Joke?' Tad says hopefully into the silence. I smile thankfully, and there's a flurry of activity as the table is laid and the food brought in from the kitchen. As soon as I push the wheelchair up to the table I realise Tad won't be able to reach his plate. Ruth, as part of her home-decoration campaign, has bought a tall table with high stools: very chic, and very impractical. When I sit on my stool, Tad's face is just visible above the level of the table.

'Perhaps you can use a stool.'

He eyes it doubtfully. 'It looks awfully high.'

The only other table is the coffee-table, too low unless we sit on the floor.

'How about eating on our laps?' Both Ruth and I look at Tad's withered legs, no lap to speak of.

55

'Cushions?' he suggests.

Ruth puts two cushions under him as I lift him up, but still his chin is only on the level with the table-top. I mentally curse Ruth for buying such a stupid table. Tad is insistent that he'll manage and so Ruth serves the food. I'm feeling sick with guilt.

'Shall I cut up your food for you?' Ruth asks.

'He's not a baby, Ruth.'

'Neither am I dumb, James,' he says quietly. 'Thank you, Ruth. I can manage.'

Please, I pray, midway through the meal, if there is an intelligent Being up there, please forgive us the humiliation of serving such a fussy little rat-bird as a quail to someone who had to raise his arms above his head just to cut it up. We didn't know, we had no experience of disabled people, but ignorance is no defence. We invited another human being to our home and from nothing but laziness and lack of imagination, subjected him to trial by knife and fork.

Tad rises to the challenge and makes a joke of his clumsiness, but he's clearly uncomfortable. He's doing quite well, but Ruth is horrified.

'Do you go out to work, Ruth?'

'Yes. I work in an art gallery.'

'Oh, how lovely! I love art don't you?'

'Yes.'

Bullshit. Would she have bought a table and stool such as these if she was an art lover? She enjoys working in a gallery no more than I enjoy working in a library.

'Who is your favourite artist?'

'Gainsborough, probably.'

'So English!'

'So boring,' I say.

'Who do you like, James?'

'Egon Schiele,' I say. It's not true, but I know it'll annoy Ruth.

'Surely not,' Tad protests. 'Who would want to subject themselves to looking at all those mutilated bodies – ugh!'

I catch a flicker of surprise on Ruth's face. She's so predictable: I can read her mind as clearly as if she'd spoken out loud: who is this little person to talk about mutilation? She clearly finds him grotesque. Her eyes keep returning to Tad, studying him when she thinks he's not looking.

Dessert is no easier for him to eat. Though there is only six inches between his plate and his mouth, the angle he has to hold his arms makes it almost impossible to spoon anything successfully to his mouth and he declines to finish it. 'I'm a very light eater,' he says. 'Being so small.'

Conversation is hard going: I realise how much of Tad's and my time together is spent talking about sex. He's another person off his home ground: almost shy. He tries hard, solicitously asking Ruth questions, but she fields them with the minimum of effort and all three of us are waiting for the evening to end. Three-quarters through my charlotte russe, I unexpectedly cough, spraying droplets of dessert over the table-cloth. Ruth dashes into the kitchen for a wet cloth, relieved no doubt to get away for even a minute, and Tad and I look at each other. 'Sorry about this,' I say.

Coffee is a little less embarrassing, but Tad is clearly hurrying through it, and when he asks to use the phone to call a taxi, I can hear the relief in Ruth's voice when she says she'll do it. I have to take the wheelchair downstairs, which means installing Tad on the settee. I can't understand Tad's instructions at first, and I make dancing movements with my arms as I try to find a way to lift him out of his chair. I finally lift him by his trunk while he wraps his arms round me, swivelling himself so he can sit on my arm like a ventriloquist's doll. I can feel his tiny buttocks on my forearm. Tad is lighter than I thought, and I lower him on to the settee as though he might shatter at any moment.

'I'll just take this downstairs.' I rattle the wheelchair hopefully, but the whereabouts of the catch still remains a mystery so I wheel it on to the landing and bounce it down the steps. I can see from Ruth and Tad's relieved expressions when I return that all conversation has dried up in my absence. I lift Tad from the settee and Ruth sees us to the door, her smile fixed and glassy. 'Please

57

come and visit again,' she says. 'We'd love to see you.'
It's a transparent lie and we all know it.

'Thank you so much. I've had a gorgeous time.'

We say nothing for the first flight, but the closeness of
our faces is too much to bear in silence and we both begin
talking at once.

'You go first— '

'No, you— '

'I was going to say thank you for the evening.'

I stop at the bend in the stairs and rest a foot against
the banister. I suddenly realise how dependent Tad is
on my goodwill. There is nothing he could do to prevent
me dropping him over the edge down the stairwell. I
push the thought away. 'I'm sorry about the table,' I
mumble.

'That's all right. The food is what matters, and that was
wonderful. Proper home cooking.'

Putting Tad in the back of the taxi, he kisses my cheek
briefly. 'Now, you'd better go and face the music,' he
whispers. 'I'll see you soon.'

I wait until the taxi pulls away, and then wipe my cheek
on my sleeve.

'Don't ever do that to me again.' It should be a line from
Tad, but no – not Tad speaking. It's Hostess of the Year,
Ruth Partridge. Yes – that is her name.

It's hard for me not to hate her, but that's as much my
embarrassment and shame as her loathsomeness. I don't
want to row so I take my glass of wine and go upstairs.
Ruth follows me into the bedroom and we undress in
silence. I may be prepared to suffer in silence; Ruth,
however, still has some exorcism of her soul to do.

'I've never been so embarrassed in my life.'

'You expect me to care about you after what we've just
done to Tad?'

'Tad? What about me? How do you think I felt?'

I sling my clothes into the corner and get into bed. 'I
don't care how you felt.'

'It was awful,' Ruth persists. 'I could have died when
he couldn't reach the table.'

I wish you bloody did, I think. 'Anyway, it wasn't so bad. He liked the food.'

'He hated it.'

'At least it made a change from your boring friends.'

She paused in her undressing. 'That's it – turn it round like always.'

I hate you! I mouth at her back.

'Anyway – what do you mean? Boring friends. Who?'

'Alex, Mandy, Vanessa.'

'Just because they're normal people, doesn't mean they're boring.'

'Tad *isn't* a freak!' There's something in that word *freak* which dynamites a breach in my damned-up feelings. Relieved of the pressure of being held in, my emotions gush out into the room. I'm angry now, and it's all going to come out. 'You're so bloody conventional, aren't you! You make everything so boring!'

Ruth looks over her shoulder in surprise. 'What's going on? First you say that the food we eat is boring, now you blame my friends. What is it really?'

I don't say anything. Figure it out yourself, stupid cow.

'Come on. What is it – sex?'

'Bingo! It's as though we're married, but with none of the advantages and all of the disadvantages.' It's a line I've been toying with for some time, and it sounds like it.

I watch for her reaction but she turns away and takes a nightdress out of the drawer. Whenever Ruth wants to punish me in bed, she wears a nightie. She climbs into bed, pulling the duvet on to her side of the bed. 'What's that supposed to mean?'

I tug the bedclothes back. 'Our sex life? Are you happy with it?'

'I don't believe I'm hearing this. You actually want to know how I feel?'

I cross my arms over my chest and stare at the bulge of my feet under the bedclothes. I start counting the number of squiggles in the pattern of the duvet-cover. I hate myself for it, but I can't stop.

'I haven't been happy with our sex life for years,' she says.

A muscle on the side of my jaw twitches. 'Well, neither have I.'

I count thirty-eight squiggles before Ruth finally says something else. 'Is that it?' she says. 'End of conversation?'

I half turn towards her. 'It's just that you're so unadventurous.'

'*I'm* unadventurous?'

'Okay – *we're* unadventurous. We've got to do something.'

'So, make some suggestions. I can't read your mind.'

Words stick in my throat. My wishes are locked in a box located somewhere between my belly and my Adam's apple.

'Well?' she says.

'Hell? What are you talking about hell for?'

'I said *well*.'

'Ah.' I return to the squiggles of the duvet. 'I don't know what I want. What do you think?' I don't know whether I'm scared or just bad-tempered.

She takes a hand-mirror from the bedside table and studies herself as she smooths her eyebrows with a forefinger. 'I'd like to be tied up.'

'What do you mean?'

'You know – bondage.' Pause. 'Are you shocked?'

Shocked. My anger disappears as though it has never existed. Shocked? Of course I am. I feel as though I've been struck on the head with a cartoon frying-pan, stars and tweety birds circling my head; I can even hear the reverberations as it vibrates like a tuning-fork. I turn to look at Ruth, but she's still studying herself in the mirror. I'll never cease to be amazed at how little I understand women. I thought I knew everything about her. But tied up? Ruth? I try to compose myself before asking the next question.

'What do you mean, tied up? How?' I've never given bondage any thought. I'm not sure how it works.

She addresses her reflection in the mirror. She's not

quite as calm as she's trying to appear. 'You know, on the bed, with leather straps or something.'

'You want to be dominated, is that it?'

'I don't know. It just seems like an interesting thing to do. I've always been turned on by strong men – you know that.'

'So, you don't think I'm man enough without tying you up?'

'Do you want to talk about this, or do you want to fight?'

'All right, all right. I'll tie you up, if that's what you want.' Like hell I will, buster. It's sick.

'We don't have to do it. It was just an idea.'

'We'll do it,' I insist. I could just tie her up and leave her for good.

'What about you?' she asks.

'I don't know,' I say as vaguely as I can.

'Don't lie to me. What do you want to do? Tell me.'

I think back to the food fantasy, but decide against it. That's too far from home base: Ruth would only laugh at that. 'I thought of maybe having, you know, someone else . . .'

'A threesome?' She laughs. 'James – you surprise me.'

'Why?' My cheeks are suddenly on fire. Damn her – why does she always have to undermine me? I take *her* seriously.

'That's a very bold thing to suggest. I didn't think you'd have the courage.'

'Well, why not? What's wrong with that?'

'Don't get all defensive.'

We're going to get back into a row if we aren't careful. Ruth returns to her mirror and I study the water stain on the ceiling.

'If we did – who would you like the third person to be?'

My God, she's serious! 'Oh,' I say, vibrato, 'I don't know.'

'You *do* want to do it, don't you?'

Yes. Yes. Yes. Yes. 'I don't know. Do you?'

'I wouldn't mind.'

I have to concentrate to keep a straight face. I can't

61

believe what I'm hearing. Is there no limit to the depravity of this woman? Does nothing shock her?

'So, who shall we ask?'

'Someone you like, obviously.'

'Peter's nice,' she suggests.

'*Peter?*'

'Why not?'

'But he's a man!'

'I certainly hope so.'

'But I thought . . . I can't do it with another man.'

'Oh – you want a woman? What is it – can't stand the competition?' I know from her smile she's intentionally antagonising me.

'It's disgusting!' My toes curl under the bedsheets just at the thought of it. Sex with another man? Ugh! 'And anyway, what about Aids?'

'All right – how about Wendy, then?' she asks.

Wendy's a lesbian friend of Ruth's I met once at a party. Not a bad idea; she's not a gorgon as far as I remember.

'Would you like that?' I ask.

Ruth gives her answer with a quick two-step of the eyebrows. Would I *like that*? it says. Would I hell! It takes a second for the realisation to seep upward into my face. It hits my brain like a clapper hitting a firebell.

'You don't . . .' I grope for another word, but there isn't one, '*fancy* her?'

'Why not?' she says simply. A little too simply. I can tell from her shining eyes she's not as confident as she's trying to seem. But she presses her advantage. 'Why are you so shocked?'

'My girlfriend turns out to be a lesbian, and you think I shouldn't be shocked?'

'I'm not a lesbian just because I fancy another woman.'

Ugh – that word again. 'How long have you . . . fancied Wendy?'

'I don't know.'

'Come on, tell me. Since when?'

'Look. I thought you wanted this.'

'Not as much as you do apparently.' Ow! Don't we say foul things when we're scared!

'So you're blaming me just because I'm not as neurotic as you?'

'No.' I am of course. Blaming her and hating her and wishing I could be as blasé.

'If you're so surprised, then why did you suggest a threesome in the first place?'

That's a point. I don't answer.

'What did you expect – eh? Two women slaves serving their lord and master, King Dick?' She finds this enormously funny, and explodes into laughter.

I say nothing. That's precisely what I'd imagined.

7

Ruth phones me at work a couple of days later. 'Wendy has agreed,' she announces. 'As long as you don't come inside her – she said she couldn't stand that.'

Barely two days later: not even a blink in the life of the universe, and I find my fantasy in the hands of two other people, and out of control. 'She said that to you? My God! How could she be so brazen?' Shock, shock, shock. My heart is taking a hammering. I lower my voice, cupping my hand round the mouthpiece of the telephone. 'And anyway, what does she mean – *come*? Ejaculate?'

'She doesn't want you inside her. Your penis.'

'Because she's a lesbian?'

'Because she was raped when she was young.'

Even though I'm light-headed with fear at the thought of making love to Wendy, I bridle at the injunction against actual intercourse. What's wrong with my prick that another woman doesn't want it?

'So, she's coming to dinner?' I ask.

'Nothing special. Just a light meal to break the ice. Some wine, some music. Clean sheets on the bed.'

'Are you sure we want to do this?'

'Don't back out of it now, James. Take a chance for once in your life.'

I say goodbye and put the phone down. A chance? It's all right for her to speak – what are they risking? It's me who has to supply the penis. All they have to do is lie on their backs with their legs open; no performance anxiety for them. Ruth has no idea how big the risk is. But how could I expect a woman to understand how nervous and unreliable an erection is? The proud standard of honour the man leads into battle is likely to flag at the first obstacle. And performance anxiety is a fearsome obstacle.

One part of me knows that neither woman is all that interested in my penis. The fact is that Wendy finds the male member ugly and frightening, and Ruth is so looking forward to her first lesbian experience that she gives my sexual performance not a single thought.

Two preparatory glasses of wine only serves to numb me, so that when Wendy finally arrives I'm incapable of anything except an inane smile and a string of banal *non sequiturs*. Ruth, typically, has to choose that moment for a friend to ring up, and is on the phone in the bedroom, leaving me and Wendy to wade through a conversation with the consistency of treacle. I don't realise it until later, but it's not the alcohol that has stunned my brain into neutral: it's shock, plain and simple.

I'd anticipated struggling through the formality of the meal, but to my surprise I find myself enjoying it. Not the food – bean salad and crusty bread is not one of my favourites – but the company. And not Ruth's. Wendy it is, with her spiky blonde hair and her baggy Peruvian jumper and her track-suit trousers, who I find myself gradually opening to. And a surprise too: a feminist lesbian and me, face to face across a table; I should have been prickly and guarded as hell, but there's something in her bright face and easy manner that disarms me. She's far too nice to be one of Ruth's friends.

We're getting there: drinking steadily, relaxing well, but still on best behaviour by the time we've finished eating. I have to keep reminding myself why Wendy is here, the meat and potatoes of our dinner party. It's too bizarre, this sex business. What are we supposed to do? Dab the corner of our mouths with our serviettes, clear our throats and say, let's get on with it? I'd happily shelve the whole idea if somebody had the courage to bring it up. But that somebody would have to be me, and courage is not mine at this moment. And so for the millionth time in my life, the little toy boat that is me is sucked along in the wake of more formidable ocean-going liners. I just hope it isn't going to end with me being sucked down the plughole.

Ruth gets up from the table and dances one or two steps into the lounge, indicating for Wendy to follow. She does so, joining Ruth in front of the sofa, and there they are, hands on each other's hips, swaying to the music. I take a deep breath. This is it, then. The point we get serious. Gulp.

'Shall I make coffee?'

'Good idea.'

I pour coffee grains into the water compartment of the percolator by mistake, and have to wash it out and start again. By the time I've made a pot of coffee and put it on a tray with three cups, the lounge is ominously quiet, and I hesitate from going in. It's too quiet for anything else to be happening, and when I carry the tray through, sure enough, they're kissing on the sofa. I can hear the very walls, the carpet, the furniture all groan the same message: *it'll end in tears*. And there I stand, a tray of coffee in my hands, like a eunuch at an orgy.

'Do you take sugar?'

Ruth lifts her face from Wendy's. 'James, don't be an idiot.'

'No, thank you, James.' Wendy disengages herself from Ruth and takes the coffee cup from me. She takes a nominal sip. 'Mmm. Nice.'

I put the tray on the table in front of us, the tight knot in my chest melting a little from Wendy's kindness. Ruth is ignoring me.

'Would you like to dance?' She sees my hesitation. 'Come on.' Wendy gets up and takes my arm. 'I love this song.' She knows the words, and sings them softly into my ear

65

as we smooch. We shuffle in slow circles, eyes closed, like familiar lovers. I'm a bit drunk, but that's not the reason I'm clinging to her so closely. I'm just glad to have someone I can hold and not have to justify the touching. Wendy, in my opinion, is far too nice to be mixed up in such seedy goings on.

The song finishes and we hold each other at arm's length, assessing. I don't know what Wendy's thinking, but as I smile genuinely for the first time this evening, I find myself hoping the attraction is mutual. This is the sort of woman I need. I'd be happy to have sat together, finished the bottle of wine, chatted, maybe held hands. Just the two of us. But Ruth wants some action.

'Bring the coffee upstairs, James.' She reaches for Wendy's hand and pulls herself up off the sofa. Just five words and the secret friendship that me and Wendy have conjured flees like a flock of starlings stalked by a cat. She leads Wendy upstairs: man to her woman.

And guess who's left downstairs? I could no more walk up those stairs at that moment than fly up them.

Dammit! What to do? I decide to give them a chance to warm up. I look at the clock above the kitchen sink. I'll give them five minutes, then I'll go up. Or maybe ten minutes. I can hear laughter from the bedroom, first Ruth then Wendy. Is there any sound more excluding than that of shared and unexplained laughter? I slump on the sofa, certain that I'm the source of their merriment. Women – who would want them? Let them get on with it together, giggling away like a couple of schoolgirls.

'Bring the coffee up!' Wendy, God bless her, shouts from upstairs. I'm at the top of the stairs, coffee cups rattling, inside five seconds. I push open the door and slide into the candlelit room. They're lying on the bed, still – to my immense relief – fully clothed, and talking. There's nowhere for me to sit, but Wendy shifts over and pats the mattress beside her. She's on her belly, propping herself up on her elbows, Ruth is on her back. They're talking about a mutual friend of ours – Kate – who's having some sort of affair with an old Irish man. I remember hearing about her from Ruth some time before: apparently she burnt all her lover's paintings. I remember at the time citing *Hedda Gabler*, a reference Ruth hadn't understood. Apparently she's pregnant now.

I'm not the only one trying to act nonchalantly. Sprawled across the bed, arms and legs touching, Ruth is talking to the ceiling while Wendy listens, unhooking a strand of Ruth's hair from her dangly earring. The scene has a contrived feel to it: we're like models for an unknown Manet painting: *Déjeuner sur lit*. Certainly not the participants in an orgy.

Wendy has absentmindedly taken my hand, linking her fingers between mine as she carries on chatting to Ruth. I begin to relax, and the more I do so, the harder my erection becomes. I try to focus on their conversation, but the child tyrant is straining against my pants, clamouring to be let out. I try to control the throbbing in my groin, but to no avail.

We finish our coffee; we're running out of distractions. Soon there won't be anything for it except to get down to business. But who's going to make the first move? Not me.

'I'll go and put some music on,' I hear myself saying. I get up from the bed, slipping my hand in my trouser pocket to hide the bulge in my crutch, and go downstairs. I squat in front of the record rack, taking my time with my choice. My hand hovers over Sinatra's 'Songs for swinging lovers', but I decide against it. The pun would be lost on them. Mendelssohn's violin concerto wins in the end: a rather obvious choice perhaps, but it's passion, not subtlety that's called for. I put the volume up high and then go upstairs with our wine glasses and a fresh bottle of Mosel. And there they are: naked, as friendly as can be. I'd apologise and back out of the room if my hands weren't full, but I stand my ground, my jaw clamped shut. They're taking up the whole bed, so I sit in the wicker chair and watch them. Wendy is playing with Ruth's nipples. *My* nipples, I protest inwardly. Two bodies: Ruth's familiar slim and brown form, Wendy's bulkier, rounded like a Henry Moore sculpture. At first sight, it seems as though they're wrestling: it's just arms and legs and a sort of innocent tussle.

67

Wendy, to my disappointment, has the sort of body I don't like; large and lardy with almost invisible areolae. Ruth's enjoying herself, pinned under Wendy, who is now nibbling on those nipples, both of the women apparently unaware of my presence.

How do you react when before your very eyes you have the enactment of a long-cherished fantasy? Two women feasting on each other, the pages of *Playboy* come alive, your horniest blue movie in living Technicolor, smell thrown in for free? How do you react? You try hard to look nonchalant and bored. At least, that's what I do.

I endure it for about thirty seconds before I have to get up. I tell myself I'm leaving to get changed, and true, that's what I do, washing under my arms, brushing my teeth, changing into my dressing-gown, but it's a retreat. I've withdrawn from the fray, and even though I go back into the bedroom, I know the evening is over for me.

In the five minutes I've been out of the room, Wendy has worked down Ruth's body, until her head is between Ruth's thighs. I stand by the door, my dressing-gown tied, and watch the candle-light gleaming off Wendy's broad white shoulders as she performs her mysterious mouth-to-mouth resuscitation. Mendelssohn is working himself up into a frenzy downstairs and Ruth is groaning obscenely.

I go downstairs and take the record off. It's getting too frantic and complicated; I want something angry. The Stones. I put it on loud, but I'm halfway up the stairs before I realise what I've done.

I-I can't get no-o sa-tis-fac-

I'm back to the record-player in two bounds, zipping the stylus off the record with the sound of tearing cloth. There's silence except for the hum of the hi-fi and the rising scale of orgasmic shrieks coming from upstairs. Ruth has hit the jackpot and wants the whole world to know it.

Wendy comes downstairs five minutes later. She's wearing her trousers and Ruth's blouse. I'm surprised to see her so soon. Isn't she going to get a turn? She sits beside me on the sofa and lights a cigarette. She offers me one, and though I haven't smoked for years, I take one.

'How was it?' I ask, nodding at the ceiling.

Wendy runs her index finger along my jawline to my lips, and then taps twice. 'Why did you want this, James?'

'I don't know. Why did you agree to it?'

'I like Ruth.'

'As simple as that?'

'It's only bodies, James.'

'Is it?'

She takes my hand. 'I don't think this was such a good idea, do you?'

I want to tell her it was Ruth's idea, but I remember it wasn't. It was mine, and how many other men in this world? *Lesbian girls in love*, Randy Ruth just can't get enough. Watch as willing Wendy goes down on her again and again. Fully uncensored hot action.

I take my hand back from her. 'Ruth said you were raped when you were young.' Damn! Why did I have to say that?

'I was raped and sodomised by my father when I was seven.'

It's as though I've been punched in the stomach: the caught breath, the sudden tears in my eyes.

'Was he found out?' I say at last.

'I never told anyone. He said that if I did, he'd sew up my vagina, so that I'd explode because I wouldn't be able to go to the toilet. I believed him – after all, he was a doctor.'

I close my eyes. 'How could someone do that? And your father?'

Wendy shrugs. 'Abuse breeds abuse.'

'But your father?'

'James, please, let's not talk about this now.'

'I'm sorry.' I take her hand and squeeze it. *But your father?*

'Come up to bed. You're tired.'

I lead the way up the stairs. At the doorway of the bedroom, I stop. 'Do you really hate men?'

'Not any more – just rapists.'

Ruth's sprawled asleep across the bed, snoring quietly. Looking at her untidy body I realise that if I ever loved her, it was so long ago and so brief it might as well never have happened. There's nothing there now for me. She's an oddly masculine stranger lying in my bed. I sleep in my dressing-gown that night, Wendy's body between mine and Ruth's.

8

'Tell me about last night.'

I sketch out the basics of the previous evening, and then fall silent. Tad had rung the library in the afternoon to hear the news of the orgy, as he insisted on calling it, but I'd side-stepped his questioning. At first I hadn't wanted to see Tad after work, but I'd allowed myself to be persuaded. Even though stones and fishes might fall out of my mouth when I speak, I have to talk to someone. And so here I am; an evening with my father Confessor.

'A more spectacular flop than your first attempt, by the sounds of it.' Tad is in a cheerful mood; if I'm seeking sympathy, I'm clearly in the wrong place.

'Thanks for the encouragement.' I scowl at him. It's been a bad day: even before I'd opened my eyes in that strange bed, I'd felt the familiar taint of a blighted day ahead. It was only an act of will that had held the floods and earthquakes at bay.

'How did Ruth like last night?'

'Very well, apparently.' I'd woken at dawn to find the two women asleep in each other's arms, Ruth still snoring. I'd slid out of bed, dreading them waking up, and fled the house, unshaven and unbreakfasted. I had to spend two hours in the park before the library opened.

'Do I detect a note of resentment?'

'Bugger off, Tad.'

He smiles and bats those long eyelashes at me. 'Tell me, Jimmy boy – the very worst. What's going on inside your dear little head?'

'Not a lot.'

'Oh now!' he says camply. 'You don't expect me to believe that.' He waits for me to say something, but I'm staying resolutely silent.

'You look just the teeniest bit put out,' he says after a minute.

'Do I?'

'The last time I heard from you it sounded as though the penile roadshow was coming to town. Lock up your daughters – here comes my bullet!'

I snigger in spite of myself.

'And now?' He pulls a long face, presumably in honour of me.

'It didn't work out like I'd thought.'

'What were you expecting?'

'I don't know.'

'How was it? Seeing two women together.'

'Okay,' I lie.

'That's why you joined in with such gusto, is it?'

I shrug.

Tad throws his hands up. 'This is like getting blood out of a stone. Help me, James – I'm beginning to talk to myself.'

How did I feel seeing two women together? Disapproving? Disdainful? More than that. I'm appalled at myself – I've got a degree in Sociology, for heaven's sake. Lesbianism is fully respectable, almost fashionable. So, why the . . .

'I was disgusted,' I hear myself say.

'At yourself?'

For once in my life I wish I could say yes, but the truth is, I'm still reeling from seeing two women so contentedly feasting on each other.

I shake my head.

'So the idea's fine, but the act isn't?' he says.

'You weren't there.'

'A pity.' Tad watches me in silence for a moment. 'It sounds as though you're jealous because Ruth had a good time and you didn't.'

That's the killer: that Ruth should have enjoyed her freedom so completely, whilst I cowered with slack penis

71

behind the settee. 'I can't believe that women could be so – '

Tad waits for the word and when none comes, he suggests his own. 'Horny?'

'Immoral.'

'Your brains are in your balls, James. You've ceased to make sense.'

'But – '

'But you can't stand not being wanted. Do you know why most men hate and fear lesbians? Because lesbians refuse to worship at the shrine of God's greatest creation – the penis. In the androcentric universe the only approved function of the female sex is the serving of the phallus. And, James my dear, the phallus is far more than the male organ.' Tad looks at me slyly. 'Admit it – you're jealous.'

'Bollocks,' I say simply. Not that I don't agree.

'And to add spice to the soup, it sounds as though Ruth might have doubled her sexual options since last night.'

'She's a complete mystery to me. I have no idea what she wants any more.'

'Apart from being tied up, that is.'

'Give me a break, Tad.'

'What was it Freud said to Marie Bonaparte?' Tad lifts his eyes and recites the quote as though it's written on the ceiling. *The great question that has never been answered and which I have not yet been able to answer, despite my thirty years of research into the feminine soul, is "What does a woman want?"'* His gaze drops to look at me. 'What does a *man* want? That's what I want to know.'

What does a man want? Quite simple: to impregnate as much of the universe as he can. Whether this is actualised by sperm or sublimated by phallic space-rockets, the idea's still the same: he who fertilises the most is the winner. Hence the number of spermatozoa: one per ejaculation for every man, woman and child in the United States. Twenty-five ejaculations and you have the population of planet earth.

So, ladies – never trust a man who says he just wants to be your friend. *Just*. Unless he's irredeemably gay, the winking one-eyed God tyrant will have its designs on your uterus. And don't be concerned about your attractiveness: all females of child-bearing capability are attractive to a man with an erection. If a man calls you sister, beware: his overtures are incestuous. Some men will deny this. Some men will deny the existence of the sun if they think it'll get them laid.

There's a message on the answer phone from Ruth. *'I won't be home till late. I'm at Wendy's. Don't wait up.'*

At Wendy's? What the hell's going on? I replay the message and listen to the tone of her voice, but it gives nothing away. I've never visited Wendy, but I know her house by reputation: communal living arrangements, four or five women – lesbians, I presume – living in organic sisterhood. It's not Ruth's style: far too sincere for her sceptical sensibilities. So, what the hell is she doing there?

I open a can of baked beans and sit in front of the television with a fork, shovelling them into my mouth. I watch an American sitcom for a few minutes and then jab the remote control, flicking from channel to channel. All boring. I turn the sound down and wander around the ground floor with my can of beans, humming to myself. I nose around the bookcase, pausing to sniff at the bowl of pot pourri. It's supposed to smell of roses, but to me it has the unpleasant aroma of air freshener. I wish Ruth wouldn't waste the housekeeping money on such rubbish. I wander into the tiny hall and open the corner cupbord, munching on my beans. Bending at the knees, I squint into the corner. There's a pair of shoes I thought I'd thrown away, and an old tennis racket, now warped beyond use. I consider picking it up and having a trial swing, but my hands are full, so I push the door shut with my foot and go through to the kitchen. The kitchen walls need washing: Ruth likes a clean house, but not enough to scrub the walls or floors, and I don't care one way or the other. Over the years, grease spots have formed an abstract expressionist mural above the cooker, not unpleasant in appearance if you don't consider the nature of the pigment. I finish the beans and drop the empty tin into the bin. Pausing to burp, I open a bottle of lager and go upstairs to the bedroom.

Strange; three years we've lived together, three years in this house, and I've never really looked through her chest of drawers. It stands in the corner, its surface cluttered with make-up and a whole forest of spray cans, enough CFCs there to burn a hole the size of Tasmania in the ozone layer. This, if ever one exists, is the locus of Ruth's private life. I more or less know the contents of the top drawer; I sift through them, however, looking with a new eye: a large pink hair-drier, an unused powder pack, a bottle of scent, emery boards, a sequined dress purse, and a paper bag from the clinic containing her contraceptive pills. Ruth and I had relied on condoms for the first year of our relationship, but now she's taking no chances. Accidentally pregnant once, she's determined it won't happen again. Now she takes her nightly pill as devoutly as I used to kneel by my bedside to say my prayers.

The second drawer contains her underwear: pants on one side, bras and the rest on the other. I rummage through the silky material, enjoying the coolness between my fingers. Thrusting both hands into the drawer, I pick up a handful of underwear and bury my face into it, smoothing the material against my cheek. So feminine and mysterious. I select a silvery-white pair of underpants and stare at the faint stain in its groin before dropping them back with the rest. A strip of black lace catches my attention and I tug at it until a suspender belt appears. When did she get this? Ruth with stockings and suspenders? She's never worn anything like this for me. I study it to see if it has been worn, but it looks new. I hold it against my waist, and then hide it at the back of the drawer.

I skip the third drawer: skirts and jumpers, and go on to the bottom drawer: miscellanea. I sit on the floor and pull the entire drawer out. This is the real stuff: the emotional flotsam of a lifetime. There's a pair of child's ballet shoes, a stiff-backed envelope with *Certificates* written across it. I find three airmail envelopes addressed in my hand to Ruth.

They're postmarked Detroit, San Diego and Cheyenne, dated October 1985. My holiday in the States. As I slide the letter out from the first envelope, a dried leaf flutters on to my lap. I ignore the leaf and read the four pages of blue onion-skin paper, struggling occasionally with the tiny handwriting. I had loved her, this person from 1985. I read the other two letters; wordy travelogues for the most part, and gushing with homesickness and romanticised lust. This was when the relationship was at its best: new and exciting; like our lives. I'm surprised that Ruth has cared enough to keep the letters all this time. At the bottom of the drawer is a snapshot of us both, pulling faces at the camera on a beach; on the back, written in biro, the legend, *Brighton '86*. I dimly remember the picture being taken. I study the faces: they seem to be having a good time, whoever they are. Were they still in love then? A lacquered Japanese box contains stubs of opera tickets: *Così fan tutte*, a silk hankie, an out-of-date bus pass, a five-peseta coin. What does this say? I check the price of the opera seats. Rear amphitheatre: cultured but poor.

I save the sheaf of curled black and white photographs to the last. They're held together by an elastic band which snaps when I try to slip it off. I spread the photographs on the floor. I haven't seen these before: Ruth as a little girl, hardly recognisable now. There's a shot of her on the back of a pony, hair tucked into her riding hat, the unbroken and confident smile of a privileged child. A picture of her in some ski resort, Mummy and Daddy and a couple of others standing around in silly hats. These are the roots she had grown from: Home Counties money, private school, winter holidays abroad; the roots she's more and more heading back to. She had self-consciously slummed it with me, but her real colours are showing through now: this present life isn't her, and neither is Wendy. There are two-dimensional people and there are three-dimensional people: Ruth is all surface; when I look into her eyes I see nobody at home. Wendy, on the other hand, has an extra dimension: the dimension of suffering. Ruth has never really known suffering; not that her life has been a particularly smooth ride, but there is an absence of imagination in her that precludes empathy. Life is straightforward and follows clearly defined rules: you try to get what you want, tread on as few toes as possible, and nobody is to blame but yourself if you fail. Her parents had done a good job; another no-nonsense, Conservative-voting child of minor aristocracy to join her insufferable brothers and sisters. She was always pretty, though, this other person.

What the hell did she see in me? And why stay with me for so long? I shuffle the photographs together and then put them back in the drawer. I'm a librarian, not a commodity broker. No money, no prospects; there's a nice flat, thanks to Mother's will, but precious little else. It wasn't always that way. Once, I could have passed for one of them. Not any more.

I try to replace everything where it had been, but I can't remember the order, so I just stuff the contents back randomly. I want to stay up until she comes back, but at two o'clock I can't stay awake any longer and go to bed. I wake in the night, and reach out to feel the bed beside me, but it's cool and empty.

9

I'm called to the phone the next morning. It's Ruth. 'Where were you last night?' I ask her, suddenly indignant. 'I was worried.'

'I stayed at Wendy's.'

I feel a weight drop into my intestines as though something inside me has sagged. 'You could have let me know.' Nothing. 'I stayed up half the night waiting for you.'

There's a studied silence: Ruth's not going to apologise, no matter how much time I give her. 'Why didn't you come home last night?'

'We went for a meal and then it was too late to come back.'

'Just you and Wendy?'

'And a couple of others from the house.'

Resentment and fear and jealousy are all jostling for attention, but it's self-righteousness I select. 'Well, I hope you enjoyed yourself.' Like hell I do. I hope she has got food poisoning. 'So, will I see you tonight?'

'Of course.' I hear an intake of breath, more a sigh than a gasp, and then she says, 'James— '

I cut her short. The tone of that single word – *James* – I'd heard before: ominous, heavy with portent. 'There's someone waiting to be served,' I lie. 'I've got to go. See you later.' I put the phone down before she can say anything.

For the next few days we have an unspoken stand-off, the unfinished sentence hanging between us like a disconnected telephone wire. I could have supplied the missing words for her: *James, we've got to talk*; but both Ruth and I feign unawareness of any incompleteness. And meanwhile, I suspect that whatever process Wendy has set in motion, is still at work.

I make sure that we see little of each other, arranging it so that I don't get home until eight thirty, by which time Ruth is usually in front of the television. Wendy isn't mentioned, and neither is our night together. I'm dying to know how it was for Ruth, but I can't bring myself to ask her. What if she enjoyed it more than she expected? Where would that leave me?

The messages, however, are clear enough. She's off sex. I know I'm not imagining Ruth's coolness in bed, the way she makes a point of not touching me. I want to reclaim her, mark my territory inside her again, but she has posted a 'keep off sign'. And trespassers definitely *will* be prosecuted.

I can feel the needle of my internal barometer swing towards 'stormy'. Something is on its way. I just hope that it will pass without too much devastation.

When I come home from work on Thursday, I find Ruth in the bedroom, getting changed.

'Going out?' I ask.

'A group of us from Wendy's house are going to a nightclub.'

I can hear the rumble of distant thunder. 'A nightclub?'

'You know. Music, dancing. Fun.'

'Tonight?'

'Yes, James,' she says sarcastically. 'Tonight.'

'And will you be home?'

'I don't know. Don't wait up for me.' She shimmies into her tight-fitting raw-silk dress, smoothing the material over her thighs, assessing her reflection in the mirror. She looks stunning.

'You're seeing a lot of Wendy.'

Ruth doesn't answer. She's having trouble with her earring and I watch as she fiddles with the butterfly clip. Her dress is undone, exposing a V of her back down to the top of her buttocks.

'Did you sleep with her when you stayed last time?'

She's got her earring in, and she turns towards me. 'You're paranoid, aren't you? If you don't trust me, come along with me – there's nothing stopping you.'

'Except an invite.'

'Don't be so pathetic.'

'Anyway, isn't it just women only?' Lesbians, I mean.

'Of course not.' She struggles with the zip of her dress. I wait for her to ask me to help, but she's determined to manage on her own, so I go downstairs. The telephone is just waiting there for me, so I dial Tad's number. He's in, and delighted to have me come over. I tell him I'll be half an hour, and then leave the house without telling Ruth. Let her worry for a change.

The relief of being with Tad is immediate: I have an ally, someone I don't have to share with Ruth. But I'm uncomfortable as well. 'Something's going on,' I tell Tad. 'She's seen Wendy twice this week.'

'And you don't trust her?'

'No, I don't.' I don't tell him why. I'm barely aware of the reason myself, but there's something threatening in the exclusive femaleness of Wendy's world. Two women together, and you have a sorority, five women together and it's a conspiracy. 'She's been so offhand since the weekend,' I say. Not offhand, I suddenly realise, *assertive*.

'Poor James.'

'We were doing fine until Wendy came along.'

Tad laughs. 'You were doing appallingly.'

He has changed the picture on the wall, and I stand up to study it; a Renaissance Madonna has taken the place of Karen Finley, a fat and disproportionate child Christ in her arms, looking more like a tiny middle-aged man than a baby. I frown at the vapid expression on the Madonna's face: I've seen that look before somewhere. I suddenly remember: the icon in the school chapel. I turn to Tad. 'Do you think Ruth's turning into a lesbian?' I say.

Tad shrugs.

'Why else would she be seeing Wendy so much?' I suddenly realise I'm afraid of Wendy, of her power over Ruth. 'I don't know what to do.'

'Ban Ruth from leaving the house?'

'I'm serious!' I feel nauseous with humiliation at the prospect of Ruth having an affair with another woman. 'I mean, if she's bored with me, perhaps it's sex.'

'Perhaps you could buy her a bondage suit, you mean?' Tad says.

'I wish you'd drop that, Tad.'

'I doubt that the problem's between your legs, James my dear. And ditto the answer.' He smiles. 'Time to grow up, James. Twenty-nine, nearly thirty – time to face the devil.'

'What devil?'

Tad holds a spoon out and I bend forward to look at my reflection in its convex surface. I stare at the ovoid head and bulbous nose and say nothing. But as I sit back down in my chair, I decide there's nothing left for it. I have to seduce her.

I wake up the next morning to find her asleep next to me. I didn't hear her come in; she must have been very late. I watch her, propped up on one elbow, and plot my next move. I'm losing her, I know it. Unless I do something soon, I'll lose her completely.

I get dressed and then go downstairs for breakfast. I need to bring the romance back into our lives. That's it: cook her a meal, buy her some sexy underwear, some flowers. Talk more, listen better. Not once do I ask myself why I should want to keep her. The answer, had the question been asked, is simple: security. I'm afraid of being alone. If Ruth leaves me it would be like living in a house without a roof or walls. I would be able to function more or less as I had done before, but it would all be in a different context. There would be no human scale to my actions; it would just be me and the enormous night sky: draughty, exposed, susceptible to rain. Without the perimeter of another person, my life, my future would be unbounded. I would be free to fuck who I wanted, to murder, to go crazy. And that scares me.

At ten o'clock I take up tea and toast to her. She doesn't want to wake up, and I have to shake her.

'Rise and shine, darling.'

'What's going on?' she mumbles.

'Breakfast.'

She stretches and yawns and then opens her eyes. 'What's this in aid of?' she says, indicating the breakfast tray. It's at least two years since I've brought her breakfast in bed.

'I just want us to be nice to each other for a change,' I say.

Ruth frowns and pushes herself up in bed. I make her sit forward while I plump up the pillows. She lies back in them and I brush the hair out of her eyes as though she's ill and incapable of doing it herself. 'There.' I pour out the tea and smile at her. I'm enjoying this, playing doctors and patients.

I ask about the nightclub: she enjoyed herself, got the night bus back to Hammersmith at about three. I can tell from the redness of her eyes that she'd drunk a lot the night before. She sips her tea. 'We've got to talk, James.'

I knew it. 'What about?'

'Us.'

'Go ahead.'

'I've been talking a lot to Wendy.'

I hold my breath. I have no idea what's coming next, but I brace myself for it anyway. She carefully puts the cup down on the tray. 'I don't know if I can take any more.'

'More of what?'

'This relationship.'

I say nothing.

'It hasn't been right for ages.'

'We get on all right.'

'We don't. We put up with each other. I don't want to live like this any more.' There's an edge to her voice, tears behind her words.

'It's not so bad.'

'It's dead, James, admit it.'

'We can do something about that,' I say, meaning the breakfast in bed, the plumped-up pillows, the attentiveness.

'But you don't want what I want. I don't think you ever have. We lead separate lives. We hardly share anything any more.'

It feels as though there's a mist around my head, obscuring my thought. I try squinting, but it doesn't help. 'I don't want this relationship to end,' I say eventually.

'But, James, it has been at an end for years.'

'Not at an end – just boring.' I can hear the anxiety in my own voice. 'What will I do if you leave me?'

'It won't be the end of the world,' she says.

'But how will I live?'

'You've got the flat.'

'But how . . . ?' The shopping, washing, housework? Cooking? A hot flush of panic surges into my face. How do people manage on their own? 'We just need to try a bit harder, put the romance back into it, and everything will be okay.' It's a weak line, and we both know it. 'We've had our bit of freedom. Let's not rock the boat.'

She shakes her head, covers her face with her hands for a moment. When she lowers her hands and looks at me, there's a new seriousness in her eyes. She means what she's saying.

'Eat your toast,' I say. 'I'm going shopping.'

I take the bus into town and spend the rest of the morning shopping for the final onslaught. I buy sexy underwear for Ruth: a pair of black satin pants and stockings to go with the suspenders I found. I'll wrap the package properly when I get home: it is to be a secret, a present, a lure. I'm desperate; I must be to endure the embarrassment of shopping for women's lingerie.

We'll have spaghetti bolognese, candle-light, red wine, carnations in a vase. I realise I should have told her to keep the evening free: I should have learned by now the danger of surprises.

When I come home I find Ruth's suitcases side by side in the hall like obedient dogs waiting to be let out. She's in the bedroom, and I bound up the stairs, two at a time.

'What's going on?' I ask. I know damn well what's going on.

'I'm going to stay with Wendy.'

'For how long?'

'This is it, James.'

I can't say anything. There was always a possibility that she'd do this, but not at such speed.

'There's a spare room at Wendy's. She offered and I accepted. I'm leaving.'

'Just like that?'

'I'm sorry,' she says, but I can see from her face that she bloody well isn't.

'So you're going to live with Wendy, is that it?'

'Not in the way you mean.'

'Pull the other one.'

'Grow up, James! I'm not going to start a relationship with Wendy. I'm not going to start a relationship with anyone. I've had enough of relationships. I want to live for myself for a change.'

I know I'm being absurd, but I can't stop myself. 'Bullshit! You can't wait to get into Wendy's pants, that's what it is.' I know it's not true. I know I'm being brattish and ugly, but the temptation to hurt her is too great to resist.

'Nothing is happening with Wendy and me.'

'Then why are you going?'

'Why do you want me to stay? Eh?' She's angry now, and I'm glad. 'We've got nothing.'

'That's not true. We've been together four years – doesn't that count for anything?'

She casts her eyes irritably over the room as though following the erratic path of a fly. 'I just can't stand your self-indulgence any more.'

'What?'

She turns to me. 'You're a child, James – you've never grown up. You want the whole world to dance attendance on you.' She's so angry, she's almost crying. 'Well, I've had it. I'm a human being too. I've got rights – I deserve more than this.' She's got her overcoat on. She's ready to go.

I follow her downstairs, wanting to protest, but incoherent in my shock. She's not the only one who's angry. It would be so easy to push her now. I see her falling, bouncing, hitting her head against the bottom step. There isn't enough of a drop to be fatal, so I would have to finish her off, strangle her, or beat her head against the wall until her skull caved in. I imagine her eyes on me, her hands round mine trying to pull them away from her throat.

'Can't we sort this out?' I say.

'It's too late to save it, James.'

I follow her to the door. 'I can change.'

She shakes her head without turning to look at me.

'What do you want from me, Ruth?'

'My freedom.'

'Well go,' I snap, suddenly vicious. 'I'm not stopping you. Go on – bugger off!'

I watch her as she bends to buckle the suitcase, ready to pounce on anything she says, but she's not going to feed me lines any more. She's serious, she's made up her mind. I can't believe it: she's going to leave me. *Leave me*.

'I'll share you with Wendy,' I hear myself saying. She ignores me.

'I've taken as much of my stuff as I can carry. I'll have to come back for the rest some time.'

I just want her to go now, be rid of her.

'I'm sorry, James.'

As she opens the door, her suitcase becomes trapped and she nearly falls over it. I leap forward to help; not for the sake of her safety, but to speed her departure.

10

I pour myself a Martini and sit on the rim of the bath while it fills. My mind is working too quickly to keep up the pace. I'm scared, I know that much, but excitement is in there somewhere. Though the larger part of me is appalled at the prospect of being alone, one part of me is glad she has gone. My emotional synapses are burning out; I can't think straight. I stare into the rushing water and try to evaluate my altered social landscape. I can have girlfriends. Hurray! I'll have to make new friends. Boo! I can eat when and what I want. Hurray! Who will cook for me? Boo! I can rent pornographic videos and watch them all day if I want. Hurray! Who will be there at the end of the day? Boo!

I'm tempted to blame Tad for precipitating this change: if it hadn't been for him and his interfering, I would still be with Ruth, as happy and mundane as ever.

Happy? I've forgotten the meaning of the word. I'd been with Ruth for four years, and somewhere in there numbness had crept up on me unawares. I feel nothing keenly any more: happiness, enthusiasm, challenge; I'm living a muted grey-brown existence and for want of something to compare it with, I thought this was just the process of maturation: the muddying of my bright tangy colours into a nutritionless gravy. My rage and my grief had been so well reined in, that if they show their heads at all, it is only as disappointment and irritability. My life is still here, of course it is, as desperate and vital as ever, but I have disengaged myself from myself, lowered my sights, and dug in for the duration. All in the name of growing up.

I had turned Ruth into a commodity. We both had. If either of us were to salvage our decency and dignity, she needed to go. I needed the slap in the face of being left, she needed to be with people who demanded respect.

I had only stayed with her because I was afraid of the work involved in engineering a worthwhile life for myself. For as long as I was attached to Ruth, my enjoyment of life could be safely vicarious.

There is a certain species of angler fish, the male of which attracts a mate with a sort of luminous bait that hangs in front of him. Once coupled, the male attaches himself permanently to the side of his mate, and for the rest of his life he lives off her bloodstream, ceasing to act or fend for himself.

I had become that fish.

Sunday was always a struggle between me and Ruth: she was for activity and housework; for me it was a day of complete withdrawal and indolence. Now as I stretch my legs into the vacant half of the bed, I realise I can do exactly as I please. Let her go off and live with her coterie of dykes and their pink bloody triangles and their Greenham Common mentality. James Morrison, this is your life, and I'll do as I bloody well please.

Toast, coffee, and the Sunday paper – could life ever be so simple and satisfying again? The spring sunshine springs through the slatted blinds, the birds twitter in the branches outside the bedroom window. God is in his heaven, and I have the paper all to myself.

I read the whole thing; starting at the book reviews and working back to the front page. By three o'clock my eyes are smarting with the effort, so I break for lunch: toast and marmalade and a pint of fresh coffee.

I watch the afternoon film in bed on our old black and white telly: *Wuthering Heights*. I can feel the tears wanting to come within minutes; Olivier, his hair dyed black, tormented by his love for Cathy, is everything I could be, am in fact. There is that in me: windswept, fatal, desperate. Love, someone to love as greatly as Romeo loved Juliet, Orpheus loved Eurydice, Anthony loved Cleopatra. The phone rings just after four, but I unplug it: today is for me only. I want to weep and wail when Cathy dies at the window, limp in Heathcliff's arms, but the most I can achieve is a moistness around the eyes. I haven't cried since I was a kid, not even at Mother's funeral. It's as though all the tears have been locked in a metal chest, and I've lost the key.

I drift in and out of sleep for the rest of the afternoon, trying to avoid the obvious agenda. There would be the whole palaver of informing our friends of our change in status. Let Ruth do it – most of our friends are hers. Who have I got exclusively for myself? Jerry in Australia. Bernice in the States. Patrick in Manchester. Mine only because Ruth has never met them. But I haven't seen Jerry for six years; Bernice occasionally phones, but not often enough to be of any use. Patrick has probably forgotten me. Why are my friends all so far away? Why have I sabotaged my social life?

I sink deeper under the duvet. This is it then: freedom. What about girlfriends then? Now *that*'s a word I haven't used for a while: with Ruth it was 'the relationship', she was 'the woman I live with', or 'my friend'. Most of the time I side-stepped classifications. But now that I'm on my own again, the whole ritual of courtship would have to start all over. How did it work? Boy meets girl: the chase, the wooing, struggling to undo unfamiliar bra straps, the thrill of the first magical contact with secret places, the final anxious bedding. But I had seen white hairs recently, few enough still to be plucked out one by one, but soon there would be too many to ignore. I'm getting older – it has to be faced. Three months from thirty. Alone again, no prospects, no money. A *frisson* of panic dispels any last sleepiness. Thirty. Keats had been dead five years by the time he was thirty. Rimbaud had been burned out for ten years, Shelley was breathing his last.

How did the relationship get off the ground with Ruth? Introduced by mutual friends – Jason and his ugly sister, wasn't it? That's right, their parents were away, it was a sunny Sunday and we were barbecuing in the garden. The kids running wild, treading the border plants to smithereens, somebody breaking a greenhouse pane with a cricket ball. Gosh – jolly japes with the upper crust. A long time ago.

Where are our parents now? Half of the couples that peopled that scene are parents themselves now. Mummy and Daddy, as Ruth called hers, were in fact the Right Honourable, Sir Robert and Lady Jean Partridge: far superior breeding to the humble Morrison clan, even though we probably matched them pound for pound. Bob and Jean, I called them, much to Ruth's chagrin. They were nice enough in their own out-of-touch way, decent and harmless, the very best of the English upper-middle classes. They led charmed lives, as did their darling only-daughter, Ruth, the Bitch of Basingstoke. Fresh-faced graduates: Ruth from Oxford, me from a yellow-brick Poly, we were both at our flirtatious, intellectual best when we met. She was a bright, hard star and I was her willing satellite. I remember the introduction, the immediate attraction. But how did the wooing start? Who made the first move? Ruth probably. That's right – she asked for my phone number, and I cringed because my bedsit had no phone and I daren't give her Mother's number, even though they were virtually neighbours in Hampstead.

But somehow we managed to get in touch. And then the cinema, more parties, our first night together. All the dancing around we did. Spending an hour in front of the mirror, and a whole week's wages in an expensive restaurant. The posturing and straining into heroic shapes like a prima ballerina and her principal. Can it ever happen again? Can I ever endure such a test again? I can see it now: I would die a bachelor and a masturbator.

I wake at dusk, the light from the TV flickering across the ceiling like shadows from a log fire. I lie for a few minutes straining to catch sounds: a distant ambulance, the muffled roar of traffic from the Shepherd's Bush roundabout, next door's water cistern filling. She'll be back; surely. We've been together too long for her to just walk out like that. We have problems, of course we have, but who doesn't? I reach beside the bed and plug the telephone back in. Perhaps she had been trying to phone earlier; perhaps she wants to reconcile. I hold my breath and listen again. Nothing.

I get up and put my dressing-gown on. I'm still groggy from my nap and sit down at the foot of the bed and stare at the TV screen. Even with the sound off, I know the programme – *Songs of Praise*. I recognise the stance: righteous faces tilted heavenward, mouths opening and closing as though chewing on manna. The camera roves through the pews: picking out the most photogenic of the choirboys; dwelling on Mrs Pewit in her new hat, focusing on proud Mr Bradford, church warden, belting out the hymn with everything he has. The camera lifts from the congregation to the stained-glass window of the nave: beatific angels gazing upwards at a risen Christ. The camera zooms in until the face fills the screen. Pretty Jesus, the Lamb of God.

With my index finger I stab the off button and watch the holy image implode and disappear into a white dot, and then I go and run a bath.

I settle down with my third round of toast: melted cheese this time, and munch through my Sunday dinner while, at the foot of my bed, David Attenborough tells me about dinosaurs. Truly bizarre, the imagination behind these preposterous shapes: crests and horns and frills and spikes; and all that time ago. One hundred and ninety-eight million years before ape-like Adam. Just think of that. I don't want to believe in God, but sometimes I'm tempted.

I've seen the film that comes on afterwards, and two of the other channels feature serious men talking politics or business or something. Channel Four has a limp comedy that Ruth had occasionally watched, so I leave it on while I leaf through the colour supplement.

Bodies, that's all it is. The food articles, the adverts for cars and jewellery and whisky and fitted kitchens: all things to put in your body, or on it, or things to put your body in, or things to transport your body, or make it feel better, or look better. And looking good counts for a lot. They *are*

88

pretty, some of these models, but from the other side of the camera it's all safety-pins and hair-spray. If such girls really exist, how come I've never met one? Why don't I know anyone as gorgeous as this girl in the perfume ad? The truth is, women always seem more beautiful at a distance. Close up, they always spoil the impression with bad teeth, or a grating voice. I turn from advert to advert, comparing the women. There's a definite image: sophisticated, rich, successful; just fantasies: no more real than the Madonna. And the men: aftershave wearers, squash players, yuppies. If these are the test of manhood, I've failed.

I get out of bed and assess the image that stares back at me from the full-length mirror by the door. Clothed properly, with a good haircut, and seen through squinting eyes, I could pass for one of them. And thirty isn't so bad; the mature look is in: brogues and corduroy and a slightly unusual hairstyle. A house in the country, an open-top sports car, a DJ for the occasional night at the opera. Cuff-links, twelve-year whisky, a CD player, J. S. Bach, Miles Davis and Kurt Weill.

I'm sinking on that Sunday afternoon and I don't even know it.

I would have slept well last night if I hadn't been so hungry, and the crumbs in the bed hadn't been so annoying, and if my mind hadn't been so busy and if I'd been tired enough. As it was, I hardly got a wink.

If the gauge of a man is the company he keeps, I would be calibrated at zero. For the next few days I see nobody, not even Tad. I've yet to tell anyone at work that Ruth has left me. It's business as usual at Flat 2 except for the removal of the roof and walls. I have occasional phone-calls from Ruth's friends – *our* friends, we had called them, but if side-taking is going to happen, there's no doubt which team they will plump for. They phone up for Ruth and surprised she's not there, it's up to me to explain the situation. I can taste the lies on my tongue as I tell them it's a mutual arrangement, and not likely to be permanent anyway. It's a good idea for us to be apart for a while, I tell Vanessa, watching my toast burning under the grill. And I almost believe it – we've been getting on top of each other recently, that's all. It's a good thing all round for us to have some time and space for ourselves. I scrape the charcoal off the toast and ponder the truth of it. Perhaps I'm right.

I should feel miserable. I should feel upset. Relieved. Something, *anything*. But my body is numb from the neck downwards. I'm constipated as well.

But I'm busy. By Monday afternoon I've booked an appointment at a classy hair salon Ruth had talked about; by Tuesday morning the bathroom has been redesigned; by Wednesday p.m. I've been to the dentist, hired a video recorder, bought a new lamp for the bedroom, repotted the rubber plant in the hall, relined the kitchen cabinets, and finally finished *The Trial*. I have trouble with Kafka, I'm not sure why: I either don't understand him, or understand him so well that my subconscious takes fright. I always find myself struggling through his stories as though I'm trying to run in a nightmare, but there's something that makes me persist until I've finished. I must admit I had a certain sympathy for Joseph K., arrested on his thirtieth birthday. Perhaps I'm afraid that's what will happen to me: except, in my case there would be no mystery about the charge. James Morrison, you stand before the court charged with wasting your life. How do you plead?

Guilty.

But no – I'm going to make bachelorhood work for me, and if Ruth wants to come back I might or might not take her back. So there.

But where *is* she? And why hasn't she phoned? I've got Wendy's phone number, but I can only stare at it and imagine what's going on. Lesbian orgies, nightclubbing, company, communal meals? She's having fun, the callous bitch, and look at the mess the kitchen is in. I haven't washed the dishes for four days now, and the fridge is emptying alarmingly quickly. One more meal of fish fingers, a tin of baked beans and then I'll have to shop for myself. I turn the radio up loud and run myself a bath. One advantage of being alone: I can catch up on *The Archers* after a four-year gap.

11

Just two inches closer and her left breast would be in my eye. I try to focus on the pyramid of starched material hovering tantalisingly close, but it's too near. Her body is rocking very slightly with the movement of her arms and I will her to move just that little bit nearer, but she keeps her distance. I give an inaudible growl as her fingers comb through my hair, scratching gently at my scalp with her nails. Warm water trickles down my neck, a tongue working its way under my shirt. I never know what to say to hairdressers, especially the young pretty ones with clear complexions and strong fingernails, so I just gaze up at her face. She *is* lovely: eighteen, fresh and innocent as a buttercup, and wholly unaware of the effect she is having on me. She smears a second palmful of shampoo into my scalp and slowly rotates her fingers over my head. I try to interpret her expression, but her face is blank except for a professional concentration in the eyes. This is just a job to her; she is giving me the best massage of my life and I could be a dummy with a wig for all the notice she takes of me. She could ask anything at that moment, and I would give it to her. She's eighteen, at the peak of her power, and she has no idea.

I never know how to handle these hair-washing basins: my six feet two inches can never be fully accommodated by these silly low chairs, and this one has some sort of ratchet device that complicates matters further. The girl – Mandy – and I wrestle for a second as I struggle to sit up, and then she wraps a towel round my head. I try to look dignified in my lilac housecoat and acid-yellow turban, but inside I'm screaming with humiliation. When Mandy offers me a couple of magazines: *Elle* and *Cosmopolitan*, I decline them in a gruff voice, and feign interest in the light-fittings above my head. I knew it was a mistake to come here. I should have stayed with my strop and cut throat regular: an Italian short back and sides job, pictures of racing cars on the walls, the back-to-front clock so you can read the time in the mirror. A man's world where you can buy condoms and discuss the racing news.

I'm the only man in the salon except for two stylists. I have a clear view of a mirror in front of me but I daren't look: I know how ridiculous I must appear. I shut my eyes and try and drift off, but all my senses are on alert. I eavesdrop conversations between client and cutter; they all seem to know each other: *and how is Paul nowadays? . . . Pop back tomorrow and I'll trim it for you . . . So I said to her, I said . . .*

The queen who owns the salon drifts from one client to the other, proprietorially caressing bobs, offering coffee to me for a second time, calling across to his white-coated apprentices. I watch the woman in front of me as she subjects herself to a process that involves gooey stuff being pasted on to her hairline. It's a serious business this hairdressing lark: the making the best of oneself, the I-just-had-to-give-myself-a-treat.

If I'd been scalped by Sweeney Todd himself, I'd still nod approvingly as the mirror is held up for me to check the finished work. It looks okay: shorter than I wanted, but I'm past caring: all I want is to get out on to the street and ruffle my hair into its normal shape again.

'It looks very nice,' the cashier says, smiling.

'Thank you.' I offer her my credit card. I bet she says that to everyone.

'That's forty pounds.' She takes my card from me, her smile not faltering for a moment.

I can feel myself redden as she fills out the receipt. Forty quid? For a haircut? I sign the slip, pretending I do this sort of thing all the time. Forty bloody quid?

'See you soon.' The queen holds the door open for me with a smile. No wonder he's smiling so much. I'd smile too if I was raking in what he did. 'Don't leave it so long next time,' he admonishes.

'All right,' I reply lamely. Why the hell don't I just tell

the fat poof to piss off? I turn left instead of right, and by the time I realise I'm going in the wrong direction I'm halfway down the road. I double back, crossing over so I can't be seen from the salon. Forty quid! I ruffle my hair. Just think, some people pay that regularly, every week or two. I pause outside a shop and look at my reflection in the window. Not bad though. I turn my collar up and square up to my reflection. I've always assumed my hair could only grow in one style, but somehow they've made it look different: I've got the Sunday-colour-supplement look. It still isn't worth forty pounds, but I can see what they were getting at.

I haven't been to the King's Road for over a year: I'd forgotten how seriously fashionable it is. I dawdle its length, eyeing my silhouette in the shop windows, openly admiring the classy well-dressed shoppers. I have a cup of *cappuccino* in a marble-floored café, pretending to smoke a toothpick, bored and beautiful and decadent, or so I hope. I have a couple of hours before the shops shut: I want to treat myself, buy something. Clothes of some sort – perhaps a pair of shoes.

I suppose it says something that I immediately recognise quality when I see it; however, seventy pounds for a shirt is going too far. I leaf longingly through the silk ties: these are Gauguin colours, Rousseau colours, rich and intoxicating.

'Can I help you, sir?'

You've got to be joking; thirty-five quid for a tie? 'No, thanks.' I walk away from the assistant to the corner of the shop and browse through the sales clothes, one eye on my new haircut in the smoked mirror. Some trousers? I try on a pair in the ridiculously small changing room. Not bad; I caress the curve of my bum appreciatively. Twenty quid – I'll take them.

I buy a baggy blue shirt a couple of shops down; a pair of Italian shoes over the road. I'm trying to resist the temptation to buy a mustard-coloured jacket, but the salesgirl flatters me into it, and I give in. It suits me, there's no doubt, but a hundred and fifteen pounds? Money, money, money – I sign my fourth credit-card

93

receipt of the day and leave the shop, suddenly hot and anxious about the amount I'm spending.

And money is going to be an issue. With Ruth paying half the bills, we just about managed to eat and dress ourselves, but on my own? I daren't estimate what that would leave me from my monthly pay. I've still got a couple of thousand in unit trusts, but that won't last long if I carry on shopping like this. Something is going to have to happen. I either have to find a rich woman, or win some money on the football pools. Either would do.

I change into my new jacket on the pavement, bundling my old one into a carrier bag. James Brown is pumping out of a cruising car. *I feel good, oh so good*. I glance left and right down the street, and then give a wiggle of my hips to the music. Look out world – here I come. A number 11 bus slows for the traffic lights and I run for it, just managing to pull myself aboard before it draws away.

I settle into a window seat, smiling out at the street. It has been a good day. I stare out of the rain-spattered windows at the lights of World's End as if I'm a child and it's Christmas.

Tad's in the television room watching the early evening news. The sound has been turned up much too loud, even for me.

'Where have you been, my dear?' he shouts in greeting. 'I expected to hear from you.'

'I've been busy.' I frown at the blaring TV. A young girl in a wheelchair near the television has turned and is staring at me.

'Let's go to my room.' His motor buzzes and I have to dodge the chair as it spins round. 'See you, Sally,' he calls, but the girl hasn't heard. She watches us leave the room, blinking a smile at me as I cast a last look at the TV.

Tad doesn't speak again till the door is shut behind him. 'But don't you look wonderful! Turn round and let me have a look.' I do as I'm told. 'I like the hair.'

'So you should. It cost enough.'

'And new clothes?' He jerks his head back indicating for me to come closer. His hand lifts to mine, but instead of taking it as I thought, he pulls at the label dangling from the sleeve. 'There are scissors in the top drawer.'

I find them and snip the plastic thread and then drop the label into his bin.

'So, how are you, James my boy?'

'Fine,' I reply automatically. 'Ruth has left me.'

'Oh,' he says sharply. 'I'm sorry for you.'

'It's okay.'

He buzzes closer and tilts his head to look up at me. 'Are you very sad?'

'No,' I say with a shrug. I don't know how I feel, but whatever it is, I'm going to keep it to myself.

'I'm afraid in my opinion I think you're well shot of her,' Tad says. 'You were a child to Ruth and she wasn't even a good mother.'

I consider his verdict but say nothing.

'I could never understand what you saw in her. She was so hard.' He's talking as though he's known her for years. I can feel my bottom lip tighten with resentment. 'You're far too nice for her.'

Any more of this and I'm going to get depressed. 'Let me show you the rest of my clothes.' Tad wheels himself over to the bags and I open them for him. I hold the shirt up against myself.

'Wrong colour for you. Nice cut, though.' He nods at the second bag. 'What else have you got?'

He makes me try on the trousers and shoes. As I'm changing, I feel his eyes on my skinny legs. Even in front of Tad I'm ashamed of my body.

'Are you managing to eat all right?'

I pull a face. Is it obvious I've been living out of cans since Ruth left? I button the trousers and do a turn in front of him.

He claps his hands in delight. 'So this is the new-look James? Very nice.'

'I've decided to get myself together. Find a new girl-friend.'

'Already?'

'Why not?' I decide to keep on my new things and so I fold my jeans into the carrier bag.

'Careful, my dear,' Tad says, watching me, 'there are bachelors out there who'll give you diseases.'

I raise my eyebrows at the catch of bitterness in his voice. He's angry about something. He's about to say something more when a bell sounds in the corridor. Dinner.

'Come with me, will you?' he says.

I open the door for him and then I have to stride down the corridor after him to keep up. The dining-room is clean and bright, the curtains shut even though it's hardly dusk outside. They've tried to make the room as pleasant as possible, but they can't disguise the fact that this is a large, multi-purpose parquet-floored hall and not a dining-room at all. I can't put my finger on it, but something here reminds me of St Jude's. Perhaps the clatter of cutlery from the serving hatch.

'You can go now,' he says. On the next table, a member of staff is spooning potato into the mouth of Sally. Our eyes meet for a fraction and then I look away, casting blindly over the broken and busted bodies. 'Come and see me soon, James?'

I don't know if I'll ever get used to the vacancy of the flat. It's not just the silence, the darkened rooms, the things exactly as they've been left: the dirty plate on the sofa, clothes strewn over the bedroom floor. There's something else, another sort of vacancy. Ruth's departure has created a psychic vacuum.

I switch the TV on in the bedroom. I only glance at the screen – a man and a woman arguing in what looks like the corridor of a derelict block of flats – before going to the bathroom to run the bath.

I've had a recurring thought over the last couple of days: the similarity between houses and boxes. I've never seen it so clearly: living spaces as repositories, receptacles, boxes to hold a body and prevent it falling or things falling on it. There are streets and streets and streets of boxes in this town and somewhere in that lot sits I, in my own little box I call home. Some of these boxes are placed one on top of each other, as in my case; some are packed so numerously and closely together they form giant filing

96

cabinets. And beneath all this is a whole other world – a spaghetti junction of pipes and tubes and cables. Pipes for gas, for electricity, for water, for sewage, and below that the Central Line tube. I've read somewhere that wherever you are in New York you are never more than forty feet from another person. I don't know what the distance is in London.

I sit on the edge of the bath, inhaling the rising steam, trying not to imagine the Dutch couple who live in the downstairs flat. But at least I've met them; what about all the strangers on either side of number 24 Ellsbirch Avenue, living their lives as though I didn't exist? Eating their dinner and making love and going to the toilet and all barely the width of two bricks away from where I sit?

Occasionally when it's very still I can hear someone pissing in the toilet next door. Odd that; it's never conversation, or even music, just the sound of cascading water and then the complaining cistern when the toilet is flushed. Perhaps it's something to do with the acoustics of bathrooms.

I don't bother to get dressed again after my bath, but stay in my dressing-gown and lounge around the bedroom, half watching the television. I keep returning to the mirror. It's not bad, I agree with my reflection. Not bad at all. I go into the bathroom so I can see my haircut from all angles. He's done a good job, I have to give him that. Somehow he's made me look different. Almost handsome. I run my hand over my chin, enjoying the rasp of two days' growth of beard. For a moment I don't recognise myself, seeing just the image in the mirror: tall, dark-haired, anxious. Perhaps I *do* stand a chance in the egg and spoon race of life; in fact, I shift focus and follow my reflections down the corridor of mirrors, I'm quite an eligible bachelor: presentable enough, intelligent, witty. I know some women fancy me – Ruth was always pointing them out to me. Hilary from work for instance, I think she likes me. And there was that American girl I met a couple of months ago at Phil's party. The American dream on legs, she was the sexiest little sophomore you could wish to meet. If Ruth hadn't been there I'm sure a North Atlantic alliance would have been on the cards.

97

I lather the shaving stick and contemplate my chin in the mirror. What was her name? Sandy? Chloe? *Connie* – that's it. We danced nose to nose and she pressed those stupendous tits into me as though she was making potato-cut prints on my chest. Ruth gave me hell when we got back to the flat, but – I grin at my lowered lids in the mirror – was it worth it!

The route I take around my face when I shave never varies. Beginning on the throat, I work up to the chin and then shave first the left cheek then the right. I complete the sideburns and then move on to my lower lip which leaves me with a white Zapata moustache, which I finish off amid much smirking and face pulling. This time, something makes me hesitate, razor poised above the foamy upper lip. Well? I smear some of the soap away until I have a shape I like. Why not? Let's grow a moustache. I scrape away at the edges with the razor and then splash cold water over my face. I assess the effect in the mirror. Hard to tell how successful it will be, but it's worth a try.

I keep my eyes on the carpet as I take off my dressing-gown and slippers, trying to recapture the look and feel of the wonderful Connie. I was drunk, not obscenely, but just enough to carry me into conversation with the busty American in the corner. Within the hour I was whispering, though hard to believe it now, 'Sweet little Connie, you can con me any time,' into the girl's ear. Ruth was justifiably enraged, but not until we got home.

Where are they now? Where are all the colleens who are ready to lay themselves open for me, nymphets who would lead me into performing acts of gross indecency with them? They exist – I know that: schools and discos and offices and colleges are full of them. But why don't I know any of them? That's the trouble with a four-year monogamous stretch: suddenly you find yourself with no back-up and a rusty line in repartee.

Wendy and Ruth – *that* could have gone differently. Perhaps if I hadn't been so wimpish Ruth would have stayed. Perhaps by now I could have been sultan of a *ménage à trois*.

The scene is as vivid as a hologram in front of my eyes. Nosing between Ruth's legs, Wendy snuffling like a great white whale. Ruth groaning, her back arched, squeezing her own breasts as though they were lemons. One week too late, the cyclopic fiend stirs and quickens. Oh no . . .

12

I could be naked and painted with vegetable dyes if my response to her is anything to go by. She's blue-black, silky skinned, a wild hog amongst piglets. I bristle as she stands in the doorway looking around. She's not sure whether to come in or not and I watch her from behind my desk like a hunter silently willing his prey into a trap. She takes one step towards the desk and my grip tightens on my spear: she's in. I watch her out of the corner of my eye as she stands irresolutely. She's African, uncomfortable in her garish and unco-ordinated Western clothes, as though she has been dressed by somebody else. She makes up her mind and strides towards Jeff, our weak-wristed assistant Head Librarian. I can't hear what she's saying, but it's something to do with the newspapers, because he takes her round to the racks, and for a moment they're out of view. When he comes back to the desk I flick a sideways glance at him. Does *nothing* get to him? Does he really not notice the magnificence of that woman? I keep my eyes on the racks and in a minute she reappears and I have a chance to see her face to face. Not pretty, not even beautiful, but there's something there; something that my two-billion-year progamming responds to with flashing lights and sirens. She's a character from Rider Haggard: majestic, bestial and fatal. I imagine her, skin shiny with sweat, grass-skirted, beads around her wrists and ankles, all dangerous muscle and fecundity, being worshipped by

99

a tribe of heathens, me – the dark side of me – head priest, chief executioner, main sacrifice.

She casts around for Jeff, and then seeing him at the desk, comes up to us. She puts a notebook on the desk, and they both consult it, Jeff craning his neck to read the upside-down print. As she reaches forward to turn the page, so her dayglo sleeveless cardigan opens at the armpit to reveal a triangle of black flesh. I twitch as though a tiny electric shock had passed through me. She's not wearing a bra. Pretending to check the microfiche, I position myself to gain an optimum view of her. Sure enough, and bless that careless designer, I can see a three-quarters breast, my view of it stopping just short of the nipple. I feel faint with lust, an internal convulsion starting somewhere in my belly and rippling up and out, ending in a slight shudder on the surface. Take her away, Jeff, I silently beg – I don't know how much more of this I can take. As though he has heard me, she follows him to the filing cabinet of microfilms and opens a drawer. I look at the clock: it's lunch-time, or as near as dammit, so I pack up the books I'd been working on and turn to go downstairs. I take one last glance back at the African Queen to see her watching Jeff thread the film into the machine, biting her bottom lip in concentration. A tiny moan escapes me.

Oh hell, the runaround our hormones give us. That and our imaginations. I can't see beyond the tip of my quivering prick. I'm blinded by this hammering in my head: the sound of my blood asking to be let loose. Lud-dup, lub-dup, love-fuck, love-suck, rub-suck.

I'm as red-faced as if I'd been slapped, which I have been in a way. I'd been sitting on my favourite bench on the Green, legs stretched in front of me, hands in pockets, having just finished my lunch. It's a prime site for world watching: young mothers with their kids, office secretaries with sandwiches, building workers kicking foot-balls around; I often come to sit here when the weather is mild. I'd been scanning what was on offer, unconsciously seeking legs, breasts, long hair. Two women – girls really

– had been talking about ten yards from me. The girl with her back to me was dressed in a mini-skirt and bomber jacket, unstockinged legs, pink and naked, ending in cheap high-heeled shoes. I'd been wondering if she was a local prostitute, gazing at her bare legs, trying to imagine them wrapped round my neck. The other girl must have noticed my stare because she said something to her friend, who had looked over her shoulder, and then turned a fraction so her back fully faced me. I should have taken the hint, but I was under the sway of the great god Priapus, and my eyes came back to the legs. Again the girl motioned to me, and this time the friend turned round. 'What are you lookin' at, you dirty old man?' she said in a loud Irish voice.

I jerked my head away, flushing with embarrassment. The girls turned and walked along the path in front of me, sneering as they passed.

I stay on my seat for another minute before I get up and move. Am I turning into some sort of voyeur, getting my kicks out of spying on women? Am I? In one word – yes.

It's as though I have a Geiger counter between my legs. Every time I approach a radioactive source, it begins its excited chattering. And these days the world seems to be aglow with female radiation: not just human beings (becoming worryingly younger – I mean *twelve* years old? Have you no shame?), but shop mannequins, lingerie advertisements, sculpture, certain vegetables, items of ladies' underwear, eggs (*eggs*? I swear, I'm certifiable), candles, golden syrup, just about any area of bared flesh on just about any girl. I'm a driven, hunted animal.

Saturday, the next day; the day I promised to take Tad to the post office. This is only our second time in public, but I'm quickly getting the hang of it, even beginning to enjoy the stares we attract. Dr Schweitzer and the crippled vessel of his largesse, I'm feeling righteous and not a little holy, proud of my incapacitated companion. Tad, meanwhile, is about to get us into trouble.

Waiting in line at the post office, minding our own

business, a young Black man barges past us to the front. This is Shepherd's Bush; the front line, and no place to object if a Black brother treads on your toes. That is, unless you're Tad.

'Excuse me,' he calls after him. The kid takes no notice. 'Hey, Sambo!'

It's like a Sam Peckinpah film when time stops. The word hangs in the air, and we know everybody had heard, including the kid. I can feel the skin on my face tighten as he turns round and comes back to us. He's eighteen and has the sort of body that might have won a design award from the Sport's Advisory Council. A classic mesomorph with good muscular definition: his skin is milk-chocolate, as smooth as if it has been poured over his body. I can feel my body already assuming a stance of studied indifference. If this guy is going to hit someone, that someone would be me. I take a quarter-step away from Tad towards the little old lady in front of us. Tad, though, is looking up at him, taking in every square centimetre of this brown satin flesh. And there's a lot of it showing.

'Does he belong to you?' he grunts at me, nodding down at Tad. A flutter of fear fibrillates my heart. This kid lives on white bread, milk and marijuana, hasn't done a day's work outside a community service rap, never exercises apart from frequent sexual intercourse with a variety of female partners, and look at him – he's invincible! A carbonised Achilles. He makes me feel thin and weak and white – which is what I am.

I keep my mouth shut, but my body speaks whole sentences: I'm here just buying stamps. Him? Never seen him before in my life.

'Excuse me,' Tad says. 'Notice the absence of collar here,' he says craning his neck. 'No lead. Contrary to your apparent observation, I am not a dog, but a wheelchair-bound human being.' The kid stares down at Tad who grins grotesquely as though a spasm of pain has taken over his body. 'Right,' he continues brightly. 'Now I've got your attention, you can call me a cripple and we're even on the insults stake.'

'Whaddyou want?'

'Go on – you owe me one.'

'All right. Whaddyou want you fucking cripple?'

I watch him, scared and fascinated. He's an animal – no doubt about it: splendid and fit and dangerous.

'Perhaps you hadn't noticed, but there's a queue of people here. An orderly line. Waiting in turn.'

'So?'

'I was wondering what your special dispensation was.' Tad waits for a response. Nothing. 'Perhaps because you're a member of an ethnic minority?' he suggests, 'or just bigger and tougher than everyone else? Or perhaps it's because you're just an ignorant bag of pig-shit?'

'Get fucked,' he says turning away.

'Hey!' This is loud; too loud to ignore. The whole queue is waiting for what's to follow. There will be blood spilt soon, I can feel it in my waters. 'Turn your back on me again,' Tad says, 'and I'll break every bone in your body.'

'You? How?'

'With this.'

He holds up his middle finger in an up-your-arsehole gesture.

'Is he crazy or what?' he asks me. Not a flicker of mirth on the face of this black Adam. A sense of humour obviously doesn't come with the package. I shrug.

'All right,' Tad persists. 'So you found me out. But I do have one weapon I'm prepared to use, and that's my tongue. So . . . Naaa!' He sticks his tongue out and crosses his eyes. The kid backs off as though Tad is infected with a dangerous disease. He turns and walks to the front of the queue. I can see that Tad has shaken him: there's more bravado than conviction in his swagger. I breathe for the first time in five minutes.

'Oh but look at his tight little bottom,' Tad groans. 'With a body like his and a mind like mine, we'd be unstoppable.'

'I'll just be a couple of minutes.' Tad bumps his bedroom door open and wheels himself into the corridor.

'Ah, Fergie,' I hear him call before the door swings shut.

I've been aware of that glossy stack of porno magazines every time I've visited Tad, and alone in his room for the first time, it's only seconds before I've got one on my lap and I'm flicking through its pages. Ten years of Catholic boarding school has ensured a profound and lasting fascination for bared flesh of any kind. Purely academic, of course.

The first magazine is no different from those I had seen in the sex shop: posturing muscle men with conspicuous dicks and nowhere to put them. I try another magazine, Scandinavian judging from the look of the language. Ah-ha! This is the *real* stuff: erections, penetration, oral sex; I turn to the last page, spunk. I backtrack to the beginning of the sequence of pictures: two men together, a bit of wanking and sucking, and then one climbs on top of the other, only a section of prick visible before it disappears into the other man. I was expecting this, but I'm still shocked at what I see. This is as illicit as you can get, a whole other world of sin and Sodom. I can hear Father O'Leary's voice as he tested us on the catechism: what are the four sins crying to heaven for vengeance? There was never any difficulty remembering the first and the last: wilful murder, and the sin of Sodom. And here it is: a textbook example.

I look closely at the men's faces. There is no pretence at love-making here: this is fucking, pure and simple. Hardly even that: substitute a club for the penis and you have one man beating another.

I turn the page, feeling myself sinking deeper into hopelessness. The top man is now slapping the bum he's fucking, his arm raised above his head, teeth gritted into a snarl. The man underneath has his head thrown back in mock pain.

I slide the magazine back into place on the shelf. Is this it then – what man has made of man? I stare at the magazine spines and then sit down. Why would anyone want to do such a thing? Allow themselves to be fucked – presumably painfully – up the arse? Being spanked by someone who clearly hates them? Do we all hate ourselves so much? Do we all want to punish ourselves, is that it? I feel suddenly nauseous.

There were two tiers of beatings at school: with trousers for venial sins and without trousers for mortal sins. Father O'Leary, our insane headmaster, was the only teacher allowed to cane us, and though he probably believed it really *did* hurt him more than it hurt us, it was us who left his study with red weals on our buttocks. He used a thin bamboo cane, bent from years of use, which was designed to whip round you to inflict maximum pain. He was an old man, and his aim was poor, often catching the top of your thighs, which hurt even more. I was sixteen when I was last caned. I had skived off Mass on Sunday, been caught by Sister reading in the dorm, and after lunch summoned to the headmaster's study. I might have escaped with detention if I hadn't argued with him, but though I knew the danger of protesting, I couldn't stay silent. Aren't I old enough to decide my own religious expression? *In loco parentis*, that was the favourite phrase; I am your mother and father in their absence, he said. I am responsible for you until you leave school. I had the sense not to tell him that Mother never went to church in her life. Without Mass, without Holy Communion he said, we are all at the mercy of the devil. If we did just what we wanted, where would we be? It was a rhetorical question, but he answered it none the less. In hell. James, he smiled a watery smile at me, it is human nature to be sinful and lustful and lazy. We must fight ourselves with all we have. The sun came out at that moment, and the room was filled with spiralling dust motes. It was then that I saw him for what he was: a thin, old bachelor, cemented into his beliefs as solidly as a plaster saint in a niche. Somehow the pronouncements of Vatican II had passed him by: this was a man who had once told me that girls should sleep with their legs crossed so that the devil wouldn't get into them at night. I couldn't believe him any more, his last shred of credibility had gone: this was the [7]twentieth century, I was sixteen years old, people were playing American football on the moon, and he was telling me about the devil? I remember my reply precisely: Why should I go to church when I don't even believe in God? That was it; the final undermining of his authority. With God went Christ, went Our Lady, went the Church, went school, went everything. Without God there was no cement, just sand. He gave me six lashes. The humiliation of taking down my trousers and bending over, exposing myself to him and his bigotry is still keen. I don't know whether he was trying to beat the devil out of me, but he gave it all he had. I can't believe he wasn't aware of the irony as he whipped me: God, he said between gritted teeth . . . is . . . love. He tried to lecture me when I pulled up my trousers, but I was in too much pain to hear him. I wanted to cry, it hurt so much. I ran to the toilets to examine the damage. The trickle of blood down the inside of my thighs was nothing compared to my rage.

I stand up and walk to the window. It was so long ago, and so fresh in my memory. Father O'Leary would be retired by now, or dead, and how many lives would he have marked in his fifty-year ministry? I was forced to go to church on pain of expulsion, but from eighteen I had never been inside one again. Even when I was in Chartres, I stayed outside the cathedral while Ruth went in. So much for the gospel of love.

The door bangs open, and I turn to face Tad, manufacturing a bright smile for him. 'Are you all right now, Peter?' the orderly says. He's Irish, and I know for a fact that Tad fancies him.

'Thank you, darling.'

'Do you want this tidied up?' He nods at a discarded newspaper on the floor.

'Please.'

'Peter?' I query as he shuffles the pages together and dumps them in the bin.

'Piotr,' Tad explains. 'It's as close as you can get in Irish.'

'But why not Tad?'

'He calls me Peter to dominate me.'

'I call you Peter because I can't get my bloody tongue round Pio – whatever it is. And Tad is just plain daft.'

'See what I mean?'

'And why is it you call me Fergie?'

'Feargal,' Tad says in a passable Irish accent. 'Whoever heard of such a name? 'Tis absurd.'

He grins at Tad. 'Now, anything else I can do for your lordship?'

Tad shakes his head and waits till he has left. 'Perhaps a blow job?' he says to the door. He turns to me. 'What's wrong?'

'Nothing. Why?'

'You look a bit – ' he shrugs. 'How are you managing on your own?'

'I'm quite enjoying it.'

'And how's your sex life? Found anyone to play with?'

'Not yet.'

'Poor James.' He seems to find this highly amusing. 'You'll have to get a grip on yourself.' He flexes his right hand.

'Har, har.'

'It's a shame Ashley has left – he was always handy in an emergency.'

'Who's Ashley?'

'A good-looking boy I used to know. As blind as a bat and the greatest polysexualist I've ever met. Very keen on the old hand job, he was. I've known him for years, my first sexual partner in fact.'

Something inside me tightens with astonishment. A sexual partner? Tad?

'*Le petit mort* nearly became *le grand mort* once when Matron came in and discovered him with a palmful of my seminal fluid. He didn't know who it was, and just sat there while Matron changed colour, and then turned on her heel and fled.'

I try to laugh but it's a poor attempt.

'I'm sorry, am I shocking you?'

'You know you are.'

He lifts a finger to his lips. 'Shh.'

Tad's right. Masturbation is the great unspoken amongst men. Proper sex, manly sex, is outward looking, a phallic imperialism. Real men collect women like butterflies which

107

they pin to cork with their penises. Masturbation is just wanking.

Solitary and secret and sinful.

I'm unsettled. I pour myself a drink and watch television with the sound off while the bath fills. It's an American drama by the look of it, a father and son talking in a studio kitchen. Tad's got me at it now: I can hear the characters as surely as if the sound is up: 'Now that you're sixteen, son,' the father's saying, 'you can give up masturbating and start to have *real* sex.' The boy doesn't look too happy – he probably knows he's about to lose the most understanding sexual partner he will ever have: his hand.

I leave the television and go into the bathroom to try and hurry the bath up. I enjoyed my day with Tad, but alone again, I can feel the tentacles of my depression clutching at my ankles.

'I need someone,' I tell myself in the mirror. I'm doing a lot of that lately – talking to myself. I'm doing it now.

'Shut up, James.'

'All right, James.'

'Fuck off, James.'

Stop it, stop it, stop it. I purse my lips to stop the words coming out and sling my clothes into the laundry basket. When am I going to have time to go to the launderette? I'm beginning to run out of clean clothes.

I test the water and then get into the bath. Perfect. I groan loudly as the water rises up my body.

'Oh God, send me somebody.' It has been two weeks since I've made love. From my toes to my nose, I can feel the pressure of unspent sperm building up inside me. Two weeks of celibacy and soon these tiny tadpoles won't care what environment they burst into.

The *Oxford English Dictionary* of 1959, the year I was born, defines the verb 'masturbate' as 'the practice of self-abuse'. Thirty years later the accepted definition is more specific and less judgmental: 'to produce an orgasm by stimulation of the genitals, not by sexual intercourse'.

There is a chance, I suppose, that the children born in 1989 will wonder what all the fuss was about. Stimulation, if somewhat mechanical, at least is free of the taint of negativity. For earlier generations, however, self-abuse was about as charged with poison as you could get. And pretty dangerous stuff it was too:

  it would stunt your growth
  it would make you blind and/or deaf
  it would ruin married life for you
  it was physically damaging
  it was the mark of a sexual deviant
  it would turn you insane
  it was sinful

I don't know how many of these I ever believed, but now of course, I see them for what they are: guilt-induced fantasies. When my hearing started going, there were a lot of jokes about wanking, but nobody ever took that seriously. I don't suppose any of the Brothers believed it either.

None of the fears about masturbation are true. Even when I was first aware of them, I didn't believe them. And largely, I still don't. Except of course the equation of masturbation with sin. Between them, St Paul and St Augustine have ensured that any wilful pleasure in the irregular motions of the flesh has been swiftly followed by crushing guilt. Being brought up by medieval monks didn't help. There's nothing wrong with s-e-x, Brother Edwards, our housemaster, told us one memorable evening, hands wringing each other behind his cassock. But if you are tempted to play with your private parts, you must resist; the Pope doesn't do it, and neither should you. We weren't really clear what he meant: self-pollution, as he called it, sounded as though it had something to do with oil slicks. We were eight: it had never occurred to any of us to play with our private parts until his proscription.

Somewhere in my forgotten past I'm sure I was innocent and immaculate, but then as surely as my voice broke, it happened. I fell from grace. My moral garden was planted, watered and took root, and then sucking sustenance from my environment, I succumbed to the knowledge of good and evil. The Brothers had done a good job. I was a good Catholic: at least for a while.

I am an adult now; I can think for myself. Ha! I have long passed the age of malleability: I am, and will always be, the prepubescent James. My beliefs were planted early in the spring and took root well before summer: by the time I began looking around, I was in a jungle. Try hacking your way through that. My Damoclean sword is a penknife and there are vines as thick as my arm to cut through. And the thickest and deepest root, forcing its way through all layers of consciousness? The belief of beliefs – we are all guilty until proved innocent.

There's a battle going on between my ears when I think of masturbation. My ego might say yes, my id might say yes-yes, but my super-ego says you touch that button, buster, and I'll blast you to kingdom come.

I'm not alone. There has been enough corporate toe-curling guilt to have replaced the tainted term 'masturbation' with 'self-pleasuring'. We live in enlightened times now: the stimulation of one's own – or even another's – genitals has been declared as innocent and healthy as taking a hot bath; recommended by psychologists, discussed on television and in magazines, slipped (not quite so easily) into conversation. An age-old activity has been rehabilitated.

Like hell it has. Every Catholic knows it'll spin you to hell quicker than you can say 'I am a man/woman with feelings and I deserve to be satisfied.'

The best I can do is have masturbation as an unfortunate necessity: only halfway decent if done at night, with the lights out, and acceptable only as long as I don't enjoy it too much. But with someone you love? I sit up in the bath so I can see my face in the mirror. 'I love you,' I say. No answer.

I go to bed strained and miserable that night.

13

Sunday, bloody Sunday; the seventh day of my bachelor-hood and another miserable sunny morning. I scowl out at the street, wanting to see black clouds and wind, the leaves of the trees ripped from their branches, umbrellas turned inside out. I want to throw open the windows, empty the flat of its stagnant air, slap some life into the floral wallpaper. It's going to be a long and lonely day, I can feel it; even the paperboy is late.

I go back to bed and spend the rest of the morning staring at the ceiling. When the phone rings on the bed beside me, I leap as though I've been electrocuted. I let it ring a couple of times before I answer.

'Hello?'

'James.'

'Ruth!'

'I'd like to come round today to collect the rest of my stuff. Is that okay?'

'Fine!' Some company – anybody. I'd have sat with Vlad the Impaler if he'd called round.

'Can I come over in – ' She pauses and I swear I can see her hitching back the sleeve of her shirt to look at her watch. ' – about an hour?'

'Fine,' I say again.

'See you later, then.' She hangs up, catching me with my mouth open. What was I going to say? I don't know. Come back to me? Help?

Things are looking up: a reason to get out of bed – my first guest. A shame it's my ex-girlfriend, but better than nothing.

I'm halfway through the washing-up when I decide to leave it: perhaps she'll relent and come back to me if she sees me struggling. I won't shave either, ruffle my hair

111

as though I haven't slept for a week; perhaps she'll melt. Like hell she will: this is the cow who left me with ten minutes' warning.

The intercom buzzes. I press the button to open the street door and take one last look in the mirror before opening the flat door.

'How are you, James?'

'Fine.' I stand back to let her pass as though she's a guest. There's something different about the way she looks.

'I won't take long.'

'Take your time,' I say lightly. I walk through to the kitchen and she follows me. 'Coffee?'

'Thanks.'

'So. How are you getting on?' I suddenly realise what has changed about her. 'You've had your hair cut.'

'You too.'

My hand goes up to my fringe, smoothing the hair back. I forgot I had it cut.

'It suits you.'

'Thanks.' I shouldn't ask, but I can't stop myself. 'How's Wendy?'

'Fine.'

'Everything all right at the house?'

A week apart and we're talking like strangers. I watch her reflection in the kettle as I fill it at the sink. We *are* strangers. Not just the haircut, there's something else, some other change I can't put my finger on. I can't believe this is the person I spent four years of my life with. I've never seen her before.

'And you? Are you managing okay?' she asks. She has avoided my question.

I shrug and let out a sigh. I'm going to play this to the hilt, even though I'm suddenly not sure if I want her back. I want her sympathy, I do know that.

'Come here.' She holds a hand across the divide to me and I take it, stepping into the arc of her arms. She hugs me. I'm astonished: ten days apart and she learns to hug. Sure she did it when we were together, but not like this.

'Are you really okay?' A practised hugger perhaps, but she's no more perceptive than before. Am I really okay?

112

Do I look like it? Is this kitchen evidence of a happy family life?

'I'm missing you,' I murmur. Even as the words leave my mouth some part of me flinches at their falsehood. I'm not missing Ruth, this stranger. My sentence has no object, has no room for A. N. Other. I should have said 'I'm lonely' or even 'I'm missing'. It was a lie to include Ruth in the equation. I miss her body perhaps, I miss the physical comfort of another human being, but that's not Ruth. It could be any body: any body which was willing to mother me.

The reassuring squeeze Ruth gives me before she pushes me away is not what I want. This isn't playing the game. 'I'm missing you' is a close cousin of 'I love you': it demands an echoed response: 'I'm missing you too', 'I love you too'. Instead all I get is a sisterly squeeze and a determined silence.

The kettle has boiled and switched itself off. Ruth glances over my shoulder. 'Coffee?'

I stretch both arms either side of her head until my palms meet the refrigerator. I've seen it done in films, a classic stance. The girl trapped.

'No, James.'

She ducks out of my arms and takes two steps away from me. I turn and reach a hand out, palm open, inviting.

'No, James. I'm not interested.'

My fingers fold like petals of a flower, until it's a fist I'm holding out. I can't believe she has left me. Not the physical absence, but the changed allegiance, the emotional desertion. I have no claim on her any more. I've been cut out of her life; my place taken by somebody else.

I'm convulsed by anger, a sudden manic flash of murder before my eyes. I hate her. I barge past her into the sitting-room. In my hurry to put my jacket on, I try to push my hand through the breast pocket by mistake.

'Don't be here when I get back,' I shout at the kitchen door. 'Go off and fuck your lesbian friends for all I care.'

My anger fuels me as far as the tube station, and then as suddenly as it appeared, it has gone. I pause to take a couple of deep breaths: I shouldn't have lost my temper

113

with her. She can be vindictive; I can't be sure she won't take it out on me. She's in the flat on her own, she could do anything. I pause by the phone box: should I tell her to keep her bloody hands off my stereo? And there's the television too.

I push the thought away and buy a 90p ticket. Where am I going? I walk down the escalator to the platform. East into town. It's Sunday, the sun is shining. I'm young – ish – I have a life to live. I ride the train, chewing on a piece of imaginary gum, strap hanging like a New York hoodlum. I put my shades on so I can stare at the girls without them knowing. I'm in a foul mood, and just asking for trouble.

I get out at Tottenham Court Road, scowling at the buskers at the bottom of the escalator. I step out of the grimy tubeway into the glare of Sunday-afternoon Oxford Street, pretending to be a pop star, frowning against the light, a photographer on the top step to snap my picture.

Oxford Street is scattered with Sunday shoppers, young couples and groups of Italian school-kids with matching knapsacks looking into the shop windows. A gust of wind harries a ball of newspaper towards me and I step to one side to let it pass. I can feel the grime of the place; it seems to be in the air, inescapable. If I had an arm the length of a tennis court, I'd sweep these crowds, the taxis, the courier bikes like crumbs from a table. But I don't, so I turn right into Charing Cross Road.

I'm genuinely unaware of my motive for taking that street for the first hundred yards, but by the time I've passed Foyles I know damn well where I'm going, though nothing short of bamboo splinters under my fingernails would have made me admit it to anyone. It's something more than gravity which is propelling me down that dreary hill, my pulse quickening with every step. I'm going to Soho, home of the sex shop. Peep-shows, dirty films, porn shops: in lieu of a real live girl, I'll get me a celluloid one. I'm going to expose myself to an occasion of sin, and burn though I may, I can't stop my legs moving one in front of the other.

114

I'm blinded to the street by the clamour of protest inside my head: this is different to buying magazines for Tad. This is me in control, James Morrison guilty of perpetuating the flesh trade, supporting the degradation not just of women, but men too, keeping the whole tyranny going with my pounds and pence, just so that I can feed my beast. My face and hands are prickling with dread: I can do what I wish; I *am* free.

Free? I'm a fish on the end of an expertly cast line: I have been caught, and wriggle as I might, my moral floundering is only compounded. Hook, line and sinker I have swallowed the myth of materialism; the myth that tells me this ache can be assuaged by consumption. Pornography is only one of the ways, every advertisement hoarding and every glossy magazine tells me of others. As long as I have enough things, the pain will go away. My actions may be my responsibility, but the impulse was taken out of my hands long ago. My lust is an industry now.

Money and sex, shopping and fucking: this is my religion now, the religion of flesh. I was eleven, perhaps twelve, when I realised exactly what was under the robes of Our Lady. It was seeing my first dirty magazine that did it. Details of the memory are blurred but one picture stands out: a shot taken under a woman's skirt. It was far from explicit by today's standards, but the black fuzz of hair and fleshy lips that were just visible was the most mysterious and exotic sight my young eyes had ever seen. I learnt more from that one picture than the entire children's *Encyclopaedia Britannica*.

That was the first time I formulated the tenets of my secret religion. Here, the cunt was the holy grail; the object of objects, the most precious, the most mysterious thing of them all. If understanding lay in that tear-drop shaped orifice, the logic went, then the closer I examined it, the closer to the truth I would get. And so I studied the most intimate pictures I could find; pictures of women spreading their legs to display as much of their bodies, short of surgery, as they could. Of course, I felt as guilty as hell and would have to hot foot it to confession sometimes two or three times a week. Later, flesh and blood replaced images, and I stopped going to church, but the quest remained the same: if only I could burrow deep enough into the body of a woman, I would find what I was searching for. And what is that thing? Peace, completeness, integrity. And needless to say, the Holy Mother of God, *semper virgo*, Queen of Angels, Tower of Ivory, Gate of Heaven, fell by the wayside.

I know, tumescent as I am, that this is insanity; the idea that escape somehow lies in the visual consumption of bared flesh, but I can't stop myself. As the Yiddish saying goes: *ven der putz shteht, ligt der sechel in drerd*. When the prick stands up, the brain gets buried in the ground.

I pause outside an amusement arcade and look in. A misnomer – amusement – if ever there was one. Amid the clamour and flashing lights are grim-faced robots leaning against machines, eyes fixed on screens, wrists tapping buttons. I haven't been in one of these places since I was a kid, and I step inside to look around. This is a power-house of psychic energy: there are a few middle-aged men, and one old lady with her shopping bags feeding coins into a fruit machine, but it's mostly young men, boys really. The days of the one-armed bandit are on the wane: half of the machines here, you have to climb into. Motorcycle riding, formula one racing cars, spaceships, the entertainment is kinetic now, the noise overpowering. And in the middle of it, these kids, masters of the universe. I watch a gaggle of Arab boys clustering round a machine, urging on one of their friends. He's tapping the controls of the machine with the speed of a touch typist. Whatever it is that is being destroyed – space invaders, cuboid monsters that eat their way through walls, robot birds programmed to kill everything in sight – they're dropping like flies, their demise signalled by a bip! from the machine. I study his face, lurid under the lights of the machine. I can see the adrenalin flushing into his bloodstream: his pupils dilating as the game hots up, his capillaries gorging with blood, all senses on alert. His friends are whooping their encouragement, but what is his future?

All his quickness of brain and sinew is just pissing in the wind: the kid is brilliant, an Olympian of the computer games, and he doesn't stand a snowball's chance in hell outside these four walls.

I turn to go and pause to study the silhouette in the doorway. Just look at him. Jeans ripped at the knees, gold earrings, a tattoo of a bluebird on his upper arm. Mean and moody, sexy as hell, propping up the doorway: the classic pool-hall punk. I adjust my shades and wander past him and then down the road to buy a can of beer from a pub. I sip it slowly, enjoying the sunshine, and take one of the side-streets. They've cleaned Soho up: I remember it as being far sleazier than this, almost every other shop being a sex shop. I can see the pink façade of a peep-show and I cross the road, but I know I won't have the courage to go in. I glance through the open doorway as I walk past: a young woman, long legs disappearing into a tiny skirt, is sitting on the edge of a desk. She looks nice: pretty, respectable, probably a student earning extra money. What must she think of us? A hand-written sign, *Poppers for sale*, has been pasted on the window. Poppers? Amyl nitrite? Surely not.

I wander back to the amusement arcade to take my place in the doorway. James Dean is still there, a study in beautiful boredom, a cigarette hanging from his lips. I wish I'd worn my cowboy boots now.

What the hell do I want? Sex? The rubbing of one body against another?

'Hi.'

I snap out of my reverie and focus on the man standing in front of me. 'Hello.'

He's about twenty-five, bearded, glasses, Indian.

'Are you busy now?'

'Well . . .' I look casually left to right like any streetwise dude, wondering just what the hell he's on about.

'How much?'

'What's that?' I return my eyes to him. He has a soft plasticine face, babyish under the beard.

'I want to suck on you. How much?'

'You want to . . . *what*?'

117

'Suck you off.'

'Uh,' is all I can say. 'Uh . . . uh.' The kid with the ripped jeans is watching us. 'Try him,' I croak.

I drop my can in the bin and sway off, my ears buzzing with outrage. Suck on me? *Suck* on me? Ugh!

When we are young we see as through a glass darkly; but now we see face to face. Ugh!

I'm still shuddering when the mulatto girl steps into the carriage at Marble Arch. She takes the seat opposite me and returns to the ice-cream she's eating. The attraction is immediate: there's something foreign about her, un-English in the way she's licking and nibbling her cornet. She's not eating it so much as giving it a blow job: rimming the outer edge with an erect tongue, and then pouting her thick lips to take the whole tip of it into her mouth. A blob of ice-cream has smudged on the corner of her mouth without her realising, and it trickles down to her chin. Goddammit – I don't want this. I've just had a shock; I need to disengage for a moment, take a few deep breaths. But grinning devils are pursuing me, poking their little tridents into my groin. She reminds me of someone, but I can't think who. It's the full lips, the solid arms, the frankness with which she's eating this ice-cream. She pauses for a moment as if she's thinking the same thought too, and for a second, our eyes meet. Her eyes are blank. She's eaten too much of the stuff: her brain has turned to ice-cream.

I can't take my eyes off her. I put my sunglasses on and let my head sink on to my chest as though I'm staring at the floor. I shudder as she goes down on the ice-cream once more. And then it comes to me. Connie – of course. Our friendly neighbourhood American. I catch myself licking the tips of my teeth. Connie – why didn't I think of her before? I could give her a ring, see what she's up to, entice her over and . . . the next word is 'rape'. I recross my legs and watch my reflection in the window. I wouldn't of course – rape someone, that is – and of course I would. Physical violence is out of the question but what do I care for another person's consent? I'm not concerned with mutual recreation. I'm seeking to slip my dick unnoticed into some accommodating vagina, that's all. After all, that's what I've been doing with Ruth for all these years. Rape by default. But Connie? I rifle through my diary. Yes – I have her phone number. What's stopping me? But would she remember me? I can't just phone her up, ask if she fancies a fuck. But those breasts, those solid thighs. One glance at the little mulatto girl is enough to have me fumbling in my trouser pocket for a ten-pence coin for the phone.

14

The phone box outside Shepherd's Bush station smells as though it doubles as a urinal after dark. Sticky labels cover the windows: local prostitutes advertising services for sale. Their marketing has become increasingly sophisticated over recent years: no longer just numbers with Lola or Cathy written in green felt pen, now they have professionally printed stickers, pictures and all. One sticker advertising bondage, *Mistress Discipline*, has a passably drawn illustration of a dominatrix in leather boots and whip. I glance over them as I struggle to get my diary out of my pocket. *New eighteen year old*, one of them says. *New?* What are you when you aren't new any more? Second-hand? Used? I flick through the pages for Connie's number. *Forty-year-old model available – one owner, good condition*. Love for sale? You've got to be joking: this was bodies for rent, nothing more. I hold the receiver at a hygienic distance from my mouth and begin dialling. Three digits into Connie's number and I rest my hand on the handset, cutting off the signal. Hold on a sec – how am I going to do this? I haven't spoken to her since the party, and that was two months ago. I put the phone down to think about it. Would she remember me? I know we made no secret of our lust for each other, but we were both drunk, and it was a party after all. People do that sort of thing at parties – it doesn't mean anything. I can feel the muscle in my jaw twitching as I redial. I hold my breath as the phone rings, once, twice, three times and then:

C: Hello?

J: Hello Connie. Ha – ha. (*Don't laugh, you fool!*)

C: Who's this?

J: James (*one . . . two . . . three*) We met at Phil's party. Remember? (*. . . four . . . five*)

C: Oh, hi. How are you?

J: (*Thank God.*) Fine thanks. And you?

C: I'm fine.

J: Good, I was just wondering how you've been. (*You've asked that.*)

C: I've been fine. Hold on a second.

J: Good. (*Go for it, Jimmy boy.*) I thought maybe we could meet some time. You know, if you're not . . . busy or anything . . . er . . . (*Come on, Connie – say something!*) . . . er . . . Hello?

C: Sorry about that – the milk was boiling over.

J: Milk? (*Milk?*)

C: I caught it just in time.

J: Oh . . . good. (*Oh . . . shit!*)

C: What were you saying?

J: Just phoning for a chat. (*Liar.*)

C: Uh-huh.

J: Umm . . . (*One more time.*) I thought maybe we could meet some time.

C: Sure. But what about your girlfriend – what's her name?

J: Ruth . . . ? Oh, that finished ages ago. (*Oh yeah?*)

C: So you're on your own now?

J: (*Don't just nod, say something.*) Are you seeing anyone?

C: Not really.

J: Would you like to . . . ? (*Umm . . .*) Umm . . .?

C: Why not?

J: What are you doing now?

C: Drinking Horlicks.

J: (*Whore licks?*)

C: I was going to have a night in.

J: How about coming over here? (*Yes, yes, yes!*)

C: Where do you live?

J: Shepherd's Bush. (*Please God, let her say yes.*) Do you know it?

C: Sure.

J: I'll come and pick you up. (*Why did I say that?*)

C: Okay.

J: Oh. (*Idiot!*) The car's . . . umm . . . out of order . . .

C: I'll get a cab.

J: All right. Then maybe you can . . . (*Don't say that!*)

C: Say what?

J: (*Stay the night.*) Tell him my address. (*Groan.*)

C: I don't know your address.

I can feel the sweat sticking my shirt to my back as I tell her my address. I gingerly replace the receiver and stare blindly at the code-list in front of me. I'd been absent-mindedly picking at the corner of one of the stickers on the door and I smear it back into place. Golden Showers, it says. *Golden Showers?* People *paid* other people to piss on them? I wipe my fingers on the seat of my trousers and push the door open. Well, I'd done it. Scored, I think the expression is.

But Connie? *You get me into trouble over this, and I'll slam you in a car door, you one-eyed son of a bitch.*

I have no time to tidy up the flat apart from straightening the duvet and plumping up the cushions on the sofa. I'm halfway through hiding the dirty saucepans under the sink when I realise I'd better arm myself before she arrives: it has been years since I've used condoms, but I think there are some in the bathroom. I find a packet in the medicine cabinet, one corner of the box sticky from cough-syrup. When was the last time I used one of these? I check the use-by date: April 1988. I take one out and put it on the shelf over the sink. Only a year or so out of date, it would have to do.

'Please God,' I say to the mirror, 'don't let her be having

her period.' I smile experimentally at myself, and then decide to brush my teeth. I study my reflection, foam bubbling out of my mouth. 'What's that thing under your nose?' I say to myself. 'It looks like a caterpillar.'

'It's a moustache.'

'Well, shave it off – it looks ridiculous.'

'But I haven't got time.'

'Shave it off.'

And of course, I nick myself in my hurry to do just that. I have to answer the door with a little flag of toilet paper fluttering from my chin. 'Hi!' I say, a little too brightly. Thank God I recognised her straightaway.

'Hi.'

'Let me pay for your taxi.'

'Thank you.'

Ah. 'How much was it?'

'I was joking.'

I smile back at her uncertainly. 'Let me take your coat.'

'I don't have one.'

'What's this?' I indicate the orange denim thing she's wearing.

'It's a jacket and I've got nothing on underneath.'

'Oh. Come in.'

'Thanks.' Two steps into the sitting-room, I remember the Durex I left on the shelf above the sink. Oh shit. I consider making a dash for the bathroom, but decide against it. 'Would you like a drink?'

'What have you got?'

'Gin. Martini. Vodka.'

'Got a beer?'

'Take a seat,' I say, but she already has. I go to the drinks cabinet and pull the flap down. I frown and then bend to look inside: it's empty. 'I don't believe it? She's taken all the booze!'

'Who?'

'Ruth – she came over today to pick up some of her stuff.' Oops, she's supposed to have left ages ago. I open the sliding door and check if there's any wine left. No – she's taken it all. She's even taken the glasses. 'Cow!' I

122

mutter under my breath. Connie is watching me, surprise on her face. 'You'll have to drink it out of the can I'm afraid.'

'That's okay.'

'I'll get your beer. There's one in the fridge, I think.' I hope.

I move out of her range of vision. The fridge: one week of living alone and it already has a desolate look to it. A wedge of mouldy liver pâté, a plate of congealed spaghetti, an open pack of suspiciously pink bacon, two eggs, an empty margarine container. No beer. It looks as though an unfinished meal has been hurriedly stuffed into the fridge.

'Ah,' is all she needs to hear.

'Don't worry,' she calls through. 'Actually, James?'

I poke my head round the corner. She's flicking through the evening paper, and looks up with a smile. 'Have you got anything to eat? I'm starving.'

'Sure, we've got a full freezer.' I catch the 'we', and bite my tongue. It's 'me' from now on – remember that. 'What do you want? Lasagne? Ice-cream? Fish fingers?'

'Lasagne. Would that be a hassle?'

'No problem.' I turn back into the kitchen to prepare it for her. It takes me a few seconds to realise the gap in the sideboard is the exact spot where the microwave oven used to be. I stare stupidly at the space before my brain has a chance to catch up. Ruth – she can't have. 'I don't believe it! She's nicked it!'

Connie comes into the kitchen. 'Nicked what?'

'The microwave.'

'Was it yours?'

'No,' I protest. 'But that's not the point.'

I look around the kitchen for the first time. The kettle, the toaster. Gone. I fling open the cupboard doors. Plates. No plates.

Connie watches me uncertainly. She has the sense not to say anything.

'Let me tell you, Connie. That bloody woman was the barrenest, meanest – ' I catch myself and stop. Let's not put Connie off before we've got started. But damn Ruth

123

– even after she's left me, she insists on screwing things up. My first date and look at me!

Connie wisely chooses to change the subject. She swings open the fridge door. 'What's that?' She points at what looks like a giant green amoeba on the bottom shelf. It's the jelly rabbit, still crouching there, perpetually on its guard against jelly foxes.

'Jelly.'

'Great! And . . . cream.'

A pot of single cream left over from the food orgy. I hold it under my nose and wince: it looks like Edam and smells like Stilton. 'Off.'

'Top of the milk?'

Persistent girl – I'll give her that.

She goes back to the sitting-room, leaving me to serve the jelly. I bring it out and set it on the table in front of her. By some sort of molecular slippage, the rabbit's features have melted back into its body, and uncannily, it now resembles nothing so much as a perfectly formed, green, female, breast.

She looks up from the paper and stares at it. It wobbles as though nodding hello at her.

'But it's a boob!' she exclaims, delighted.

'It used to be a rabbit.'

'What happened?'

'Myxomatosis,' I say dully.

She cuts into the breast with a spoon, a sucking sound as she mastectomises it. 'I always think jello's so sexy, don't you?'

Did you hear her? Sexy, she says. Two weeks it has been waiting in my fridge to have that compliment paid it. My timing is definitely off; as off as the cream.

But listen to this: we talk and talk and talk. Fancy that – this rather short, rather busty girl with the interesting accent and disarming honesty is like a fascinating foreign coin I've found in the loose change in my pocket: she had been there all along, just waiting for me to reach in and pull her out. It's not just wanting to get her into bed that makes me sparkle. I genuinely like the girl.

124

We talk about elephants, what musical instruments neither of us play but wish we did, our mutual distrust of machinery. She tries to explain the American school system to me, and I tell her about Miss Bryant and the infant-school uniform I used to wear. We compare memories of travelling, broken bones, camping in Virginia (she) and Cornwall (me). She's younger than I thought – just twenty-three; she still has that peachy, flawless skin of a teenage girl; hair as shiny as a horse's mane, good teeth, an easy laugh. She's been in England nearly a year, staying with her uncle, a cellist with the RPO. She's working as a groom in a stable in – of all places – Kensington. I tell her I never knew there were stables in London, and I get a short lecture on the history of the horse in London. From the outside looking in, it probably doesn't look like much, but from where we're sitting we're as cosy as a pair of jacket potatoes.

We're gravitating closer and closer towards each other on the sofa, until I can smell her scrubbed smell. I show her the photos from my trip to Paris. The Champs-Elysées, the Latin quarter, the Eiffel Tower. Big deal. Neither of us is interested, but what do we care? My arm brushes her breast as I lean across to turn a page of the album, and she doesn't move away.

Four hours of this, and the question can't be avoided any more: I'm gorging myself on her, and could happily eat and eat and eat, but my eyes are getting heavy. One of us will have to make a move – I have to work in the morning.

I decide to broach the subject. 'Uh,' I say. 'Another cup of coffee?' Please stay. I love you.

'No thanks. I'd better go soon. It's nearly two o'clock.'

'You can stay if you want.' I cringe at my clumsiness, but she raises an eyebrow at me.

'Where can I sleep?'

I pat the sofa. 'This is fairly comfortable. Or . . . uh . . .' She smiles, deciding not to help me out. 'There's a double bed upstairs.'

'I'll sleep with you, James. But *sleep* is all. No funny stuff.'

125

All right! I tidy up the coffee cups so she can't see the grin on my face. All . . . right! 'Let's go to bed – I'm knackered.'

I show Connie the bathroom and give her my dressing-gown so she can change in the bathroom. I remember the condom on the shelf, but it's too late, and anyway, a little more focus on the sex won't do any harm. I'm glad I shaved my moustache off – to tell the truth, it was far from successful.

I lie on my back on the bed, waiting for Connie to finish in the bathroom. So, how am I feeling? I ask myself. Scared, certainly; tired, you bet. But excited. Sex seems to be out of bounds for tonight, but I'm not going to protest. Whether we make love or not, this is a night to remember. There *will* be other nights? I hope so. I hadn't anticipated enjoying Connie's company so much. I hadn't anticipated enjoying Connie's *anything* so much. I want more of her. I'm so excited I give a little victory wiggle on the bed.

She comes through from the bathroom and stands at the foot of the bed. 'That's quite a bathroom.'

'Oh?'

'The mirrors.' She doesn't have Ruth's height, and wearing my dressing-gown, she looks even shorter than ever. She's not my body type, but that doesn't stop a little moth of lust fluttering up my windpipe.

'Ruth's design – I had nothing to do with that.' I swing my legs off the bed and stand up. She's waiting to be kissed. We stand smiling, toe to toe, and she lifts her head while I bend my neck. We hesitate mouth to mouth and then she stands on tiptoe to kiss my forehead. She can see the question in my eyes as we separate. The forehead? Connie laughs aloud and I find myself grinning back. I'm going to enjoy this girl.

She holds up something between her thumb and fore-finger. At first I have trouble seeing what it is.

'You'd better throw this away, James.'

It's the condom.

'It's an antique. I hope you weren't thinking of using it?'

I take the thing from her and toss it into the bin. 'Perish

the thought,' I quip, making a mental note to buy some more: the girl is asking for it.

I dig out an old pair of Paisley pyjamas from the airing cupboard, and change in the bathroom. I haven't worn these since I was a kid, and it looks like it. The legs stop midway down my calves, the arms likewise mid-forearm. The buttons strain across my chest, but I manage to do them all up. My movements are restricted, but I manage to scrub my teeth without any buttons popping off. I wish my ten thousand reflections good luck, and then head for the bedroom.

Connie shrieks with laughter when she sees me. I grin in what I hope is a rueful manner and hop into bed beside her. My sudden action is too much for the cotton and there is a loud ripping sound from under one of the arms.

Connie is having hysterics. 'I said – no funny stuff. Come on – take it off.' She sits up to help me and the sheets slip down to her waist revealing a frilly lilac bra, filled to the brim with female breast. I gag slightly as she tugs the jacket over my head, catching the material round my neck. Those lifted arms: the sweet deodorant, the proximity of those lilac-clad . . . things. I'm close to swooning as she tosses the ripped jacket on to the chair, and already there is a stirring in my groin.

We snuggle down, four hands in unison pulling the sheet up to our chins. How the hell am I going to sleep next to this girl with an erection like this?

'Are you sure you don't want to change your mind?' I ask hopefully.

She must have known what I was thinking about because she answers with not a second's hesitation. 'No.'

I'm not going to ask, but the word just pops out. 'Why?'

'I'm having my period.'

Damn you God!

'You can wait can't you?'

I've melted inside: I'm a pool of syrupy butter. *You can wait, can't you?* There's going to be more: it's Christmas eve, we've hardly started yet. She seeks my hand under the sheets and gives it a squeeze. 'That's best isn't it?'

The child tyrant nods from within my pyjamas, though somehow I doubt that it's a nod of agreement.

Have you tried getting to sleep next to a stranger? And one with so much bared flesh? Connie had apparently dropped off as soon as the light went out, but do you think I can sleep? I'm buzzing with adrenalin. I shuffle discretely until my thigh is against Connie's. Is she wearing underpants? I can't make it out through the pyjama material. I listen to check that her regular breathing hasn't been interrupted and then turn on my side with a sleepy groan, letting my hand fall against her crotch. Yup – I can feel it, the same lacy material. Without warning, my hand is lifted and dropped on to my side of the bed. 'Hands off,' Connie whispers.

The worst things that can happen to you: number one in an interminable list: waking in the night to find you've ejaculated all over the person sleeping next to you.

I slip off my pyjama trousers and try to wipe it off Connie, but she moans and turns over with her back to me. I estimate that her left thigh has taken the brunt of the blast and I gingerly trace the extent of the sticky patch. My God – where does it stop? Two weeks of semen at close range – it's a mess. The top sheet is already beginning to stick to her thigh and I'm feeling sick with anxiety.

I slide out of bed and creep to the bathroom, praying that Connie is a heavy sleeper. The light in the bathroom is so bright that I can't open my eyes more than a slit. I grope my way to the sink and wash my groin and thighs with hot water.

'What have you done, you stupid bastard?' I whisper at myself. She'd wake up in the morning, a shiny patch on her thighs and she'd know damn well what happened. Suddenly I see the whole thing: a stranger asleep in my bed, the seed of my loins drying on a thigh I'd never even seen, let alone caressed. The end of a beautiful friendship.

'You stupid bastard,' I hiss at the white face in the mirror. I shove the trousers into the laundry basket and stand, all ten thousand of me, thin and guilty, looking at myself.

A line of William Blake's comes to mind: *The invisible worm that flies in the night has found out thy bed of crimson joy*. What *does* that mean? Errant sperm?

'Oh rose, thou art sick,' I say to myself in the mirror, checking my tongue as a doctor might.

It's hours before I get back to sleep, and then what seems minutes later, I'm wakened by someone shaking my shoulder. At first I think it's Ruth, and wonder what she's doing back in my bed, but then I remember. And then I remember last night. But Connie's already up and dressed. I can't meet her look: if she has discovered the evidence, I don't want to know about it. I would deny my own mother at this moment if I thought it would help.

'Sleep well?' I ask her over the muesli and tea. Still no sign from her: she either hasn't noticed, or has decided to save herself the embarrassment. She needn't bother, I'm embarrassed enough for both of us.

But it's off to work we go. A little less hi-ho-hi-ho in my step than there might have been under different circumstances, but a fifteen-minute walk through the morning park with another person does something to lift the spirits.

15

I'm abstracted all morning. My body may be consistently at my desk, but the luminous ball of my thoughts is bouncing between Hammersmith library and the Kensington stables with unsettling speed. What's going on with Connie? We parted at the traffic-lights without saying anything about future meetings. She kissed me politely, waved when she'd crossed the road, but no indication that she wanted to see me again.

Absurd – of course she wants to see me again. Didn't she say as much? And no matter what happened in the middle of the night, we *did* enjoy ourselves. It was the best evening I've had for years; ruined only by the child tyrant. I run through the morning's conversation: was there any indication that she'd realised what had happened? She'd slept well, she said, commented on the lack of cereal bowls, asked me how long it took me to get to work. But her look: the sly smile on her face when I came downstairs, what had that meant? She might not have spotted the crusty sheets, but the plasticky patch of dried semen on her thigh would be there until she washed it off: if she hasn't found it yet, she would by tonight. And if she asks me about it, what can I say? A slug got into the bed last night?

Oh, but that body, those breasts, that sexy smile! I can feel the thrill surging through me, sparks flying out my fingertips. I'm getting that hungry feeling again, a delicious yearning located not so much in my groin as in the pit of my belly. There's something missing down there: something the shape and flavour of Connie. There's no doubt about it – I'm in lust.

What a night, and what a cock-up. Every time I remember what I've done, it's as though a stick has been shoved in the spokes of my freewheeling bicycle. It's a bad dream, it has to be. Nobody ejaculates over a first date. 'A thousand thousand slimy things lived on,' I quote under my breath, 'and so did I.'

I hear clattering footsteps down the stairs, and a middle-aged man rushes past me, coat tails flapping, tie flying over his shoulder as he runs out. I don't have time to wonder about him when someone shouts, 'Stop him!'

I look from the disappearing figure back to the stairs. Hilary is in hot pursuit. She skids to a halt by the desk and pulls me by the shoulder so she can hiss in my ear. 'A flasher! Catch him!' I hesitate but she's propelling me from behind my desk and so I trot to the exit. Heads are beginning to turn.

I look both ways down the road, but there's no sign of the man. I run a hundred yards towards the tube, but I can't see him, so I walk back to the library.

Hilary is in the staffroom with a young girl. The girl is sipping a mug of tea, steam fogging her glasses.

'No luck,' I tell them.

'I've called the police,' Hilary says. 'Did you get a good look at him?'

'Not really.'

She takes me to one side. 'Apparently he was wanking behind one of the shelves, and then flashed himself at this girl.'

'Sorry?' I haven't heard, and she has to repeat herself.

I look at the girl: thirteen or so, a local schoolgirl judging by her grey uniform. She's taking the tea in tiny sips, not lowering the mug from her mouth. Fright more than anything, I expect. What's a swollen prick in this day and age? 'Do we really need the police?' I ask Hilary.

'James. She's been sexually assaulted.'

'He didn't touch her, did he?'

'No, but that's not the point.'

I look at the girl again: she's younger than I thought at first. I see now that she's clinging to the cup in order to hold back her tears. Her eyes don't leave the floor. I suddenly want to apologise to her. I don't know what I'd say, but I feel guilty because this girl's afternoon has been shattered by a man with an erection. I want to wipe away the event, go back to half an hour ago so that I can steer the girl away from the nexus of her and this man. I don't want it to have happened. I don't want it to continue to happen.

The policeman asks me for a description of the man and then tells me to keep an eye out for him. 'We're getting a lot of this sort of thing now. Not a lot we can do about this one. We won't catch him now.' His tone is businesslike, resigned.

I'm subdued for the rest of the afternoon. Somehow the issue of Connie seems less important now. Perhaps it was a dream after all.

However, the urge starts up as soon as I get home and I dither for half an hour before I decide against phoning her. Without a good enough reason, I may look too keen, and that would only scare her off. Or so I tell myself. I'd hoped she'd left something behind at the flat by mistake, so that I had a legitimate excuse to ring her, but I search the bedroom and bathroom in vain.

By nine o'clock I can't stand it anymore, and find myself dialling her number. She sounds pleased to hear from me, and I breathe again. 'How are you?' she asks. 'I had fun last night, didn't you? Did you have a nice day?' Her accent is more American on the phone.

'Fine. And you?'

'So-so.'

'Any chance of meeting up tomorrow?'

She pauses. 'What time do you take lunch?'

'One.'

'Want to have lunch together?'

Is the Pope Catholic? Do bears shit in the woods? 'Great!'

I suggest meeting in the Angel for a drink, but Connie would rather be outside, so we arrange to meet on the north side of the Green for a sandwich lunch.

I'm never comfortable about using the phone. Not being able to see the speaker's lips, I often lose half the conversation, but for once, I'm happy to talk until there's nothing more to say. It's nearly ten o'clock before I put the phone down, pleased with myself, the world, Connie.

I skip down the steps at lunchtime, twisting my ankle on the bottom step and nearly falling into the path of a pushchair. Careful, James, I tell myself. Don't get too excited. I smile at the young mother's startled expression and indicate for her to go first. I still can't believe my luck. Who would have thought that a girl, hardly on the periphery of my vision a couple of days ago, would today be standing at the very centre of my attention: young, cheeky and interested in me? I'm so excited, I want to run all the way to meet her, but I force myself to walk slowly. I buy sandwiches for both of us at Joe's and then trot the rest of the way.

It's another scorching day, and the Green is busy with sunbathers. The grass is browner than last week: soon there will be nothing left but dust and weeds. I see somebody waving in the distance and realise it's Connie. Keep your cool, I warn myself; look before you leap, knock before you enter. I deliberately slow my pace as I approach her. We don't know how to greet each other, and my hands flap around as though I'm using semaphore. I spread my jacket on the ground and offer it for her to sit on.

'You're such a gentleman,' she says, parking her bum neatly on to it.

I smirk my flirtatious smile and drop next to her on to my outstretched arms. I used to do that a lot when I was a kid but I don't remember it hurting my wrists so much. I secretly clench and unclench my hands as I watch her unwrap the sandwiches. Those slightly podgy fingers picking at the Cellophane, the business-like way she's wedged the second pack of sandwiches between her arm and her bosom: ah! I take the soggy bread she hands me. I want to be her teddy bear, sleepy and sunny and loved.

We eat our sandwiches in silence and then lie back and watch the clouds. I can see one that looks like the profile of a pig and I point it out to her. Connie snuggles until her head is on my shoulder. There's that smell again: her perfume or shampoo or something. I slide out from under her and prop myself up on one elbow and look at her.

'What is it?' she asks.

There's a piece of grass in her hair, and I brush it out. I continue to smooth her hair; I can't believe how shiny and blonde it is, and I tell her. The sun is catching her eyes and I can see speckles and stripes in their depths. And then the world seems to fragment, slowing down to individual frames as I lean over her and hold my lips above hers and inhale the warmth of her mouth. Our lips brush each others, dry, and then moist as we press gently. Our tongues meet, tip to tip, and then deeper. We part for a moment and she whimpers quietly before we kiss again. A new touch, a new taste; lips as soft as clotted cream. I'm in heaven.

We separate and I lay back while Connie rests her head on my shoulder again. What a kiss! The girl can barely contain her passion; I could feel it in the hungriness of her touch. I grin up at the sky. Sometimes I wonder what I'd do if

133

the three-minute nuclear-attack warning sounded. Run for shelter? Lie down and wait? Panic? Lying there next to Connie, I have no doubt. Five seconds into that wail and we would be stuck groin to groin, our pants around our ankles. Something sags inside me at the thought: three minutes of that would be worth dying for.

I close my eyes and let Shepherd's Bush recede until the roar of traffic is the crash of waves on a beach. I feel drugged by the heat. We lie like that until I hear the time signal on a transistor radio. Two o'clock. I force myself back up on to one elbow and look down at her. 'Wakey wakey.'

She opens her muscovado eyes and stretches her arms above her head. The suggestion pops out of nowhere. 'Would you like to go out tonight?' I ask. 'Go for a meal somewhere?' As soon as I see her flicker of hesitation, I know that it's lost. I begin to retract the offer, but we're both talking at the same time.

'Of course, if you— '

'I'd love to but— '

'No problem— '

She doesn't voice her regret, but the face she pulls is enough apology. 'How about Wednesday?' she says after a moment.

'Fine!' I leap at the suggestion as though it's a far better idea.

'I'll give you a ring to arrange the time.' Standing, our height differences mean I have to duck to hug Connie goodbye. She brings her face up to mine, her lips open. I can feel the pressure of her body straining for more, her tongue forcing open my lips and flicking over my teeth. I can hear that siren start up. Suddenly she breaks off, smiles, and then without saying anything, turns and leaves.

I follow her with my eyes until she reaches the road and disappears behind the traffic. I can still taste Connie on my tongue; still feel those solid breasts pressed against my chest. It takes me back to my schooldays: snogging with girls from the local convent school, their mouths tasting of chewing gum and cigarette smoke. But that

134

was child's play compared to this. Those were girls, this is a woman.

I carry the warmth of our embrace back to the library as though it's a fluffy little chick in my pocket. I can't wait to be alone and examine this little ball of down and see exactly what manner of bird has hatched.

Tad phones in the afternoon. I have the unpleasant feeling that he's keeping tabs on me. I tell him I can't chat, so he asks if we can meet after work. I'm not finishing till late, and I want an early night, but I tell him he can come shopping with me for a bit.

Shopping? Top of the list is condoms. In the chemist I look through the shaving cream until Tad buzzes off behind an aisle and then I go to the prescriptions counter: I don't want him to see what I'm up to. I look at the range of condoms in front of me: there's something for everyone here: supersafe, coloured, packets with sunsets and silhouettes, others that look more like fashion accessories than anything else. Sign of the times, I suppose.

'Can I help you?'

Who is it that designs the layout of chemists so that the shelf of condoms is always just in front of a young female attendant? How many unwanted pregnancies in the world because of the unhappy mix of insensitive design, embarrassment and sheer bad luck? There's such a bewildering selection, I'm tempted to buy vitamin C tablets instead, but I pick up the nearest packet and give it to the girl with the shaving cream. I've been spoilt by the Pill: it has been a long time since I've had to take any responsibility in that area. All Ruth had to do was pop a pill and that was it. No trouble, no risk – at least for me. It was Ruth who had to contend with daily hormonal poisoning and the threat of cancer.

'What's going on, James?' Dammit, Tad has seen what I've bought. 'Is there something you're not telling me?'

I tell him briefly about Connie. I can't see his face, but as soon as he speaks I can hear the upset in his voice.

'Do you know why contraception has traditionally been the role of the female in society? Because deep down, men

135

can't bear to see the death of all those potential clones that just pour out of him by the million. In fact, if it wasn't for women, and the indignity and pain and downright inconvenience of growing another human being inside themselves, I doubt if birth control would have got beyond the stage of female infanticide.' Outside the chemist, he won't meet my eyes. 'I'll see you around, then.' He spins his chair round.

'Tad?' I follow him. 'Hold on.' But he doesn't stop, and I watch him jiggling away at top speed. 'Fuck you, then,' I mutter, and turn to go home.

There's a message on the answer phone when I get back. It's Connie. *I can make that date after all. Can I say yes to tomorrow?*

'Yes!' My heart is a yo-yo and Connie has the string round her little finger. I dance across the room, doing a tango with an invisible partner. Things are moving along nicely. I have a bath and then fish and chips from the local take-away; a bottle of Guinness; Vincent Price on the telly: bliss. I try to watch the film, but my mind is on other things. Like l-u-r-v-e.

A plan is needed; a strategy. I scribble a timetable on the back of an envelope:

13.00 hours – book a table at a restaurant
18.30 hours – wash and brush up at home
20.00 hours – romantic dinner for two
22.30 hours – home for a nightcap and then . . .

I lower the pen and gaze at the television screen: the hapless victim is at the local inn, already being warned of the Count who lives on the hill. But would Connie's period have finished by then? I count the days on my fingers: Sunday, Monday, Tuesday – three days. Was she just starting or just finishing on Sunday? No matter – the sex isn't the main thing. No – a heart is on offer. Sex is just a commodity: any of the local sticker-clad phone boxes is proof of that. The *heart* is the thing. The living, pulsing, emotional centre of another human being.

I snuggle into the sofa and watch Count Dracula sink his fangs into his first victim: this is the life.

16

Connie had suggested an Italian restaurant she knew within walking distance of both of our places, and we agreed to meet there at eight o'clock. I should have picked her up in my sports car, I know, but it was at the garage that day, and anyway this was the age of female liberation, and anyway it was good exercise. Truth is, it never occurred to me to meet her at her uncle's place. It had been so long since I'd taken a woman out to dinner that I'd forgotten the rules of play. It has also been so long since I'd been to the launderette that the only clean piece of clothing I had was a black T-shirt, but luckily it didn't look too bad under a suit jacket. Half smart, half neat: a safe bet for wherever we're going.

I squeeze into a pair of Ruth's black jeans she'd forgotten to take with her, tuck what's left of this month's wages into the back pocket with a condom, and I'm ready. I give the flat a five-minute tidy up before I leave, cursing myself for not having prepared things better. There's still no food in the fridge, no booze in the cabinet. And when was the last time I changed the sheets? I take the rubbish out with me when I go, splashing baked bean sauce on to my lapel in my hurry.

She's late – of course she is. What woman would happily sit in a restaurant waiting for a date? By the time she arrives I've almost finished my second bread stick and the glass of red wine I ordered is two mouthfuls away from being empty.

'Sorry I'm late. Have you been waiting long?'

'Not long. How are you?' She looks great. She's wearing a pastel summer dress, her breasts straining the stitching of the bodice. Blonde hair cascades around her shoulders. I half stand and lean across the table to kiss her on the cheek. She's wearing make-up: rust-coloured eyeshadow, and her lips have been painted until they look like two peach segments. She's the very opposite of Ruth, and nice enough to eat.

I sit down and pass her the leather-bound menu. This place is more expensive than I had hoped. 'Did it take you long to get here?'

'I caught a taxi – it's only five minutes.'

'What do you fancy?' I ask, nodding at the menu. I've been through it already, but I make a show of consulting the menu once again. My eyes flick right to left, checking the price against every entry. I have thirty-five quid to spend, and my cheque-book in my pocket just in case.

I can see her finger tracing down the list of antipasto. 'Shall we share a couple of starters?'

'Good idea.'

'How about some mussels?'

'I don't like mussels. Anchovies and mussels are the only things I can't eat. My mother, too.' I take a sip of wine before I realise how the last sentence sounded. 'I mean my mother couldn't eat mussels either – '

She smiles at me, relaxed and plump as a cat by the fireside. 'I wouldn't mind a salad with some pâté. How would that be?'

'Fine.'

'You wouldn't like an avocado or something?'

'Pâté's fine.' Her tiny gold necklace catches the candle-light and I have a powerful urge to kiss the cute little mole where her neck joins the rest of her body. 'What about your main course?'

'I have this craving for some fish. The *pesce*'s good here – I think I'll go for that.'

Good girl, that's only a fiver. 'And wine?'

'A bottle of house red?' I'm doing quick sums in my head. About twenty quid so far.

I flag a passing waiter down and give our order. I stumble over the Italian pronunciation of the food and have to repeat it in English. Connie meanwhile is busy admiring the waiter. She even turns to watch him as he heads back to the kitchen. A Romeo with nine-inch hips and a toothpaste smile. I wait until she turns back to me, and then arch an eyebrow questioningly. Not that I'm asking a question – it's an expression I picked up from some film or other. It's intended to look devastatingly seductive. I don't know what Connie makes of it.

'Is your mother still alive?' she says without warning.

'No. She died a couple of years ago.'

'Oh.' She doesn't add anything. She glances around the restaurant and then examines something on the wall behind my head. 'How?' she says at last.

'She had cancer.'

'I'm sorry to hear that.'

'They had to cut most of her stomach out.' A warning bell sounds in my head: it's a while since I've been on a first date, but I know stomach cancer is not a recommended topic. 'Do your parents live in Virginia?'

'Yes.'

'That's nice.' I don't know if it is or not, but it's something to say. Where's all the familiarity of Sunday night? But she *does* look lovely.

'You look lovely,' I say.

'Thank you,' she says, surprised.

'What's that perfume you wear? It drives me crazy.'

'Ah.' She smiles full into my face. I'm on to a winner here. 'In that case I'll keep it a secret.'

The wine arrives and we wait while two glasses are poured out. There is a confusion over my first glass and the waiter takes it away even though I haven't finished with it.

'What about your father?'

'Alive and well and making a packet in Brazil.'

'A packet?' she queries.

'Of money.'

'Doing what?'

'I don't know. Business.'

'Do you ever see him?'

I can feel my hackles rise. Connie doesn't know it, but we're on treacherous ground. 'I didn't even see him when he was my father. They split up when I was young. He was always abroad on business.'

139

'And no brothers and sisters?'

This is definitely prying. 'No.'

'So, it's just you?'

'Yes.'

'*Scusa, signore.*' I look up in surprise. The waiter is bending conspiratorially low beside me.

'Yes?'

'Do you have a car number – ' He consults his scrap of paper. 'ALU one-seven-two?' He pronounces the letters ah-elle-oo.

'Umm.' I look as though I'm considering the question. 'No?'

'I'm sorry. It is someone has parked illegally and you know, the police . . .' He doesn't finish the sentence. I nod, man to man. Yes, we know the police.

The starters arrive and we both sit back to allow the waiter to make space on the table.

'What kind of automobile do you drive?' she asks between his darting hands.

I don't know how she's managing to do it, but Connie's two forays so far into conversation have been direct hits: my family and my masculinity: two of my tenderest topics. 'I don't drive. I had one driving lesson a few years ago but I had to chuck it in. It was too much like playing one of those video games. You know – where you have to sit in a cockpit and pretend to be a racing driver.' I laugh tentatively, but Connie only smiles back. 'I couldn't trust myself to take it seriously enough, so I gave it up.' It's a prepared line I have, and not strictly true. My one and only lesson behind the wheel of a car frightened me so much that I vowed never to try it again. It had been the thought of all that power that had scared me. And me, James Morrison, responsible for it all.

The equation of masculinity and the ability to drive a car is the product of a favourite unexamined belief system of mine which, simply put, means that as most men over twenty can drive, and I'm nearly thirty and can't, ergo I'm not a proper man. Patent bullshit of course, but it's a myth I've bought.

140

The flourish with which the waiter serves our food is deserving of something more impressive than two plates of spaghetti. It's as though he's performing a brilliant conjuring feat for us. Ta-ra! And for my next trick I will grate pepper you don't want over your spaghetti. Connie seems to like him though.

I try to be scintillating throughout the meal, but I can't get my brain engaged. Even as the words plop out of my mouth I know how badly I'm doing. Why have I decided to be nervous now? It doesn't help having a group of young women on the next table who are obviously having a much better time than we are. Feminists, I suppose, judging from their haircuts and the quality and volume of noise they're making. Connie is filling me in with updated news about our only common acquaintance – Phil – and though I try to be interested, the best part of my attention is on the conversation from the next table. I can only catch snatches of what they're saying, but I can see them eyeing the waiters and laughing. Is this what Ruth is up to? Plotting the overthrow of the patriarchy with her butch chums? I try tuning them out, screwing my attention to Connie, but short of plugging my ears I can't stop myself listening. One of the women has a high-pitched laugh, slightly hysterical, with which she keeps puncturing the conversation, oblivious to the disapproving glances from other tables. Eighty years earlier, they would have been suffragettes; but now what do they talk about? There's a lull in the rest of the room and I strain to hear what they're saying. 'And you know how Sal gets so ardent about the fur trade? Well, Hugo bought her one of those little furry things – what are they called?'

'A yak?' someone suggests.

'A caterpillar?'

Hysterical laughter from the woman. She's either pissed, or a full-time major pain in the arse. 'No – they're toys, about this big. They were popular in the sixties.'

'Teddy bears?'

'My Beautiful Pony?'

'What?'

'No – I know the ones you mean. It was a lion, wasn't it?'

A gonk.

'World-cup Willie.'

'World-cup wanker, if I know Hugo.'

Ha ha ha, from the one with the laugh.

'They're those things with long hair. Like a cave man. Oh, what are they called?' The poor woman is in pain. 'Donks, or something.'

'Oh, I know. Bonks.'

Gonks, for God's sake.

'James?'

My attention jerks back to Connie. 'Pardon?' Connie has ducked her head, facetiously looking up into my face.

'How's your food?'

'Fine.' Truth is I haven't tasted a mouthful of it. It's warm, that's all I can say.

'Don't you ever chew?'

'What do you mean?'

'You're practically drinking your spaghetti – doesn't it give you indigestion?'

Ruth had complained of that. It isn't as though I eat quickly: in fact I've developed a particularly languid style of eating: one elbow on the table – I rarely use a knife – I've made an art of toying with my food. Ruth had thought I was in danger of becoming anorexic, but as I told her – anorexics think they're fat: I *knew* I was thin. I don't know if there's some deep-seated psychological explanation, or whether I'm just lazy, but I never give food more than a desultory chew – especially if I think someone is watching me. I try not to order anything in restaurants that demands too much attention: soup is a favourite, pasta too. There's something faintly obscene about eating: perhaps somewhere along the line I got mastication and masturbation confused, who knows?

Connie and I chat for a minute, but my attention goes back to the other table. One of the women is telling the group about a man she spent the evening with recently, but I can't tell if it's a lover or just a friend. I shift in my seat to try to blank the conversation out, but it's too late.

I might as well be sitting on their table for all the attention I'm paying Connie. I miss most of the details of the story, but there's something obviously hilarious about the event, and when she finishes relating it, the table collapses into laughter, the hyena woman's laugh arching over the rest of them until heads begin to turn. 'He's such a show-off. I just wish he wasn't such a sexist bastard,' I hear the first woman say.

Sexist bastard? Is this what women get up to when they're together? Slag off men? I glance at Connie and she nods at the group of women. 'Did you hear that story?'

'Not really.' So *she* was listening too.

'Apparently her boyfriend got a job as a stripagram without telling her, and then took her out to a restaurant where he had his first job. Halfway through their meal, he gets up and goes over to another table, and starts singing Happy Birthday to this girl and stripping off his clothes. His girlfriend was so shocked, she ran out of the restaurant.' She laughs.

'And she thinks that's sexist, does she?'

Connie looks confused. 'What do you mean?'

'She called him a sexist bastard.'

'She called him *sexy*.'

'Ah.' I focus on my spaghetti. Idiot.

'But what is this Green Party thing?' Connie asks. 'I've been hearing a lot about it recently.' She indicates the woman who told the story: she has a Green Party badge pinned on her beret as though she's a 1990s Che Guevara.

I pour Connie another glass of wine. 'Ecologists. Surely you have Green politics in the States?'

'The only green thing that's taken seriously back home has a picture of a president on the front.'

'They think we need nothing less than a revolution. Tampering with the system won't help matters. For as long as the basis of society remains unbridled consumption, there's only one option – the dwindling into nothing of finite resources.'

Connie looks as though she has regretted asking the question, but I forge ahead none the less. 'They're right

143

of course. There's one massive question that our whole civilisation rests on, but no one thinks to ask it.'

I invite Connie to ask it, but it's clear she's waiting for me to continue. 'What will we do when things run out?' I'm aware of how pompous I'm sounding, but I can't stop myself. 'Only when we cut the last tree down and shoot the last buffalo will we discover that we can't eat money.' I have a nasty feeling I've misquoted the saying, but I let it stand.

'Buffalo?' I think Connie has realised as well.

'Or elephant, or whale. Take your pick. All economy is ecologically based: take away the natural resources and there is only one logical outcome. We'll starve.' I'm on the moral high ground: I can see for miles around.

Connie arches an eyebrow – so *she* can do it as well. 'You can't afford to lose any more weight,' she says with a smile. Is she taking the piss out of me?

'I'm serious.'

'So am I – you're far too skinny.'

She *is* taking the piss.

'*Signore, signorina.*' The gigolo is back. 'Would you like some dessert? Coffee? Ice-cream?'

'No.'

'Yes, please.'

He presents Connie with the open menu as though it's a bouquet of flowers. She glances at the page and then cranes to see the cake trolley. No wonder the girl is so fat.

'Some cake?' He seems delighted by the prospect.

'Is that strawberry gâteau?'

'*Sì*. Fresh strawberries. Very good.' He purses his lips as though he has a mouthful of the stuff.

'Okay.'

'*Signore?*'

'Nothing.'

He wheels the trolley over and delivers Connie a slab of gâteau. '*Crema?*'

'Yes, please.'

I watch stonily as he pours cream over the cake. Skinny? The waiter slides back into the shadows and fatso tucks in.

144

She concentrates on the cake as though I'm not there, as though the world isn't poisoning itself to death, as though the thousands of Ethiopia aren't starving. And with every forkful I resent her more. Especially as I wish I'd ordered a piece.

'Sorry, James. Carry on with what you were saying.'

She called me skinny. Fuck the environment. She called me *skinny*. 'It doesn't matter.'

'We'll starve, you said.'

'Forget it. It's not worth it.'

'Have some cake.' She holds a spoonful out to me. It's a peace-offering and I wrinkle my nose as though it is a lump of shit she's proposing I eat.

She shakes her head and pops the spoon into her own mouth. 'You don't *have* to be so disapproving all the time, James.'

'What do you mean?'

'Or so heavy. Remember, angels can fly because they take themselves lightly,' she says. Lightly.

'Who wants to be an angel?'

'Oh, oh, oh,' she groans in what is presumably a parody of myself. If there was any doubt before, there isn't now: the barricades are up. I watch her, tight-lipped, as she finishes her cake.

'You *can* give up control, James,' she says, licking the cream from her fork. 'You proved that on Sunday night,' she adds as an afterthought.

'Sunday night? How?'

I can see that she's regretted saying it. 'I'm not going to say anything. It's up to you.'

'What are you talking about?' She couldn't. Surely not. She wiggles an eyebrow at me, a mocking glint in her eye. Oh my God – she was. 'Is this before or after we went to bed?' I ask tentatively.

'After.'

My cheeks are a sudden beacon of embarrassment. How *could* she bring that up? 'Ah,' I say. There's nowhere to go. I have no choice but to admit it. 'You're talking about . . . er.'

'Your little accident.'

She's deliberately humiliating me. Smiling into my face and gloating over her sudden ascendancy. I can't bring myself to look at her. I'm five years old again and I've just wet my bed. 'I'd been . . . I mean, it had been ages since Ruth and I had made love and – '

'It's all right, James. I'm not accusing you of anything. In fact I was quite touched.'

'Touched?' If there was a lever for me to pull so that I could disappear from sight, I'd pull it. I'd rather slide down an oubliette than continue to face Connie across that table.

I don't know what I want to say. I twist the table napkin in my hands, wringing its neck. 'I'm sorry,' I say at last. 'I didn't mean to.'

And then Connie does the worst thing she could do at that moment. She laughs. Not maliciously or wickedly, but all the same, she laughs. 'I'm sure you didn't mean to.'

The pilot light of my subterranean rage was just waiting for this: all four gas-rings turn on at once, and I ignite. Just audible above the roar of flames, I hear myself say, 'Come on – let's go.' I hold my hand up for the waiter, clicking my fingers. I'm livid.

'I haven't finished my wine yet.'

I stare at her. I'm aware of my hands trembling on the table: Connie can't realise how close I am to standing up and turning the table over. 'Well hurry up.' Oh hell, even in my rage I know I shouldn't have said that. 'Sorry,' I mutter.

She doesn't say anything. She just looks. There are no clues to her thoughts, but I have no trouble filling in the speech bubble for myself: 'You're a jerk, James. A paranoid, stupid bastard. And you've ruined the evening.'

The waiters here are blind. I flap my hand about, not daring to look at Connie. Much to the hilarity of her friends, one of the women at the next table starts sneezing repeatedly. She must have sneezed ten times before she comes to a halt. The girl with the laugh says 'Bless you' after every sneeze. I think if she'd carried on for much longer I'd have got up and punched one of them on the nose.

146

I'm on the point of standing up and fetching a waiter by force when Connie tugs at my arm. 'Come on, James. Don't be so serious. It's not that important.'

Not important? My masculinity held up to ridicule? 'I don't want to discuss it.'

Her hand drops from my sleeve. Even in my rage I can see that she doesn't play the game as Ruth had done. I had one chance, and that was it: there would be no cajolery with this little vixen.

The waiter finally comes, and then there's an interminable wait till he brings the bill. Connie and I sit like two strangers, each thinking our own thoughts. Mine are solely of escape. If I don't get out of here soon, I'm going to start baying like a dog.

The waiter lays the bill beside my wine-glass and I unfold it to glance at the price.

'Let's go halves,' Connie says, trying to see how much it is.

'No, no. My treat,' I say between gritted teeth.

'If you insist.'

'I do.'

'Thank you.'

Outside on the pavement I offer to wait with her for a taxi. We walk towards the main road and then she stops. 'You'll have to realise one day, James, that everybody in the world isn't out to get you.'

I don't say anything. She's wrong – it's not everybody in the world. Just women.

'Look,' she persists, 'let's not leave it like this. I'm sorry for bringing it up. I didn't know it was such a touchy subject for you.'

'Oh yeah?' Meaning, bullshit you bitch, of course you did.

And then sweet little Connie parts those peach-slice lips and says: 'Fuck you, then.'

Well, that's it. The cherry on the top of the worst evening of my life. It's only by an immense act of will that I manage to stay with her till the taxi comes. Everything in me tells me to do violence to something, to get the hell away from this girl and break something.

When the cab arrives I tell the driver her address and then open the door for her. We're close enough to kiss, and for a moment we both hesitate. I'm not going to make the first move. Connie bobs up towards me and pecks me on the cheek. 'Good night.'

Shit and double shit. I watch the red lights of the taxi recede until they're out of sight. There goes my chance of having anything with her. I'd fucked up. I'd well and truly fucked up. I slip my jacket off and hook my thumb through the label. I don't want to go home yet, but there's nothing else to do so I stomp back to Ellsbirch Avenue on that balmy summer's night, my own personal rain-cloud over my head. Fuck you, then, she'd said. I suddenly remember they were the last words I said to Tad. Fuck. I try the word out, puffing my cheeks for the 'f', spitting out the end of the word. Fuck.

I couldn't have put it better myself.

17

They hate us. Women hate us men. Listen to this, from the manifesto of the late sixties anarchist-feminist group SCUM – the Society for Cutting Up Men: 'To call a man an animal is to flatter him; he's a machine, a walking dildo . . . Eaten up with shame, guilt, fears and insecurities and obtaining, if he's lucky, a barely perceptible feeling, the male is, none the less, obsessed with screwing; he'll swim in a river of snot, wade nostril deep through a pile of vomit if he thinks there's a friendly pussy waiting for him . . .' God bless you too, Valerie Solanas.

Tad's not in the common room, so I go to his bedroom and knock on the door. He hadn't sounded too well on the phone, but neither had I.

'Who is it?' comes from the other side of the door.

'James.'

There's a pause and then the door is opened by Feargal. 'Hi. Come in.'

Tad's on the bed. He looks grey and pained, and he only glances at me. Feargal goes back to him. 'Okay. Now let's get you in your chair.' One hand under his shoulder and the other under his buttocks, he lifts Tad and swings him round to the wheelchair. He looks tiny in the arms of Feargal – he can't weigh more than five stone. The blanket on the seat of the chair is rucked and he has to lift him out and try a second time.

'Let James help you,' Tad says. 'He can earn his keep for once. Not just sit there and watch the freaks.'

I squat by the chair and straighten the blanket. I couldn't care less what Tad says to me.

'That's not fair, Tad,' Feargal says.

'*Life*'s not fair,' he says bitterly.

Feargal lowers him into the chair and Tad and I look at each other. His breathing is difficult today; I can see that it's giving him pain. I step back and allow Feargal to straighten him up as best he can.

'Do you want your hair brushed?'

'Yes.'

He has to hold Tad under the chin to stop his head flopping about while he brushes his hair. I watch in silence: I've never spoken much to the Irishman.

'Careful,' Tad snaps.

Feargal takes no notice: I can see that he has abandoned trying to cheer up Tad for today. I wish I could take the brush from him and do his hair myself, but something holds me back. Tad is closer to me than anyone I know, but a wall goes up between us when I see him like this. Absurd – here is the most disabled person I've ever known, but after our first couple of meetings, his handicap was no longer part of the equation. He's just Tad, a mind trapped, like the rest of us, in a body. Only once or twice have I seen his frailty stamped this visibly; but now that it is, I can see nothing except his prison bars. It's not just selfishness or laziness or lack of imagination that holds me back. It's the fear of that suffering. Fear, not only of the physical stench of pain but of the implications of such handicap. The confinement, the limitation, the indignity of having someone lift you in and out of the bath. Open doors. Carry you upstairs. I'm glad to be Tad's friend, but for me friendship can't stretch this far.

'What's the time?' His hair is parted down one side, making him look much younger.

'Quarter to two.'

'Pass my pills, could you? Not those – the red and yellow ones.'

Feargal puts the bottle of pills on the tray of his wheelchair, but Tad makes no attempt to pick it up. 'Open it for me, can't you? Have I got to do everything myself?'

'How many is it – two?'

'Yes.'

Feargal puts the pills in Tad's hand and fills a tumbler from the tap. 'All right now? Do you want your shoes on?'

'No.'

Feargal flashes a glance at me. 'I'll leave you two then.'

I shut the door behind him, hesitating for a moment before I turn back to face Tad. I shouldn't have come today. 'Is the pain really bad?'

'What do you think?' He sighs and lets his head drop forward. I watch him for a moment before I realise he's crying, his little chest heaving with the effort. I sit on the edge of his bed. 'Is there anything I can do?' I ask after a moment.

'I've got to get out. Take me for a walk, would you, James?'

'A walk? Are you well enough?'

He smears the tears across his face with the back of his hand. I can't tell if he's smiling or if it's just a grimace on his face. 'I'll feel better if I'm distracted.'

I put his shoes on for him. They are about size five – children's shoes, I suppose. The laces are beginning to fray with wear, but the leather is unscuffed, the soles as clean as if they had just been bought.

'Stick that bottle of pills in my pocket – I'll need them.'

Outside, Tad complains that the sun is hurting his eyes, so I have to go back and fetch his sunglasses. With his shades on and his Italian hair flopping over one eye, he looks like a Mafia gangster.

'Let's go to the supermarket.' He jerks the control of his wheelchair and spins round to face the opposite direction. He speeds away from me, his maximum four miles per hour jiggling his body over the uneven pavement. I let him go on ahead: I don't know if he wants to be on his own, but I certainly do. I can feel my tolerance dissolve with every venomous look Tad shoots at the world.

He's looking a bit better by the time I catch up with him at the supermarket. He slows down so that I can walk beside him down the aisle. 'Talk to me,' he says.

'Nothing to say.'

'Come on, James. Don't be a prat.'

I don't want to talk about it, but it's the only thing on my mind. 'I had a date last night with Connie.' I don't care if Tad's going to be upset or not, I have to talk about this. 'We went out to dinner.'

'And?'

'It was disastrous.' It's difficult talking to Tad when I'm standing. Unless he makes an effort to crane his neck, I can only see the top of his head.

'Tell me more.'

'We ended up arguing.' Did we? I step to one side to let a trolley pass. 'Perhaps not *arguing*, but . . .'

'Why?'

'I think she just hates men. She just despises me.' Tad doesn't say anything. 'She didn't take anything I said seriously. In fact she bloody laughed at me.'

'So – she *laughed* at you!' He gives a wheezy giggle.

I make some noncommittal noises.

'Poor little Jimmy boy. Why did the horrible big girl laugh at you?'

'Oh . . . nothing.'

'Nonsense. Tell me.'

'She called me skinny.' Better to be thought of as a complete fool than a pervert. 'It's because she's so fat, that's why. You should have seen her stuffing her face.

151

And she was more interested in the waiter than she was in me.'

'I'll never understand what you men see in women.'

'Nor will I.' I hate that girl. I hate her, I hate her, I hate her. 'I think I might just give the whole thing a miss for a bit.'

'Give up sex? That's a little drastic, isn't it? Perhaps you could just change sides.'

'What do you mean?'

'From batting to bowling.'

'You're not serious?'

'We live in hope.'

'I'm just going to give up the game completely,' I say.

And wouldn't you know it, the very moment those words leave my mouth, my eyes light on the young woman in the pet-food section. I feel an immediate tug as though a fishing line has been cast across the space between us, the hook catching in my skin. There's no doubt about it, God's greatest act of creation is the woman. What design genius: the curve of that hip, the rounded thighs, the slim arms reaching up for the Kattomeat. Perhaps it was the devil who programmed lust into the mind, but the shape itself is nothing less than divine. Tad has disappeared round the corner, so I sit on the edge of the refrigerator and look around at the shoppers. How could I give all this a miss? There's a million women out there, all willing and able to give of themselves. It's relationships that complicate matters; sex is as simple as eating and drinking.

'Come on,' Tad calls from the end of the aisle. I follow him to the checkout. The pain has visibly worn off his face: I can see him coming alive by the minute. We have to wait for a while at the checkout, and he's impatient, wheeling around like a matador with an invisible bull, looking in people's trolleys, commenting on what they're buying.

He's only pretending not to be aware of the sea of turned heads he leaves in his wake. I suddenly realise how used I've become to Tad's appearance. I watch other people pretending not to watch him: they find him fascinating.

He pays for the handful of things he's bought and

then gives me something wrapped in plastic. 'Here. A present.'

'What's the meaning of this?' It's a baby's dummy.

'I didn't know whether to get a pink one or a blue one. I hope you don't mind pink.'

'Hah bloody hah.'

'I thought if someone laughed at you again, you can have a good suck and feel better.'

'Just what I always wanted.'

'Many a true word spoken in jest.'

I stick it in my pocket. 'Let's get out of here.'

He suggests a cup of coffee, and so we go to a place he knows round the corner. The waitress greets him, holding the door open while I jiggle the chair over the threshold.

'A seat by the window please, Iris.'

'Of course, your lordship.' She moves a couple of chairs aside so Tad can wheel himself to the table. 'How are you?'

'I must admit I was a miserable bitch this morning, but James here has done wonders with me.'

Iris and I exchange smiles of greeting. Tad parks himself at the end of the table – his chair obviously isn't going to fit behind it. 'A cup of coffee for me, Iris. And?'

'The same for me.'

The table is right up against the plate-glass window, so close that it seems as though we're sitting on the pavement itself. Tad's sitting at right angles to me, facing out on to the street. 'Sorry for being so snappy earlier on, James.'

'That's all right.'

'Friends?' He holds a hand out and I shake it.

'Friends.'

He'd bought a quarter of whisky in the supermarket and he pours a tot into his coffee when it comes. He offers me some, but I turn it down. Three thirty on a sunny afternoon is a little early for me.

'You know, this is the first time we've been out together,' he says. 'Properly.'

As I look at Tad, I finally pin down the source of the nagging memory. For the last few times I've met him I've been aware of an echo from my past; more a feeling than

153

a thought. Sitting here, stirring sugar into my coffee, I suddenly realise the last time I felt this close to another man was at St Jude's. My recollection of ten years at boarding school has darkened over the years, a principled stand obscuring the experience, but it probably wasn't as bad as I like to remember. Sure, it was a bizarre anachronism with its arcane traditions and Gothic architecture, but amid the bullying and compulsive competitiveness that seemed to be part of the syllabus, there was a genuine closeness amongst the boys. It has been ten years since I've seen any of my school-friends, but they've recently started appearing in my dreams, their faces as easily conjured as if I see them every day. I miss them. I miss belonging. Tad has supplied a connection I wasn't aware I was looking for.

'Thank you, Tad.'

'What for?'

'Being my friend.' My eyes drop to the sugar spoon I'm playing with. 'You know something? You're the first man friend I've had since school.' I look up at him. 'What are you smiling at?'

'You called me a man.'

'Well, you are.' I smile back, surprised at how much I'm enjoying his company. Tad's a broken machine, but he is a man, and we understand each other.

'I'm very fond of you, James.'

I glance at him and then down at the spoon. 'I've been wanting to ask you something for a long time.' I pause. Do I really want to say this?

'What?'

'I don't know how to put it without offending you.' He's waiting, so I carry on. 'What's it like, being handicapped?'

He laughs. 'Who's handicapped?' He glances around the café. 'Oh, you mean me? What's it like being unhandicapped?'

'I'm serious.'

'So am I, darling.' He drums his fingers over his humped chest. 'This is all I've known. I presumably feel no less normal than everyone else. I'm still me, no matter what I look like.' He frowns at me. 'But that doesn't answer your question, does it?'

'No.'

He pauses to think, suddenly serious. 'I was in an awful lot of pain when I was very young, and that was all that mattered. If I was out of pain, I was happy – it was as simple as that. I couldn't care less about being in a wheelchair, or how I looked. The trouble started when I stopped breaking bones, and discovered there was a world outside hospitals and care centres. Adolescence was a horribly difficult time for me – I kept falling in love. And it didn't help when I discovered I was only interested in men.' He takes the spoon off me, and puts it in the saucer of his empty cup. 'A few early knocks and I quickly learnt what *that* was all about. The real world was full of young men with strong arms and legs, nobody was going to be interested in poor little old me. At the time, it looked as though I had two options – give up any hope of living a normal life or fight for one.' He smiles at the memory. 'I was *so* angry and unhappy – you wouldn't believe it! I wanted to smash every mirror I saw. I hated being different. All I wanted was to be the same as everyone else. But that was a hopeless ambition, and so I used to dream of escaping from my body. I wanted an angel to come and carry me away.'

I remember the time we shared fantasies, his reference to angels then. 'But have you got over it? Can you accept yourself now?'

'Is it possible, you mean?' He tilts his head to one side, and for a moment he looks like an inquisitive bird. 'Are you asking about yourself, or about me?' I sit back in my chair to think about the question, but he continues. 'I used to envy other people's mobility, but by and large, I no longer do so. Except for the physical pain, my world seems no more full of frustration than theirs. I was born into humility – I don't know what it's like to run, or catch a bus, or kick a ball. It would be nice to try, but I'm not going to lose sleep over it.'

'But do you like yourself?'

He hugs his chest and rocks his body like a baby. 'I must admit, I do.' He laughs suddenly and unexpectedly. 'Is that a very naughty thing for a Jewish Catholic to admit to?'

'Very.'

We sit in silence and watch the passing faces on the street. A traffic warden is making her way along our side of the street, writing down all the registration numbers of the cars parked in front of the café. We both watch her. 'Look at that face,' Tad says.

'What about it?'

'Just look.'

Judging by the frown lines carved into her face there's something very puzzling in this person's life. Not actively unhappy perhaps, but whatever the enigma is, it has been with her long enough to work its way into her body. Not just the expression on her face, it's in her posture, in the hunched shoulders, the querulous movements of her limbs. She's a block of marble that life has carved its message on. Tad is thinking along the same lines. 'If that was a sculpture what would you call it?'

I think for a moment. 'Confusion?' I say.

We watch her until she walks out of sight. 'Poor cow,' Tad mutters. We dawdle over our coffee, watching the moving tableau. They're all here, characters from an ageless fable, a *Pilgrim's Progress* of the human condition: here's Hurt Pride, here Timidity. Smile At All Costs is having trouble with her shopping bag. Mr Busy has just seen the traffic warden, and is considering whether to become Protestation until he realises he hadn't got a ticket. Please Don't Laugh At Me and I'm Only a Girl walk arm in arm, pausing to look at the hi-fis over the road. It's like watching a television programme: it would have been boring had it been fiction, but it's for real, and it's depressing. These are human beings and what are they playing at? Second-rate soap operas, for the most part. I don't stop to consider what Tad and I look like. Beauty and the Beast perhaps – but which way round?

'Oh, I nearly forgot,' Tad says suddenly. 'Feargal's having a party tomorrow night. Why don't you come along?'

'Am I invited?'

'Don't sound so surprised – of course you are.'

'Are you sure? I hardly know him.'

'Don't be silly. You can be my chaperon.'

And why not? I'm a bachelor and I'm damned if I'm going to give in at the first sign of female perversity. A party means women, and getting drunk, and being young again.

We arrange to meet at eight o'clock at Innocence and take a taxi to Wimbledon. Tad can use his disablement pass for the taxi, so it will only cost a pound. We'd have a great time. Let the good times roll.

I change my mind about the whisky, and have a slug straight from the bottle.

18

'Let's at 'em, Jim boy.'

The throbbing beat of zulu jive is pouring out of the open front door and on to the street like a molasses and coconut milk cocktail. In its wash, a couple of figures in the front garden are silhouetted against the house lights. I catch the glint of metal as a beer can is lifted to a mouth. A red open-topped sports car gleams conspicuously under the street-lamp. It looks like a set for an advertisement for a fashionable fizzy drink. The kids are all right.

The wheelchair can't make the kerb and I have to back Tad on to the pavement, aware of eyes from the front garden on us. He's in a snazzy silk shirt: aquamarine and scarlet flashes, black trousers and shiny black shoes. He could have been stunning, with his silky black hair and full lips and long eyelashes, if his body hadn't been squashed by the forces of bastard luck. He's a Valentino cheated through a quirk of chromosomes. He leads me up the garden path, past the couple sagging the next-door neighbour's fence, and into the house. The crowd parts in front of the wheelchair like water before the bow of a ship and I follow in his wake.

Everybody seems to be an art student, or a socialist, or both. Street-cred points are high: just on my way to the kitchen I pass one hammer and sickle badge, a shaved head and a pair of men kissing. I've lost Tad by the time I reach the drinks table, already awash with a beer and rosé cocktail. I find a clean plastic cup and pick up a bottle of wine at random and pour myself a drink.

I listen to the chatter, the sound of laughter coming from the next room. It's as though everybody's enjoying a shared joke that somehow I've failed to understand. Everybody seems to know everybody else, and judging from all the notice anyone takes of me, I'm apparently invisible.

I sip the unpleasantly sweet wine and examine the décor of the kitchen. It isn't until I find myself studying a frying pan that I realise there *is* no décor. It's a kitchen, with a sink and two tables: a wet one for drinks, and a crumby one for food, and that's all. A student house in the middle of Nowheresville. I eat an olive and look for an ashtray for the stone but there isn't one so I bury it in the soil of a potted plant. I shouldn't have come – I knew it.

A girl comes over to the food table, and I watch her out of the corner of my eye. Mid-twenties, jeans and an open-necked shirt. Sort of boyish and sexy at the same time. She's more interested in food than in company, and scans the table with hungry eyes. Say something, say something, say something, I tell myself. Quick, before she goes away. 'Enjoying the party?'

She finds what she was looking for and looks up at me. 'Say what?'

'Enjoying the party?'

She shrugs. 'What's your name?' She's Scottish, and a bit pissed.

I tell her.

'I had a boyfriend called James, once. James Cavendish. Perhaps you know him?'

'Er – ' The name sounds vaguely familiar. 'Is he famous?'

'No, he's an old boyfriend of mine.'

'Ah.' She's more pissed than I realised.

'What do you do then?' She snaps a pair of Twiglets

between her front teeth as though they are my ulna and humerus.

I should lie and say I'm a novelist or an actor or something. 'I'm a librarian,' I admit.

She scoops a palmful of peanuts into her mouth. Crunch, crunch. She has strong teeth, this girl.

It's apparently my turn to say something. I consider the gambits that come to mind, but I can only think of ridiculous things to say. I'm aware that she's looking at me as a fishmonger might eye a box of cod he's thinking of buying.

'Casanova was a librarian,' I say eventually. It's the only thing I can think of. 'Chairman Mao too,' I add lamely.

'All those wee red books.'

'The second most-read book in the world after the Bible.'

'That so?'

She leans in front of me to tear the end off a French loaf. She dips it in a bowl of hummus and gives it to me. 'Eat,' she commands. 'You're too thin.'

I take the bread. Why do all these women think they have to fatten me up? I reluctantly nibble at it.

'Are you a student?' I ask.

'I'm a nurse.'

I nod and fill my already full cup with a random bottle of plonk. 'Have you got a drink?'

She's drinking from a beer mug which she holds for me to slosh some wine into.

'A nurse – eh? What sort?' I stub the bread out in an ashtray. This is better. I change from first gear to second.

She presses her forefinger against my lips. 'Are you here with that funny little fellow in the armchair – I mean wheelchair.' Her hand slides down from my face to my neck and then rests on my chest. She holds my gaze, her head wobbling slightly. 'What's your name? You're awful pretty.'

Oh God, a pissed Scottish nurse – just what I need. 'You haven't told me your name yet,' I say buoyantly. I can feel the smile freezing on my face.

She traces her fingers over my shirt as though she's writing something on my chest, and then comes to a full stop on my nipple. 'I'll see you later,' she says, and then she sways off.

I refill my cup and go in search of Feargal. I find him in the back garden, but he's busy rowing with his girlfriend, so I wander round the garden for a few minutes. The sky is clear and bright and I catch sight of a shooting star. I make a wish: that I was back at home watching television.

I wander from group to group, eavesdropping on conversations: the injustices of the university examining processes, the new Degas exhibition on the South Bank, gossip from the textile department, China. I have a stab at chipping in with the China conversation, but my contribution falls flat: these are ethnology students, mini-experts in their field, and from the look on their faces, I don't know what I'm talking about. I strike up a conversation with a bronzed young man – a zoology student. We range from Indonesia to the rain forests to Conrad's *Heart of Darkness*, but even though I know something about all three of these, I never get the hang of the conversation. We seem to be talking at cross-purposes. It's only later when I see him with his arm around another bronzed young man that I realise what those purposes are. Meanwhile I'm steadily becoming more and more drunk.

The front room has been put aside for dancing. All the furniture removed, windows open to the street, the lights just a glimmer and the music so loud, it's felt rather than heard. I stay at the threshold, sheltering my cup from being knocked out of my hands by the jostling. Sweaty bodies twist and shake as if in pain. Dante had obviously been to a student party: this was apparently the river Phlegethon of boiling blood and violence.

Something is happening in the middle of the room: even above the music I can hear whoops and shouts of encouragement. I stand on tiptoe to see what the focus of attention is, and just catch a glimpse of a wheelchair. I push through the bodies to see what he's up to. Tad's dancing with his wheelchair – spinning it round crazily, reversing, jiggling it from side to side. His chair's moving too fast for his neck muscles to cope, and his head lolls and bounces as he spins round. He looks spastic; awful and crippled, and he couldn't give a damn.

There's only one logical step once I've reached the front door, so I step out into the garden. The fence-sagging couple have gone, and the only other person is being sick into the roses. I watch the figure in the shadows give a final lurch and then straighten up. From the street-lights I can see that it's one of the Chinese ethnologists. I smile triumphantly: I hope he's feeling like hell. He sways with a puzzled look on his face, and then belches and begins climbing through the open window into the front room. He manages to get one leg over, but the second won't follow, so he leans to one side and topples out of sight. I stare at the billowing lace curtain for a moment and then go back in.

Tad's empty wheelchair is in the hall. I stare at it stupidly, my mind struggling to understand. Has he been stolen? I look in the dancing-room, but it's too dark to make anything out. Where the hell could he go without his wheels? I see Feargal coming down the stairs.

'Where's Tad?'

'He's upstairs. In the smoking-room.'

As soon as I smell the air, I know what sort of smoking is going on. I pause in the doorway, unsure whether to go in or not. Some people get funny about smoking dope; secretive and unwelcoming, but the nurse is there and she waves me over. I'm not too steady on my feet after a pint or so of wine, and the single red light-bulb is hardly bright enough for me to see my feet. Halfway across the room I step into an ashtray, catapulting the contents on to the laps of a couple of people. 'Sorry,' I say, but they hadn't noticed.

It's like an opium den in here: layers of sweet brown smoke hanging in the air, the muffled music from downstairs the only sound apart from the subdued voices of the figures lolling on cushions. 'Hello, James, my boy,' someone calls from the corner. It's Tad, propped against some pillows on a mattress, a fat joint between his lips. He's sitting next to a couple of girls. 'There's some space

161

over here.' I lift my hand in greeting to the nurse and go over to Tad: I'm not drunk enough to take her on yet. I lower myself into the gap on the corner of the mattress.

'This is James,' he says to the girls. Wouldn't you know it: the two best-looking women at the party and Tad has them eating out of his hand. 'Say hello, James.'

'Hello.'

One of the girls is called Sandy and the other Aviva, but I'm not sure which is which.

'James's girlfriend left him a couple of weeks ago, and he's looking for a little excitement, so if either of you would be willing . . .' He hands me the joint and blows a kiss at me. Sometimes I hate the little bastard.

Like most of her friends, Ruth had fallen midway between the coke-snorting upper class and dope-smoking middle class and had consequently been hopelessly muddled about the whole drug thing. Drugs were something other people did: people you saw on documentaries or read about in the Sunday papers, and the combination of illegality and ill health was enough for her to ban anything except alcohol from the house. It's years since I've smoked dope and by the time the second joint comes round, I can feel the top of my cranium lifting off.

Tad is showing the two girls a newspaper cutting and I ask to see it: a young woman baring a lean breast for the camera. It's a face I've seen before but I can't place her. 'Who is it?'

'La Cicciolina.'

'Ah,' I remember now. 'The porno star?' Why is it that everything to do with Tad is something to do with sex?

'That's the one – Europe's first Tantric politician, God bless her.' He takes the picture back. 'You know Tantra?'

'Yes,' I say, meaning no. All I know is that it's supposed to be sexy and has something to do with Tibetan Buddhism.

'I don't think Jimmy boy understands,' he says to the girls. 'Judging from his goggle eyes, I can see that he's got the wrong idea. Tantra is nothing to do with sex, and it's about nothing *except* sex. The goal of Tantra is *Mahamudra*.' He says the word with exaggerated care as though he's ordering an Indian take-away over the phone. 'The great orgasm. Cosmic Intercourse.'

'What you might call the big-bang theory,' one of the girls says.

'I'm the one who makes the jokes.'

'Sorry T.P.'

He sees my questioning glance. 'Tadpole,' he explains. 'Anyway, don't interrupt. In Tantra, you don't use your willy, you use your whole body, your whole mind, your whole be-ing.' His head drops forward on to his humped chest for a moment and I suddenly realise how tired he is. We wait while he gathers himself.

'La Cicciolina getting into government was the greatest act of liberation in Italy since they offed El Duce,' he says after a while. 'But it won't be long before the Vatican gets her. She'll be wearing concrete wellies in the Tiber before the year's out.'

'*Tizer*?' I ask.

'Tiber, my dear. They're going to drown her, not drink her. You see, Little Cuddly scares the pants off the Church. Why? Because she gives people back their power. How? By giving them back their sex. And there's nothing as frightening to the Church as powerful people, as James would no doubt tell you.'

Would I? I suppose I would.

Tad is warming to his topic. 'Sex is power and power is dangerous when it's in the hands of the people,' he jerks his right hand up and down suggestively and raises an eyebrow at me, 'at least, if you're the ones in charge. That's why La Cicciolina is the Antichrist – at least, anti *their* Christ. Their Christ is a castrated miracle worker, pinned up on a tree and dying for everybody's sins.'

I want to protest, but I keep quiet. Blasphemy was almost a capital offence at St Jude's. One boy I knew was nearly expelled for throwing the Bible across the room.

'The church can't stand sex because it's something they have no control over,' Tad continues. The two girls have been listening for long enough to realise no input is required from them: as long as they listen, Tad will talk. 'So, the uptight bastards outlaw sex, and then they invent sexless

163

gods so that we feel guilty if we get horny. The Church has hijacked the real Jesus for two millenia now. They've cut off his balls, and they're damned if they're going to hand them back to the likes of you and me without a fight.'

He pauses for a drag. When Tad smokes he looks like the very worst image of the addict: lips puckered up, eyes squinting as if in pain, he pulls the smoke into his lungs with a whistling gasp.

'You know, the second-century Docetists debated whether Christ actually went to the toilet. One school of thought said he only pretended to eat, so there was no waste matter. The other school said that he ate but he didn't defaecate.' He takes a second drag on the joint, holds his breath and then passes it on. 'No wonder he looks so agonised on the cross – thirty-three years of constipation would make anyone squirm.' He exhales noisily, the smoke jetting out of his mouth. 'The only point everyone agreed upon was that Jesus couldn't have done it behind a bush like everyone else.'

'Preposterous!' a female voice chips in. 'God with a rectum and anus.' There's laughter in the room. There's more than a handful of us listening to this nonsense.

'Actually,' Tad says, 'there was a third lesser-known school, the Bonnum Olfactum School of thought which said that Christ did it, but it smelt nice. And he didn't use his arsehole. Because he didn't have one.'

'Works of the devil, arseholes.' The same voice from the shadows.

'Of course they are! Diabolical things! So what happens is, when we die and go up to heaven, a little angel seals our bum-holes and cuts off our willy, and there you are – you're like God intended you to be. Girls of course are cauterised front and back.'

'No cunts in heaven.' Who *is* that? I sit up so I can see. It's the nurse. She's sitting cross-legged on the floor, trying to stick two cigarette papers together. She looks at me and winks.

I don't know how long I'm there before I start to be absorbed into the floor. The joints keep coming from somewhere: great fat lung busters that strike me forcibly between the eyes. I keep plucking at my lower lip: it has

164

gone unpleasantly numb, and when I speak, my mouth seems to be packed with cotton-wool. Tad and I have somehow slid down the wall until we're propping each other up. He's still talking though. Something about butterflies, or is it the stock exchange? My mind, I must admit, has been wandering.

'I've been thinking about starting a new religion,' I find myself saying. 'The Church of Jesus Christ the Postman. Seriously,' I add when nobody says anything. 'I've given it a lot of thought – instead of churches we'd have post offices. Priests would wear letter-box-red robes, and the Communion wafer would be a rice-paper postage stamp. We'd use red ink instead of wine. The Pope would be the Post Master General and we'd have services every day except Sunday.'

Tad laughs half-heartedly.

'I'm not joking,' I say. 'For as long as I can remember I've been nagged by the idea that one day I'll be saved by the arrival of a letter. Everything would be solved by this one sheet of paper. Everything: my past, my future, my present – all wrapped up.'

'Who's the letter from?' Tad asks.

'I don't know. God, I suppose.'

'What would the letter say?'

'*Don't worry. Everything's under control.*' I waggle my feet to check that they're mine. 'Childish, isn't it.'

'Hmm.'

I want to sit up, but I'm in too uncomfortable a position to move without breaking something.

'And no letter yet?' one of the girls asks.

'No.' I feel stupidly miserable all of a sudden. I want to pout. I probably am. 'Sometimes, God, I think you push your luck a little too far. One of these days, I'm going to really stop believing in You. And then where would You be – eh?'

'God is dead,' somebody calls from across the room.

'Not dead, just hiding,' Tad whispers into my ear.

I have to get a drink: my tongue is sticking to the top of my mouth. The more I think about it, the drier my mouth becomes until I can think of nothing except water.

I have to go downstairs for a drink. Whether I can make it or not is another matter, but if I don't go soon I'll die of thirst.

And then I find myself in the kitchen with the nurse. It must be late: there's nobody downstairs at all. The front room is empty apart from something asleep in the corner.

'Food,' I say, scanning the crumby table. My thirst has magically disappeared: I'm suddenly incredibly hungry.

'Sex,' the nurse says from behind me, her hands on my crutch.

'Food first.' There's hardly anything left: a bowl of crisps, a few wodges of bread. Two olives. I'm aware of a pleasant sensation in my groin as I try to stuff my mouth full of crisps. It's only when I see our reflection in the window that I realise my flies are open, and the nurse's hand is inside my trousers.

'Whoa,' I say, spraying shards of crisps over the table. I may be stoned, but I'm not ready for this. I pull away and zip my trousers up. 'Naughty!' I say popping both olives into my mouth. I watch while she searches the fridge for more food.

'Yes,' I say aloud.

'Yes, what?'

'Yes, I *am* having fun yet.' I hang on to the draining-board to stop my feet from sliding beneath me. It's true: I'm actually enjoying myself. I try to spit the olive stones into the sink but they fall short, one falling into the open top of my shirt. I grope around my midriff for the stone, but it feels as though I'm massaging a bowl of blancmange so I stop. The nurse has materialised some grapes from somewhere. I try to take them off her, but she snatches them back and insists on feeding me with them mouth to mouth. It seems pretty silly, and when I bite her lip by accident, she lets me take the bunch off her and split it in two.

The next thing I'm aware of is being propelled out of the kitchen and into the dancing-room. Some samba is playing, and she turns the volume up high. The shape in the corner groans and turns over. It's the Chinaman again.

166

Neither the nurse nor I are in control of our bodies enough to attempt anything more than a perfunctory jiggle, but we give it a try.

'Happy, darling?' We gravitate towards a swaying sort of smooch. If I didn't know better, I would swear we're on the open deck of a ship, cruising through the balmy night of some South American paradise. The nurse meanwhile has apparently fallen asleep.

She's a big girl, whatever her name is. Tall enough for us to rest our chins on each other's shoulders: and together we achieve a sort of equilibrium so that neither of us falls over. We sway like this for a few minutes until she straightens up and blinks at me.

'Oh, it's you!' she says.

'Is it?' For a second I'm genuinely surprised it *is* me.

'I think so.'

'Let's have a look.' I go to the mirror and squint at a fuzzy image that squints back at me. 'No it's not. I think I must be someone else.'

'Do you want a drink, whoever you are.'

I'm suddenly weak with amusement. I don't think I've ever heard such witty repartee. I find myself giggling on my own, and look around the room. The Chinaman is still there, but the nurse has gone. Ray Charles is playing and I close my eyes to listen better until I get too dizzy and have to open them again. The nurse is back and we dance opposite each other, passing a bottle back and forth between us until it's finished. I'm going to feel like hell tomorrow.

'You want to come back to my place?'

I step forward to nuzzle her ear. 'Mmm.'

'Come on then, Batman – let's split.' The floor rushes up to hit me, but the nurse steadies me.

'Okay, Robin.' There's a joke somewhere there about bantams and robins, but I'm too stoned to think of it.

19

She lives round the corner, just far enough for me to realise what I'm doing. A girl I hardly know, and here we are about to perform the single most intimate act of physical communion. I smile out at the world. This is the way it's supposed to be. Free love; easy sex. Bonking.

She has trouble getting the key into the key-hole and we giggle together on the doorstep, hands all over each other. Falling into the unlit hall she pushes me up against the wall, forcing her tongue between my teeth. She's taken me by surprise and I'm too busy staying on my feet to do anything more than just keep my mouth open. She has a powerful tongue: I think if I slipped she could pin me to the wall with it. Then her hands come into action, sliding into my jacket, round my waist. A picture behind my head jumps on its hook as she bumps me against the wall, groin to groin. She's going to have her way with me whether I want it or not. The room is beginning to sway and I focus on the coatrack behind her shoulder and manage to push her away. It's so dark I could have been kissing anyone.

Somehow we make it up the stairs to her room. It's large and confusingly organised, the bed barely distinguishable from the piles of clothes that grow like enormous toadstools around it. I catch my foot on a sewing machine, nearly falling into the open maws of an enormous wardrobe.

In the glare of the overhead light I have my first good look at her. She may be a nurse, but she looks more like a patient: sallow skin with large pores on her nose; a wide mouth with sharp teeth. Sharp eyes, come to that. She winks at me as she leaves the room. Here's a sure candidate for *vagina dentata* if ever I saw one: the toothed cunt. I scowl at the wonky poster of Rambo on the wall and lower myself on to the single bed. My mouth suddenly fills with saliva, a presage of throwing up. I take a deep breath and sit as straight as I can. Careful Jimmy boy.

Ah! Good – I turn the packet towards me to make certain. Yup – our little nurse is on the Pill. I switch on the bedside lamp and knock her alarm-clock over. God, I'm drunk, or stoned, or something.

She comes back in without her jeans and for a second before she switches off the overhead light she looks like a huge schoolgirl in her gym knickers. I suddenly remember who she reminds me of; a Robert Crumb cartoon character: thighs like boa constrictors, nipples as big as milk-bottle tops, a cunt the size of a shoe-box. She picks her way across the room and sinks beside me on the bed. She has brushed her teeth, a fleck of foam hanging on her chin. There's nothing in me that responds to this girl. I suppress a burp and wipe the toothpaste off her. It's not that she's ugly: her eyes and nose and mouth are all roughly in the right places, but there's nothing between us, no understanding, no nothing. She's a stranger. And sex? I don't know where the lower half of my body is, but it's not within a hundred yards of this bedroom. I should get up and leave, but the nurse has started massaging my ears, and all I can hear is the sound of crunching cornflakes.

She lies on her back with her feet still on the floor and pulls me on top of her, but her single bed is far too small for us both and we slide on to the floor until we're lying side by side amongst her dirty washing. I'm dizzy with the sudden change of perspective and I can't focus on her face this close, so I try and sit up, but somehow one of my arms has become entangled with a pair of tights, and wrestling to free myself I accidentally punch her a glancing blow on the side of her head.

'Sorry.' I don't think she noticed. I roll on top of her, close my eyes and start kissing her. I try to hold myself above her but my muscles and tendons have dissolved over the course of the evening and I keep sagging down on to her. She rolls us both over after I've knocked the breath out of her for the third time, and now she's on top. God, she's heavy, and there's something sharp poking in my back. She can't realise how close I am to vomiting otherwise she

169

wouldn't be so insistent about poking her tongue into my mouth. I nuzzle her neck to get away from her mouth, but then she starts on my ears again, tracing their shape with her tongue, flicking in and out of my earhole like a beetle trying to get into my eardrum.

This is taking on the quality of combat for me. I manage to push her off me until we're side by side again. Her bare upper leg slides over mine and she's half way back to climbing on to me when I push her down again and start unbuttoning her shirt. She leaves me alone while I fiddle with the buttons – obviously the best form of defence is attack. I finally get all the buttons undone and expose her powerful no-nonsense bra. I make a show of kissing her cleavage while with one eye I search for the hook, but it has been fastened at the back, so I pull down the nylon material to try to release a nipple. Whether the material won't stretch that far, or the girl has no nipples, I can't tell, but I find nothing except an expanse of swelling white bosom. I nibble at the synthetic material for a bit before surfacing to her head like a diver coming up for air. This is hard work.

But something is straining from within my underpants. Any last chance of getting away *virgo intacta* has gone: once I'm under the sway of the Priapic Prince, there's no stopping. I'm still vaguely worried about taking my clothes off in front of her – nurse or no nurse – but I'm on my back with my jeans around my ankles before I know it. I look down at the penis that points skywards through the fly of my boxer shorts. Then somehow jeans and shirts and pants all disappear and before I know it we're skin to skin under the bedclothes. And what a sensation, the first contact with another naked body. Breasts against chest, thigh to groin, hands exploring unknown shapes, the delight of hidden bonuses. And then the groping to find a common language of touch: not like this, like *this*; slow down; touch me there. And the nurse is no shrinking violet – she knows exactly what she wants, guiding my hands down to her Venus fly-trap, subtle adjustments and then 'There!'

Her clitoris stands to attention and she groans her approval. I'm on top of her, dragging my penis over the damp patch between her legs, but she puts her hand there. No entry.

'Use a rubber,' she whispers.

A rubber? My mind's blank for a moment. Oh, a *condom*. I remain poised over her, buttocks in the air. But I didn't bring them. Oh shit!

'Do we have to?'

She rolls out from under me and I collapse on to my face.

'I'm not doing it without,' she says matter-of-factly.

'But aren't you on the Pill?'

'Yes,' she says. 'But so what? I'm not going to get Aids no matter how pretty you are.'

'Oh.'

She reaches across to the bedside table and opens a drawer. 'Here.' She hands me a foil-wrapped condom as if she's offering me a cigarette. 'I can get them for nothing from work.'

She's not interested in my struggle to get the thing on. Even when I put it on inside out, and then have to take it off to start again, she doesn't break off from staring at the ceiling.

I signal I'm ready to begin the grand assault. The nausea has passed, but I still can't bring myself to kiss her mouth, so I hold myself above her as I try to move on top of her.

'No. Like this.'

She swivels round until she's lying face down. One hand gropes blindly behind her, seeking to guide me into position. I obey, kneeling behind her, my pink-suited penis bouncing with the movement. She arches her back bringing her bum up to meet me as though she's a space capsule trying to dock. She has two red spots on her left buttock and I focus on these as I lean myself forward into her. I feel as though I could slip my whole body through the envelope of flesh between her legs, disappear like a cartoon character until only my socks are left. I shudder as a surge of heat convulses through me. She wriggles until we're sealed groin to buttock. The sensation has gone now and for a second I wonder if I'm inside her, but when she begins

171

to rock I can feel my solidness still there. We pause for a moment and then I grip her haunches as though they're the handlebars of a bicycle and we begin a forward and backward movement.

Is this it; is this what all the fuss was about? Jerking myself in and out of a vagina? The bed taps our rhythm out on the wall: the Morse code of Eros. I slip my hands under her to grasp her breasts, pushing myself deeper and deeper into her. This is what I'd dreamed about, what I'd swum a river of snot for. I'm surprised to feel myself coming. I'm hardly even interested in what I'm doing, but my body has taken over. I hate myself. I hate this woman. I hate everything. My face contorts as though I'm sucking on a lemon, and then with a groan I ejaculate into her. And that's it. Less than two minutes beginning to end.

How was it for you dear? Nothing more than a release, as though I've just pissed against a tree. My nausea is returning, but as I try to pull out of her, she holds me with two hands on my buttocks and begins her hip-rotating movement again.

'Fuck me,' she groans.

Fuck you? What do you think that just was? I reluctantly begin my pumping again, feeling with each thrust my erection become more and more flaccid, until by the squelching sound I know I'm in danger of losing the condom. I have an absurd image of Eeyore putting his burst balloon in and out of an empty hunny jar.

I pull out of her and slip off the ridiculous bag of semen, dropping it beside the bed. I try and run my hands up and down the inside of her thighs, but she rolls on to her back, nearly knocking me off the bed. At first I think the buzzing noise is an electric shaver, but when I see where her hands are, I realise what she's up to. She doesn't need me now, her hands working the vibrator between her legs as she brings herself to orgasm, shrieking obscenities into the pillow.

'Oh fuck! Oh fuck! Oh fuck!' she goes.

Oh fuck! I've forgotten Tad! I said I'd take him home. She collapses, spent, on to the bed and after a moment I tentatively stroke her shoulder in apology. She's damp with perspiration, and I hadn't even broken sweat. I'd been useless, I knew it. There's a click as she switches the machine off. Drunk though I am, I'm keen to the humiliation of being vanquished by a battery-powered dildo.

But no matter. She's asleep within minutes.

I struggle into my clothes, tipping finally into the wardrobe, my trousers round my ankles. Somehow I make it downstairs and on to the street, where I stand looking left and right, feeling like a character in a bad dream. I'm sick with myself, sick with disgust, stupid from alcohol and cannabis. Left or right? I try to remember the way we had come: it was only the next street, but which bloody way?

I don't know how long I've been walking: it feels like hours. I'm as lost as I'm going to get. I don't know the name of the street I'm trying to find, I don't know the number of the house, I don't know Feargal's second name. I'm lost, Goddammit.

When I hit the main road yet again I decide to take a taxi home. I've had enough of wandering Wimbledon, talking to myself. The join between my soul and my body is beginning to unstick – much more of this and I'll leave my body lying on the pavement and go home without it.

And Tad? Let him find his own way home.

It's starting to get light when I fall into bed. The cab cost me eight quid, but at least I'm still in one piece. It was a day I wouldn't want to repeat, even if I could remember how it went.

20

Bobbing out of sleep like a cork in a stagnant pond, the light hits me smack between the eyes. I swipe at the alarm-clock, knocking it out of reach. A second stab silences it. There's a moment's blankness and then my scum-covered consciousness bobs up beside me. Saturday – do I have to get up? No. Then why set the alarm-clock?

The phone has some significance but I can't remember what it is. I try looking at it with both eyes at once, but the pillow is too close to my right eye to make any difference. It sits there on the bedside table like a riddle, looking back at me. I have to phone somebody – but *who*?

It's too soon to tell if I have a hangover. At the moment I appear to be having an out of the body experience. At least two of my senses are working: I can see, admittedly with only one eye, and if there was anything to hear, I'm sure I'd hear it; but my body exists only as a blur of sensation. I know I have a body because I can see it: it's that lump in the bed south of my head. I let my left eye shut. Perhaps I've died in the night and I'm in purgatory.

Tad – that's right. Phone Tad to check if he got home last night. Both eyes come open this time while I try to focus on the swaying ceiling. Interesting how of all my eroded faculties, my sense of guilt is the most complete. I was supposed to look after Tad: my one and only task for the evening and I blew it.

I will myself to move, almost hearing the gears grinding as my mind engages with my body. I lean across the spare pillow and pull the phone on to the bed, apparently smashing a phial of sulphuric acid in my head with the sudden movement. This isn't alcohol, it's poison. I stare at the buzzing receiver in my hand, debating whether I'm going to be sick or not. Why did I get so drunk? And

174

what am I doing with this phone in my hand? Tad. Phone Tad. I know the number, but my head has filled with industrial-strength glue during the night and all my digits have stuck together. Four seven six – no, that's the library. Two four three – no. Three four three – I try a couple of combinations in my head, but none seem to fit. I dial once and get an unobtainable tone; my second attempt is successful. I slip back until I'm lying flat again. My brain feels as though it has expanded like a mutant cauliflower and is threatening to split my skull apart. The phone rings for a couple of minutes before anyone answers it.

'Is Tad there please? It's James.'

'Hang on.'

A few minutes gap and then the same voice, 'Can you phone him later – he's only just woken up.'

'Okay. Er . . . did he get home okay last night?'

'I suppose he must have done. Didn't he go to Feargal's party last night?'

'Yes.'

'Well, he's here now.'

I ring off. Well at least he's not wheeling himself around Wimbledon. I just hope he's not too angry with me.

The reclamation of my body is now well underway, but I don't know if I want it back. I lick my cracked lips; for some reason my feet are incredibly itchy. I rub one foot against the other and discover I'm still wearing my socks. Why do I do this to myself? Poison myself in the name of having a good time? What I need is to be turned inside out and given a good scrub. I lie there, thinking about jugs of cool water and emptiness. Was it just one party or three? I try to piece together the night before. I seemed to have got drunk and then stoned and then drunk again. And the nurse. I struggle to picture her, but all I get is Connie's face. Did we really have sex? I seem to remember it was far from my best performance.

Would Connie never leave me alone? For a moment my headache has gone and Connie is standing in front of me. Why am I so hooked on this girl? She's not my type, she insults me, she laughs at me. But I like her. I watch the thoughts cross my field of vision like a sluggish game of

175

ping-pong. The truth now, James. You're missing her, aren't you. Why should I be missing her? The truth – yes or no. Yes, but what is there to miss? Nothing has even started between us, in fact a week ago you couldn't even remember her name. I stretch cautiously until I'm spreadeagled in the bed. I know exactly what I want. I want her in this bed now: deaf, dumb and blind perhaps, but I do want her. I want her sex.

The phone rings and I jump. Can it be her? Has she been tuning into my thoughts, thinking about me as I'm thinking about her? I lift the receiver cautiously. 'Yes?'

'Hey! Jim boy!'

'Oh it's you.' It's Tad.

'Don't sound so disappointed.'

'Sorry. Oh, and sorry about last night.'

'What for? I had a brilliant time. And so did you by all appearances. I see that Janet got her wicked way with you.'

'Who?'

'Janet – your nurse. You *did* know her name, didn't you?'

'Of course I did.' *Janet?* That seems to fit. 'Do you know her?'

'Who doesn't, darling boy?'

'You got home okay?'

'Aviva drove me back.'

'Aviva? Was that the pretty one?' I seem to remember they were both pretty.

'Are you jealous?' I don't say anything. It's too early to play games. 'What are you up to today?' he asks.

'I think I'll stay in bed and die.'

'That bad, huh?'

'That bad.'

'Come and see me tomorrow if you're still around.'

'Okay.' He hangs up. How can anyone sound so cheerful after a night like last night? I prop myself up on the pillows and stare at the tent my feet form under the duvet. Nine six two – how does it go? My fingers know the number even if I don't. I punch the six digits and wait. I hope I know what I'm doing.

176

'Hello, Connie?'

'No. This is Linda.'

'Is Connie there?'

'She's still in bed. Who is it?'

I glance at the alarm-clock. Twelve thirty – was I the first one to get to bed last night? 'James.'

I wait while she goes to fetch Connie. Linda – is that the flatmate? But whose is that man's voice? I strain to hear what he's saying, but it's too faint to make out. A young man, not the voice of a cellist from the RPO. So they entertain men early in the morning, do they? Two bachelor girls, men's razors in the bathroom, an unclaimed pair of socks in the laundry basket – I know the score. And why is Connie taking so long coming to the phone? There *had* been someone, now I think of it. She'd just come back from Germany or Austria when we first met, and she mentioned a boyfriend she'd stayed with there. No doubt a ski-instructor or something. I can see him now: a big blond Aryan with a big pink dick and a belly like a washboard. I hear a masculine laugh, and then Connie's voice. 'Hello, James?'

'Hello, Connie.' There's a pause while I hear the voice ask something and Connie's muffled reply as she puts her hand over the receiver.

'Sorry.' She's talking to me now. 'How are you?'

A three-inch nail has been driven through my temple and I'm aching in every joint. 'Okay. Sorry for getting you out of bed.'

'That's okay. We didn't get to sleep till late.'

'Really?' Oh didn't *we*? Who is this other person? What's his name?

'We went to the ballet last night and then out to dinner afterwards.'

'That's nice. What did you see?'

'A Black company from New York. They were amazing – very avant-garde.'

'Oh yes?' I didn't know the Hitler youth approved of modern dance. And nig-nogs too. There's a pause.

'I'm glad you phoned.'

'Yes.' I shut one eye and line my foot up with the

handle of the chest of drawers. 'Connie? Sorry about the other night. I was a bit of a pillock.'

'Pillock?'

'Idiot.'

'You were, weren't you?'

An internal voice protests over my headache: you're not supposed to say that!

'And I'm sorry for being so thoughtless,' she continues. 'I shouldn't have said what I did.'

I can feel the weight of resentment lift off me by the moment. 'I'd really like to see you today. That is, you know if – '

'I'd like that too.'

'Why don't you come over?'

Which is exactly what she does. Praise the Lord.

I'm fragile, but dressed by the time she comes round half an hour later.

'You look awful,' are her first words.

'I feel it.'

She walks into the sitting-room and pulls the curtains open with a flourish. The aspirin I took hasn't reached my optic nerves yet and I flinch as the daylight strikes the back of my eyeballs. She offers to make me some coffee, but I can't face anything else in my system yet.

'Well?' she says. Connie has brought the sun in with her: she makes sympathetic enough noises, but I can see from the smile that plays round her eyes that she's not going to take this seriously.

I sit delicately on the sofa waiting for the aspirin to go to work, listening to her recount the story of the night before. It was the first time she'd been to the ballet: she was like a child in her enthusiasm: the lead dancer was a marvel, the choreography ingenious and original. I'm glad for her, and try to follow what she's saying, but she stops after a minute. 'Poor James – you're not interested, are you?' There's a look of such tender amusement in her eyes that it almost makes a hangover worth having. 'Come on – let's go out. You need some fresh air.'

So she drags me out for a walk; she striding on ahead

178

and me following behind her like an arthritic dog. We catch a bus to Holland Park where I find myself on a bench staring at the flowers while Connie feeds the ducks with some bread she's brought. I think she's the first person I've ever met who remembered to bring breadcrumbs for the birds.

She insists on hearing all about the party, and I give her an edited version, leaving Janet out of it. She asks me about Tad. What is there to tell? He's a gay Italo-Polish half-Jewish half-Catholic atheistic cripple.

'An interesting sounding guy,' she laughs.

'He calls himself an all-round pariah. Next lifetime he says he'll come back as a black lesbian dwarf.'

'I'd like to meet him.'

'Come round to Innocence some time. I'm sure he'd like to meet you, too.'

'*Innocence?*'

– 'It's where he lives.' Innocence – I've forgotten how strange it sounds as the name of a house.

It's a hot day and the park is full of the sounds of summer: dogs and kids and footballs. And Connie rustling the bag as she empties the crumbs on to the grass for the birds. She's wearing green corduroy trousers – far too tight round the bum for her, but she looks nice squatting there by the pond. She shouldn't really wear trousers: skirts are more her style. She has the body of an Ingres model: smooth and full and clearly not designed for androgynous twentieth-century clothing.

She sees me watching her and we lock eyes for a second. She smiles very slightly and then pulls me up from the bench. 'Let's go and watch the cricket.' She links my arm in hers and we stroll to the pitch. We find a sloping bank to lie on, a perfect couch for a snooze. 'I love watching cricket, don't you? It's such a dignified, ridiculous game.'

'There's only one thing more boring than playing cricket, and that's watching it. I'm going to sleep.' I try to snuggle into a comfortable position, but I need a pillow. 'Could I – ?'

She pats her lap and I shift so my head rests on her thighs. The corduroy is soft and warm against my cheek, and she strokes my head as though I'm a cat. I'd purr if I could.

179

I watch the horizontal game of cricket for a few minutes before my eyelids sag and I drift off to sleep. I dream I'm sitting on a stool by a turnstile at a football ground, watching people as they pass through the gate. Every time the gate turns there's a click as though a counter has recorded their entrance. I'm not going to the match – I'm waiting for someone, sitting on a green stool in the sun.

'Oh, good hit!' I come back to Holland Park and Connie and cricket. I roll to face her, my nose almost touching her crutch.

'Sleep well?'

'Mmm. I thought I was asleep on a solar-powered water-bed.'

Her hand absently rests on my neck as she returns her attention to the match. I listen to the click of leather on willow, the spattering of applause. Through my half-open eyes, her trousers look like a huge field of grass. I nuzzle the material under my nose, nodding my head to ease her legs apart.

'Tell me when you want to go.'

'Mmm.' I'm as warm and safe as a joey in a kangaroo pouch – I could stay like this for ever.

The match is over: apparently it was a close-fought thing, and while the umpires collect the bails and stumps, the small crowd clap the last two batsmen back to the pavilion. Connie joins in the applause, and I have to sit up.

She stands up and brushes the grass off her trousers and tucks her blouse back into her waistband. I've never seen Connie look lovelier. 'Let me take you for a meal to make up for last time.'

She thinks about it for a moment. 'Yes – that would be nice. Thank you.'

We stroll back to the road through the woodland, the late-afternoon sun dappling us with amber and gold. It's good to walk on soil for a change. Connie catches my sleeve and we stop to watch a squirrel on a branch above us, its tail twitching. Something makes me look back at the bright expanse of field behind us, almost white after the dusk of

180

the wood, and I know the image will be imprinted on my memory for years.

But even as we walk, Adam and Eve, back to the road, I can feel the slimy serpent slither back into my mind. I don't want to ask, but neither do I stop myself. 'You must be getting bored with all this eating out.'

'Not at all. I love it.'

'Who did you go out with last night?'

'Linda and Martin.'

Ah – the Teutonic lover. 'Who's Martin?' I ask as nonchalantly as I can.

'Linda's brother – it was her birthday yesterday so he took us both out.'

We come out into the open and squint against the light. I don't think she registers the look of relief on my face.

We agree on nothing fancy for the meal. Cheap and cheerful – it's a lovers' meal: shared pizza, melted cheese forming strands from plate to mouth. The people at the next table are uncomfortable at our laughter, but what do we care? We are young and hungry and glad to be alive. Connie orders a milkshake – a big pink one, and she slurps the bubbles through a straw while I watch her over the rim of my glass of mineral water. A family has taken the corner table: a children's birthday party – giggling and party hats and 'Happy Birthday to you'. We join in, and birthday boy brings over a piece of cake on a plate.

'Happy Birthday, Tim,' Connie says with a smile. How does she know his name? She catches his arm so he can't escape. 'How old are you?'

'Seven.'

'Seven?' Connie says in amazement. 'Lucky you – that's the best age to be.'

'Why?'

'Because you're not six any more, and you're not eight yet.'

The kid thinks about it for a moment, and then decides it's a joke and laughs.

'Thank you for the cake, Tim.'

He goes back to the table and Connie mouths thanks

181

at the parents. 'I've given up telling myself I shouldn't eat this stuff. Here – ' She holds a forkful of cake to my mouth. I think we both remember at the same moment – we've been here before: strawberry cake then as now. I take the cake into my mouth, my eyes closing in a reflex action at the sweetness.

I order coffee for both of us and we talk more. And then brandy, and Connie introduces me to the delights of hot fudge sundaes with vanilla ice-cream. I have a second cup of coffee, and the family get up to go. Connie catches the boy as he passes our table and whispers something to him. He giggles and then follows his parents out.

'What did you say?'

'He'd been pretending his apple juice was wine, so I told him I hoped he wasn't too drunk to drive the car home.'

I reach across to wipe a fleck of ice-cream from the corner of her mouth. 'You're good with kids.'

'I like them.'

'So would I eventually.'

She looks puzzled for a moment and then she laughs.

'What is it?' I ask, sensing I've misheard her.

'Nothing.'

We finish our brandies and then comes the question we've both been waiting for:

'Do you want to come back to my place?'

Her gaze travels up the stem of my glass until our eyes meet. 'Yes.'

I don't need to ask more: it's all there in the look. There's no need for more, no need for pretence, no nervous jokes. Just her eyes, soft and unashamed. Something opens inside me at that moment; a brief unfolding of something with velvet petals. I've felt this sensation before, years ago with Ruth. It's too new to give it a name, but the truth is, I'm in love.

Ah, love!

It's slow, our first love-making. Her body is as warm and round as fresh-baked bread and she lies there, all of her, a mound of extraordinary womanhood across the

182

bed. She smiles and stills my quivering hands with her own, kissing my fingertips, her breath flicking my belly, my groin, down to my toes.

We're gentle and slow, tumbling over the bed in slow motion, mouth to skin to mouth, the sheets tangling our legs, our legs tangling our arms. We picnic on each other on that bed, kissing insteps, behind knees, chewing and nibbling and drinking each other.

She's golden and rich and ripe and there's all this. Calves, belly, breasts, the inside of her thighs; there's so much of her, this miracle. And the smile as she watches me kissing this and that of her.

I want to weep, I'm so happy.

It's like falling, when she opens her legs for me and I slide into her; an exquisite plunge into another person. A whole world is here; as warm and generous as the girl herself: inside her I am lying in a field of corn in the sun. And her face so close to mine. I don't know how long we last, but I stay inside her, spent, just resting. Her fingers stroke my hair and our grins meet in a kiss.

'I love you.'

21

We wake in the morning in each other's arms. From asleep to awake is so finely graded that surfacing next to a new woman in my bed is as natural as if we had dreamed together.

'Hello.'

'Hello.'

We look at each other nose to nose in silence, and then there is a little click as Connie's sleep-gummed lips part and she takes my lower lip in her mouth.

'Fleep well?' I ask.

Her eyelids brush my cheek as she blinks. 'Mmm.' She

darts her tongue between my teeth and I bite it gently. I feel as though I've slept in cotton-wool, comforted and cared for.

'Fancy some breakfast?' I ask.

'In a minute.'

We fit well, lying together as snug as matching jigsaw pieces. Almost imperceptibly we begin reacquainting ourselves with each other's bodies. I gently gnaw the fingertips she drapes over my face while she rubs her cheek against the bristle of my chin. I explore her face: the smoothness of her skin, lips puffy from kissing, eyelids drooping with pleasure. I run my tongue along the line of her jaw, down her throat to the depression in her collar-bone. After Ruth's brittle body, Connie's is a feast: there is so much flesh to hold, flesh that demands caressing. I could spend a week exploring her breasts alone. I can feel my lips wanting to form the shape of a suckling baby's. I want to consume her. I want to eat and drink her.

Her ability to abandon herself impresses me; here I am, worshipping her body, mouthing the skin of her belly, smoothing her silky pubic hair against my cheek, and she takes it all, eyes shut, body responding like a seismograph to distant earthquakes. She lets out a moan as I brush her pubic hair into a quiff and then trace the triangle of her groin with my tongue. She is perfect, even the moles that dot her body are beautiful. I can feel a convulsion building inside me as though my veins and arteries are contracting.

I have never been so fascinated by a woman's body: toenails, a tiny birthmark under her arm, the coy belly button. The more I stroke, the more she opens, arching her back, her head thrown to one side. She cries out when my fingertips find her clitoris. 'Sorry. Am I hurting you?'

She holds my hand in place. 'Don't stop.' One more stroke and she topples over the edge, shuddering to a climax. I watch her face in amazement, the teeth biting her top lip, face creased in pain.

Her eyes slowly open. She looks drunk. 'Thank you, that was gorgeous.'

I tug the sheet back up, and as we cuddle I find myself

grinning into her hair. Ridiculous, the pride in achievement of having her orgasm, but I'm glowing inside. I kiss her cheek. 'I want to make you come and come and come,' I murmur.

But when she looks at my naked body, I contract like a sea anemone. I try to stay under the sheet, but she snatches it off the bed and playfully throws it in the corner. She kneels beside my supine body and I can see the greed in her eyes as she scrutinises me. Last night we were both intoxicated with the newness of it; the lights were dim, the brandies had lowered my defences, but this is too exposed. I see myself through her eyes, cringing in the middle of the bed, a fake, a cheat. I try and read her expression. Disappointment? Disgust?

She smiles and runs a finger across my belly, but my muscles tighten as if it's a razor-blade she's holding. I can feel my hands straining to cover myself, but I keep them rigid beside me. *Relax, you idiot. She's not going to eat you.* I scan the ceiling, searching for something to focus on. *Phagophobia, the fear of being eaten.* She bends to kiss my neck and then my shoulders down to my chest. I want her to shut her eyes, disappear me. I want to be absent, to have no physical locus, not to be reminded of this clay and stick body.

I suddenly have a memory of standing in line for medical inspection at school. I'm in my vest and underpants. The nurse is going to examine us: we don't know what for, but rumour has it that she cups your balls in her hand and asks you to cough. I'm terrified I'm going to have an erection.

'What's wrong, James?'

'I'm just a bit nervous.'

'Turn over.' I do as she says, my face in the pillow. I feel her straddle my back. 'You need a massage.' She begins smoothing my skin with her hands as though I'm made of wet clay. 'Have you got any oil?'

'Cooking oil.'

'Talcum powder?'

'In the bathroom cabinet.' The pressure leaves my back and I watch her sideways as she pads out of the room. Her

185

legs are short, making her bottom look larger than it really is. It's astonishing that underneath her clothes there was this miracle waiting all the time. You mean she actually carries this body around? Inhabits it? I can't believe the richness of the girl. She is so full, so *real*. I can hear her humming in the bathroom, the tinkle of water as she has a pee. I'm torn in two: I want her so badly, but I'm afraid. Of what? Not that she'll eat me, but that she'll laugh at me.

One of these days I'm going to have to grow up.

I'm lying in the same position when she comes back in. From a distance her pubic hair is so fair it's just a shading at the convergence of her thighs, an arrowhead pointing to her feet. 'You are beautiful,' I say.

The talcum powder feels like warm snowflakes settling on my back. 'Close your eyes. Just relax.'

We planned to have breakfast in the Italian café in Hammersmith, but our arms and legs won't obey us, so we have brunch in bed: crackers and cheese and two tomatoes. I've forgotten to bring plates or cutlery from the kitchen, but no problem, Connie opens my dressing-gown and lays the food out on my belly and we spread the margarine with our fingers, breaking chunks of cheese off and feeding each other, licking the pippy tomato juice from each other as it spurts down our necks. Crumbs find their way into the tangle of my pubic hair and Connie vacuums them with her mouth. 'I love the way you look.'

'What do you mean?' My prick?

'I love your body.'

'You're not serious.'

'Honey, you're just my type.'

I can't believe what I'm hearing. 'You don't think I'm too thin?'

'Of course you're too thin.' She laughs. She must have seen my face drop. 'Not like that. You are who you are — thin and gorgeous. It's you I . . . like.'

She nearly said *love*, and we both know it. I watch her as she slides a hand down my thigh to my ankle. 'Mmm. Yummy.'

'I hate the way I look.'

'Why?'

'I'm just not built right.'

'You mean you're not built the way you'd like.' She leans over to kiss my Achilles tendon. 'Well, neither am I. Big deal.'

'What's wrong with the way you look?'

'You really want to know? My bum is too big, my boobs are different sizes, my thighs are fat.'

'But you're beautiful.'

'Thank you. I won't argue with that. Now, will you accept a compliment and shut up about your opinions?'

'Okay.'

'I like the way you look.'

I take a deep breath. 'Thank you.' Connie slips inside my dressing-gown and I hold the flaps over her, sealing her in. 'How can one so young be so wise?' I ask her.

The phone rings. I look from Connie to the phone and back again. 'Being a woman helps,' she says.

I reach across her for the phone, but she catches my hand.

'Leave it.'

'But it may be important.'

'As important as this?'

She's right. I push the answer phone button. *There's no one in right now. Please leave a message after the tone and I'll get back to you.* I turn my attention back to Connie but as soon as I hear the high-pitched voice I pull away from her to listen to the message. *James? This is Tad. Phone me back.* The machine beeps and switches itself off. Damn Tad and his timing.

We doze and talk all afternoon. 'I've got a confession to make,' she says. 'The other night when I said we couldn't make love because of my period? I was lying.'

'Click! I don't care.' I frame her body with an imaginary camera: if there's one snapshot I could take from this afternoon, it would be this: Connie lying with her arms behind her head, the sheets down to her belly.

'What are you whispering, you madman?'

'She's all States, and all Princes, I. Nothing else is.'

'Is that a poem?'

'John Donne.' I can see she's never heard of him. She brings her arms down and two tyres of fat appear round her middle. I slide a finger into the crevice but she plucks it out.

'I don't need to be reminded of my fat thank you.'

The cupboard is bare, so in the evening we make a dash for the shops and bring back some food. French cheese, garlic pâté, fresh prawns, a couple of avocados – I can see that food is going to take on a new significance with Connie.

We're back in bed by ten thirty; candles lit, food laid on a tray, the wine chilled, the music low. Within seconds of that woman touching me, I'm aroused. 'Let's eat later,' I whisper, putting the tray on the floor.

She laughs and we roll towards each other. I'm hungry again, but it's not food I'm after. And then the phone rings.

'I'm sorry, I've got to answer it.'

And of course, it's Tad.

'Hi, Jimmy boy. How are you?'

I'm in heaven: Connie is nestling behind me, her hand in my groin. 'Okay.'

'How's it going?'

'How's what going?'

'You were dying from alcohol poisoning last time I spoke to you.'

'I'm okay now.' Connie has pulled me on to my back and is sliding on top of me until she's sitting on my groin.

'How about coming over tomorrow? You're not working on a bank holiday, are you?'

'I don't know.'

'You don't know?'

'Ah.' With one hand guiding me into place, Connie lowers herself on to my penis.

'What did you say?'

'No, I'm not working.' She's sitting above me, squeezing her vagina muscles in time to the music.

There's a pause. 'Are you on your own, James?'

'Yes. I'm watching telly.' The tempo of Connie's contractions are increasing. *Hurry up*, she mouths to me. 'What time shall I come over?'

'Three?'

'Fine. See you then.' I'm about to put the phone back on the hook when Connie takes it from me and buries it under the pillow.

As soon as I see Tad's face it's clear that I've made a mistake by inviting Connie. He's visibly shaken to see another person. Connie steps forward and holds her hand out to him. 'Hello, Tad.'

'Hello.' He takes her hand. 'Who are you?'

'This is Connie. Remember me telling you about her?'

'Oh, yes.' He looks at me questioningly. 'Sit down, why don't you?'

'Can I use the john first, please?' Connie asks.

'John?' Tad says disdainfully.

'The lavatory.'

Tad tells her how to find it and we both wait until she's out of the room.

'This is *our* space,' Tad hisses as soon as the door closes behind her. 'What is she doing here?'

'I thought you'd like to meet her.'

'Your mistress?'

I grin, my eyebrows doing a little celebratory wiggle. 'She came over on Saturday.'

'And?'

I spread my hands like a comedian delivering a punchline. 'I'm in lust.' I give an appreciative shudder. 'I shouldn't find her attractive – I go for the tall, sophisticated look – but I do.'

'Well, that's quite a turn around.' Tad's chair buzzes into action, and I have to move aside to let him pass. He bumps against his desk and tries to open the drawer, his hands fumbling with the handle. He finally manages to open it and pull out a sheaf of papers. I wait for him to say something else, but he just spreads the papers on the tray in front of him and begins reading.

'What are you doing?' I ask after a minute.

'I've got some work to do.'

'Tad?'

He refuses to look up at me, and I have to squat in front of his chair. 'What's up? Aren't you pleased?'

'Ecstatic.'

'Don't be like that.' The sun is rapidly fading from my day. I want him to be happy for me.

'How should I be? You've got your little red rooster – congratulations.' He turns back to his manuscript, but then shuffles the sheets together after a moment. 'And Constance!'

'What do you mean?'

'Lady Constance Chatterley?'

'Oh, come on, Tad.'

'Starring James as the strutting Oliver Mellors, and the wheelchair-bound cuckold played by yours truly.'

'Now you're feeling sorry for yourself.'

'Or perhaps it should be Constance Wilde, the hapless wife of poor gay Oscar.'

'You're jealous!'

'Of course I'm bloody jealous! I'm tied to this bloody wheelchair while you two lovers skip off into the sunset of heterosexual bliss. How do you expect me to feel?'

'But Tad, we'll still see each other.'

'You don't understand, do you, my dear sweet James,' he says with a catch in his voice. 'I'm in love with you.'

Ah, love!

It's as though I've been struck between the eyes. I have no time to say anything before Connie comes back in and sits down.

'James tells me you work in a stable,' Tad says.

'Yes, I've been there a couple of months.'

'And how long are you staying in England?'

'I don't know. I've yet to see.'

Tad looks her up and down. 'And you're from America?'

'That's right.'

'You have exotic tastes, James.' He turns to smile at me, but I just stare back. He's in *love* with me?

'Virginia is hardly exotic,' she says. 'Not as exotic as – what are you – Italian and Polish?'

'You've been talking about me, James.' He looks from me to Connie. 'James and I are good friends.'

'I know.'

'Though I've felt a little abandoned since you came into his life, my dear.'

They both look at me, but I can't think of anything to say. I'm glad Connie isn't apologising.

'He tends to lose his head a bit over the fairer sex.' I can see from the glitter in his eyes that he's on the attack. Connie is just smiling back at him, a well-fed look on her face. 'James seems to head to Lady Jane like a bluebottle to dustbins.'

'Lady Jane?' she asks.

'John Thomas and Lady Jane. Surely you've read D. H. Lawrence?'

'No, I haven't.'

'John Thomas, prick. Lady Jane, cunt.'

He must have noticed me stiffen in my chair, because he turns to me and says, 'I'm sorry. Am I misrepresenting you?'

'Tad,' I protest. 'Come on.'

'You object to my use of the divine monosyllable? It doesn't upset you, does it, Constance?' She doesn't answer, but I can see she's confused at being targeted as the enemy so swiftly.

'Of course, the first person since Chaucer to use the word "cunt" with any sense of dignity was our Mr Lawrence. It's a shame you never read *Lady Chatterley's Lover*. If you had you might have agreed that "cunt" is anything but a dirty word, in fact in the mouth of the bard it sounds quite beautiful, don't you think?'

Connie doesn't bat an eyelid, but it's more than I can take. 'Please don't, Tad.'

'Are you blushing, James? Constance here isn't. *Cunt* apparently was one of the seven words deemed indecent by the US supreme court. If I remember right, the others were fuck, piss, shit, tits, fuck, cocksucker.' He's counting them on his fingers. 'Oh, and one more.

191

What was it? Perhaps you remember Constance, you're American.'

She says nothing. I get up to go, but Connie makes no move.

'No? Or James, you should remember this one. Mother-fucker.'

'Come on, Connie. Let's go.'

'Not yet, James.' She turns to Tad. 'What is it with you?'

'Nothing, my dear. Just chatting.'

She looks up at me. 'And you call him a friend of yours?'

Tad's head nods forward and he stares at the floor. 'I'm sorry,' he says softly. 'I've been horrible to you.' He looks at Connie and then at me. 'Forgive me please – I shouldn't have said any of that.'

'Damn right, you shouldn't!'

It's Tad's turn to be embarrassed. He tells me to sit down, and then offers us coffee. I don't want any, but Connie says yes. She has the sense not to volunteer help while he struggles to spoon coffee into two mugs.

We wait in silence for the kettle to boil. He's in *love* with me? What have I done to deserve that? And now he's trying to wreck things with me and Connie. I want to get out of here as soon as I can.

Connie and Tad make small-talk while they drink their coffee. Even with my head full of Tad's revelation I can't help noticing the different way that Ruth and Connie relate to him. In spite of his insults, Connie has apparently decided to give him a second chance. Tad meanwhile is trying hard to make up for it. He's being his charming best now, asking her questions about work, where she comes from, what she's seen of London.

'I hope you and James are going to get on well,' he says to her as we're about to leave. 'He's a fragile soul.'

They both smile at me. Is there some sort of conspiracy starting between these two? I busy myself washing the mugs, feeling their eyes on my back.

'He's tough enough,' Connie says. 'He doesn't need me to look after him.'

'Fatten him up though, couldn't you?' I hear Tad whisper. 'He's too thin.'

I apologise as soon as we're out of the room. 'I don't know what got into him.'

'He's in love with you. That's obvious.'

'Don't be ridiculous!' I protest loudly.

'Whoa, James!' she laughs.

I hold the swing-door open for her, but she doesn't move. 'How could he be in love with me?' I say, refusing to meet her eyes. 'It's absurd.'

Connie tugs my arm and we go through the door together. She keeps hold of my hand as we step into the sunlit street. 'Love between men isn't absurd, James. It's very natural.'

I allow myself to be steered to the bus-stop. Agape is natural perhaps, caritas; platonic love, fraternal love. But not this – this was *in* love.

I suddenly realise where we're going. 'Aren't you staying tonight?'

'No, James. I've—' She cuts herself short.

'You've what?'

'I was going to say I've got things to do, but that's not true.'

'So, come home with me.'

She shakes her head. 'I want to be on my own.'

I try not to show my disappointment. We've had such a good two days, why stop it now? I want to domesticate her, take her home and keep her there.

I wait with her till her bus comes and then walk back to the flat. I can already feel the steel cables of Tad and Connie tugging against me. How short-lived our victories are. Within twenty-four hours I've become tethered between two people's love, caught in the middle like a harpooned whale.

Perhaps I should have seen it coming: Tad falling in love with me? But how had it happened? What had I done to warrant it? Surely I hadn't encouraged him? I know we got pretty open about sex, but can't two men be friends without one of them wanting to stick his dick in the other?

22

Now what? Just pick up my life as though the weekend hasn't happened? Cook my meal and have my bath and climb into bed alone as if, not even two miles away, a woman lives and breathes who holds the missing piece of the jigsaw of my desire? I phoned her this morning to suggest that we meet after work, but she had a date with a girlfriend she said; she wouldn't come round afterwards either. Why, she didn't say. I wanted to tell her that I missed her, that I wouldn't know how to fill my evenings without her, but instead I bit my tongue and went home.

Why isn't she here? We're getting on well enough – better than that – we're brilliant together. Then why is she seeing friends? And what friends are these? If jealousy is a fire, then love is the paraffin that's poured on to it. And I'm beginning to burn.

But she stays on Wednesday night. I hardly recognise her when I open the door to her. She's wearing her work clothes: denim jeans, boots and a short-sleeved checked shirt. Her hair is tucked into a Yankees' baseball cap. I want to whoop when I see her eyes light up as the door opens. She must be in love with me: that look means only one thing.

'You look like a cowgirl.'

'Moo.'

She smells musty, organic; a refreshing, real smell. I wish I hadn't put my aftershave on now.

'I'm filthy. Can I have a shower?'

'If you let me watch.'

'No way!' She slaps my bum and runs up the stairs. I listen to her singing as I start the cooking. There's still so much to find out about her. I've begun the exploration of her body, but her background is still largely uncharted.

Not the biographical detail, but the person behind the facts, the person behind the glittering smile she gave me when I opened the door. She's still as mysterious to me as that horsey smell she has brought home.

'Do you like your work?' I ask her when she comes downstairs. She has changed into a cotton dress. I melt when I see that the towel she's using to dry her hair is one of mine.

'Yes. I love horses.'

'More than people?'

It's a serious question to her, and she pauses to think about it. 'More than most people.'

I want to ask the obvious question, *more than me?*, but she's unaware of what she has said.

'How about you? What's working in a library like?'

'Me?' I'm hypnotised by her. 'I give eight and a half hours of my life every day to other people and their ideas. One day I swear I'll get my own back on those bastards and write my own book.'

'Way to go!'

I can feel myself slipping; I know I'm loving her more than I should, but there's nothing missing in her; it's all there, everything I need. I'm intoxicated by her. She's cherries soaked in brandy, rum truffle, sherry trifle. I want to gorge myself on her, eat so much I'm sick.

I'm trying to impress her, and I know it isn't working. A friend from Burma had written to me at the beginning of the week, and there the letter lies, exotic stamp and all, a conversation piece waiting to happen. The music I play for her is so obscure as to be almost incomprehensible: West African cora music, minimalist piano pieces, free-form jazz. She hates it.

We make love after dinner, and then again, but still I can't get enough of her. There is a seam of sex running through her like coal, but no matter how much I dig, there's more and more to mine. Ejaculations are like explosions in my head: dynamiting open new passages. I watch her face as we make love: the sweat on her upper lip, the eyes squinting as her orgasm builds until she comes. Sex has never seemed so mysterious or so hopeless.

195

I have a new project: the seduction of Connie. The next day I copy a recipe from a Chinese cookbook in the library: dried mushrooms and bamboo shoots, I'll knock her dead with it when she comes round next. I send flowers to her home, I buy her a copy of Tagore's love poems. I write her a poem of my own, a sonnet no less: the first I've written for ten years. The first line reads: *What need have we for more than this?* And, if only I could reach the bottom of her sexuality, indeed, what more would we need?

How do I love her? Let me count the ways. I love her blousy body; her rounded belly; her handwriting. I love her smell and her smile and the way she talks. I love her humour and her simplicity. I love the way her pendulous tits bounce when we make love. And her vagina.

Oh, that devil's gateway: it is a whole house big; soft furnishings and underfloor heating and imaginative décor. It is home, and I can lose myself – and do – in those many rooms.

And her taste is of warm golden syrup and cool passion-fruit. Yeah verily, she has the sweetest cunt in the whole of Christendom.

I work late on Thursday and don't get home till half past eight. The light on my answer phone is flashing – a message from Connie? She said she'd be busy again this evening, and that she'd phone me on Friday. Is it my imagination, or is she evasive when I ask her who she's seeing? There's no hint of another man, but I still daren't ask. I feel like the pretender to the throne, insecure in my claim for her attention. She still doesn't realise just how much I want her; just how unnecessary these nights apart are.

I press the playback and wait while the machine beeps. Two calls without messages, and then Tad's voice. *James? Could we talk please? I'm not going out, so could you phone me this evening? . . . umm . . .*

I make a sandwich and go upstairs to run the bath. A spider has fallen into the bath and I spend five minutes trying to scoop it out with a rolled-up cone of paper. I can't bring myself to pick it up with my fingers and it keeps running out of the paper and dropping back into the bath, but I eventually rescue it and throw it out of the window. Do spiders float when you drop them from a height, or do they fall at the standard thirty-two feet per second? A fifty-foot drop to a spider must be the equivalent of sky-diving without a parachute. I might as well have squashed it in the bath, saved it the journey.

I sit on the side of the bath and eat my sandwich while the bath fills. What should I do about Tad? I've never been loved by a man before. I imagine the reply on a problems page.

Dear Perturbed of Hammersmith,
There is nothing unnatural about another man being attracted to you. Providing that you take precautions, sexual intercourse with somebody of the same sex can be as fulfilling as any heterosexual relationship. However, if you don't want the relationship to progress to a physical level, you must gently but firmly tell your friend that you're not interested.

So, bog off, Tad! The last thing I need is for my only two friends in the world to be competing for me. I stuff the last of my sandwich into my mouth and decide to phone him after my bath. Getting to my feet I find that two inches of my shirt tail has dipped into the bath-water.

It's eleven thirty before I realise I've forgotten to phone Tad.

But, hallelujah, Connie agrees to stay the weekend. Two whole days and nights with her; I can't believe my luck.

On Saturday we take the train to Richmond and spend the afternoon in the park, trying to creep up on the deer, skimming stones in the lake, lying on our jackets in the bracken. It's a perfect day, and we know it. I realise it can't go on forever, but we're getting on better and better. We're in love and we have the sense to enjoy every moment of it.

'Do you feel it?' I ask her. 'As though we're the only people in the park?'

She stops to listen. 'Yes,' she says excitedly. 'Like we're walking in a bubble of something.'

197

And she's right; we seem disconnected from other people, the sounds that reach us muffled as though strained through an invisible cocoon. I run on ahead of her and turn to look back. The sun is behind her, her hair like spun glass, a halo not just round her head, but her entire upper body.

Sitting on the train at dusk I can still feel the sun on my face. Connie's freckles are coming out: tiny gold flecks across her nose. We stay in for the evening, have two games of draughts – checkers, as she calls it – listen to some music, Connie doodling with a felt-pen on my arm. I'm liquid when she touches me, as sleepy and syrupy as laudanum.

She's been invited to a party in Hampstead and we half decide to go, but by nine o'clock it's clear that the spell is too special to break. *What need have we for more than this?* There will be plenty of time for parties.

'Would you mind if we stayed in?' she asks.

'Would I mind?' The only reason I venture beyond my front door at all is to find someone like you, my cream puff. I kiss her forehead. Now I have her, I'll gladly give up the rest of the world. Independence, in my vocabulary, is just another word for loneliness.

I love Connie being at the flat. The ghost of Ruth has long since gone; Connie belongs here, this is her place now. When I see her toothbrush in the bathroom mug I do a little war dance. She's staying. Now all I have to do is nail the front door shut and I've got her where I want.

I'm lying on the settee staring at the ceiling when the phone rings.

'Hello?'

'James! How are you?' It's Tad.

'I'm okay. Look I can't stop, I'm about to go out. I'll phone you back.' I lie back to study the ceiling again, glad that Connie hadn't heard. Tacky behaviour, I know, but I'm on automatic as far as Tad is concerned. The images of those men spanking each other in Tad's porno magazine have stuck to the inside of my skull with the unwelcome persistence of a piece of gum to the sole of my shoe. I know that's not what Tad wants to do to me, but do you think I can convince my subconscious of that?

Connie's period has started and so I make her a hot-water bottle and we watch the midnight movie in bed, Connie cuddling the bottle and me cuddling her. It feels so good that I wonder if this isn't what I've been searching for all along: a cuddle. We snuggle and giggle under the bedclothes until we drift off to sleep.

She goes back home on Sunday afternoon. I want my look to say it all, to say how much she's breaking my heart by leaving me, but she has steeled herself to me: she knows how much I want her to stay, and still she kisses me and leaves.

So I have my conversation alone, sitting on the settee, talking to an imaginary Connie next to me. Think of all the advantages of living together I say: visiting the launderette together, cooking for two, halving heating bills, an end to loneliness. Stay with me darling.

Monday night she's out. Tuesday night she's visiting a friend. I detect a whine in my voice as I try to persuade her to cancel her date on Wednesday, but she ignores my plea and suggests I go and see Tad.

That's still a sore point. Somebody is phoning up a couple of times an evening: Tad, I presume. The answer phone is on all the time now, but no messages are left. The only person I want to speak to is Connie, and she's bloody out all the time.

I'm called to the phone at work on Thursday morning: it's Connie. 'Hi. How are you?'

'Surprised,' I say, surprised.

'Is it okay to call you at work?'

'Fine. More than fine, it's wonderful to hear you.'

'Sorry I've been so busy this week.'

'I've missed you.'

'That's nice.'

She's so different on the phone; almost curt. I want to ask if there's something going on that I should know about, but I don't want to know the answer. I'm getting that yearning feeling again.

'Look, let's meet on Friday.'

'Can you stay the weekend?' It's not the sex; it's something greater than that, something I don't want to admit, even to myself. I can't live without her.

It feels like the first time, when we make love on Friday night. It's so wonderful to be inside her again that I forgive her for not seeing me all week. She is a miracle, this girl, a thing bright and beautiful. A Madonna.

On Saturday we catch the tube into town to buy me some jeans. I don't really want any, but Connie insists, and I give in. The train is crowded and I have to sit opposite Connie. Beside her is an oriental girl – Japanese perhaps, or possibly Korean. I begin by smiling directly into Connie's face, but by Shepherd's Bush I can feel my eyes sliding helplessly from Connie to the girl. Goddammit! Will I never be satisfied? Here I have the vessel of my desire, a whole orchard of soft fruit in Connie, and my mouth is watering for sushi. *Petite* and cute as a doll, her compact oriental breasts – one mouthful each – transfix me. I pretend to gaze out of the window, looking instead at the girl's reflection in the glass.

'Where did you go on Thursday night?' Connie asks suddenly.

'Nowhere. Why?'

'I phoned you twice and got the answer phone.'

'Oh hell! That was you, was it? In future, speak and I'll pick it up if I'm in. Anyway – I thought *you* were going out.'

'I did.'

'Where?'

She hesitates. 'I went to see Tad.'

'Tad?' I think I've misheard.

'I've seen him twice this week.'

'What?'

'He phoned me and asked me to see him.'

I can't believe it. 'So when you were too busy to see me, you were seeing Tad?'

She nods.

'But how did he know your phone number?'

'He asked me for it when we met the first time.'

'You've been seeing Tad?' My brain won't compute this information. *Error* flashes up in front of my eyes. 'Why didn't you tell me?' I say at last.

'I'm telling you now.'

'But twice?'

'Tad asked me not to say anything.' We go over a bridge and she raises her voice so I can hear her. 'He's very upset at the way you're treating him.'

'And what way is that?'

'Why are you avoiding him?'

Her voice is still loud and I frown. 'I can't tell you here,' I say, my eyes flicking to the oriental girl, wondering if she understands English.

'Tell me for Christ's sake.'

I lean forward so our heads meet. 'He's fallen in love with me – can't you understand?'

'Yes?'

'Well, he may not be able to do anything about it, but he sure as hell wants to.'

'What are you talking about?'

'He wants more than friendship.'

'Sex, you mean?' I wince, but she continues. 'I know he does. So what?'

The train squeals to a halt in a station and the girl stands up to get off. I take her place beside Connie. 'What do you mean – you know? Have you talked about it?'

'Sure.'

'What did he say?'

'He wants to make love with you.'

'Oh my God!' I watch the stroboscopic effect of the posters on the platform as they flash past the window. He really *does* want to fuck me. But how? Like the pictures in his magazines?

'Can't you be friends still?'

'Were we ever friends? I don't know.' All the talk, the probing, the confessions – was that out of friendship, or was he just getting his kicks from me? Copy for his dirty stories? I'm suddenly suspicious. 'What else do you talk about?'

'It's between me and Tad.'

'Go on – tell me.'

'It's none of your business.'

A young businessman has sat opposite us, and I watch him. Suits aren't designed for bodies like his, and he looks uncomfortable in it, trapped by too much muscle. His fingers are as thick as half-Corona cigars, blond hair curling round his wedding ring. I imagine what a punch from one of those fists would be like. 'Do you talk about our relationship?' I ask Connie after a minute.

'What happens between Tad and me is our affair.' Her tone is friendly, but her look means business. I drop it and sulk till Oxford Circus.

The first piece of grit has entered our relationship. I try and ignore it, but it's there, rattling in my shoe all afternoon. We can't find any jeans I like, so we have an expensive cup of coffee and then take the tube home.

Connie can obviously see something's bothering me, and as soon as we're indoors, she asks what it is. I'm ready for her.

'I want to see more of you. I hate you spending so much time with your friends.'

Her face darkens. 'Don't spoil what we've got.'

'But what *have* we got? Frankly, I'm confused.'

She says nothing.

'Look – I can't play this game if I don't know what the rules are. You blow hot and then cold. When I see you, you're all over me, and then in the week you're too busy to speak to me.'

'I like you a lot, James.'

'Do you?' I'm surprised to feel tears behind my eyes. 'I'm just a little shocked to hear that you're seeing my best friend more than you're seeing me.'

'I want to see who I like.'

'That's not what I'm saying. You can see Tad if you like, but aren't I more important to you than him? I feel like you're cutting me out of your life. Not even that – I

202

haven't even been admitted into it yet.' What else could I say? Don't leave me, I want to spend my every moment with you? Stay with me?

'I'm scared, James.'

'Scared?'

'I don't want to get too attached to you.'

I wait for more.

'London isn't my home. I'm going to have to leave some time.'

I take her hand and squeeze it as an apology. It's true, and I haven't wanted to think about it, but this girl is passing through, no more permanent than a tourist.

My disappearing act starts for real later that evening when we make love. I've only managed the length of a penis so far, but I know I want more: I want to disappear, arms, legs and all, through that aperture and hide in her womb. I want to bury myself in her and pull the covers over my head.

I'm lying in the crook of her neck when she asks me what I'm thinking about.

'I'm trying to remember a joke.'

She waits in silence. It was something I read years ago in a student rag. I'm not sure if I can remember it right, or whether I should tell it even if I can. 'It's not all that funny.'

'Let's hear it.'

'There was a farmer who went to a prostitute who was famed for the size of her – um – *thing*.'

'Lady Jane?'

'Precisely. Anyway, it's so big that his penis is useless, so he has to use his arm. But it's still too big, so he uses his leg. This fits about right, and he's doing fine until his boot comes off, so he climbs inside her to look for it.'

Nothing from Connie, so I continue. 'Inside, he's amazed to see a panorama of rolling hills and trees and a little river. He sees a lane which he follows until he comes to a stile. Another man is leaning against it, looking at the scenery. "Have you seen my boot?" the first man asks. "No," the

203

second man says, "but you haven't seen a horse and cart by any chance?"'

My head lifts up as Connie sighs. 'I told you it wasn't funny,' I say.

She's silent for a moment and then she says, 'Is that what men think about women? That there's this other world inside them?'

'I don't know. Yes, I suppose so.'

'I don't know whether to feel flattered or insulted. Are we really that mysterious to you?'

'Yes.' I kiss her on the chin. 'Mysterious and dangerous and wonderful.'

'Don't patronise me, James.'

'I'm not, am I?' I sit up and look at her. 'Am I?'

'I'm not a cave. And I'm not a saint. I'm me.'

I don't say anything. I feel uncomfortable when she gets this serious.

'And I'm not even your mother.'

'Why do you say that?'

'Ever heard the saying "return naked to the womb"?'

Return naked to the womb. That's it, isn't it. That's what I want. 'What does it mean?'

'It's a phrase we use back home. It means someone who screws his mother.'

I'm too surprised to say anything. *Incest?*

She's got it in one. I'm turning her into my mother. A mother I've been in search of since the umbilicus was cut. It's as though I've been stumbling and struggling and fighting all my life towards a giant female breast which hangs over me like a mythical cloud. That's all I've wanted; that's all I want now: the breast, the warm milk and deep cradle of a mother's arms. That's why the passion and the desperation and the compulsion to make love with Connie: I want to go back home.

Connie touches my lips with hers. 'I love you, James. Don't go away,' she whispers.

23

It's a couple of days later that Connie tells me about Tad's operation. She doesn't know the details – it's something to do with his breathing. He hasn't been well, and so they've decided to operate next week. Just what I need to compound my guilt about abandoning him.

'It's his birthday soon, so he's bringing the celebration forward.'

'Oh, yes?'

'They're having a party at Innocence. He wants you to come.'

I receive the invitation with a nod of my head. Tad has stopped phoning now and I haven't seen him for over two weeks. With every passing day, the chance of our reconciling has lessened, and Connie's attempts at diplomacy haven't helped either. She has seen him a couple of times recently and returned to reprove me. She doesn't press her point, but she clearly thinks I'm a shit for what I'm doing to Tad. As do I. Now Tad is ill, my status is slipping below even that of ordure.

'He's really cut up about the distance between you two. Can't you make it up?' She likes Tad a lot, and I can see the pain our rift is causing her. At first she visited him just because she was asked, but now it looks as though they've become friends. I'm jealous, of course – of both of them.

'I don't know if I want to make it up.'

'What's the big deal about Tad having the hots for you?'

'You'll just have to believe me. I can't handle being loved by another man.'

'But why? He's not asking you to suck his dick. He just wants to be your friend.'

'Who are you – my analyst?' I close my eyes while I take a breath. 'Sorry for snapping.'

'And that's what you're going to do if you don't ease up on yourself soon,' she says quietly. 'Snap.'

I've read enough oriental philosophy to know the difference between bamboo and iron: one bends, the other doesn't. The question: which is stronger? 'I'm okay,' I say.

She clucks her tongue. 'You English and your stiff upper lip.'

'The great British anal retentive.' I try and wither her with my sarcasm but she just smiles blandly; it seems she's never heard of Freud.

'But please go to the party. It'd mean so much to him.'

I think about it for a moment. 'Okay.' And I really mean it.

Connie and I agree to meet at Innocence at eight o'clock after I've finished at the dentist. I've been putting off doing something about my teeth for months, and two new fillings and the promise of one more to come proves it. I'm still intending to go to the party by eight thirty, but the novacaine is wearing off and I'm beginning to feel as though somebody has punched me in the mouth. I go to the mirror expecting to see a swollen face, but I look normal enough, if a bit sorry for myself.

I take a couple of aspirins with a glass of Martini and phone Innocence. I'll excuse myself; I'm in no fit state for a party. I give up after a minute: either there's something wrong with the line or they're having too good a time to hear the phone.

I'm halfway through watching a film when the phone rings. I glance at the clock: eleven thirty. I let the answer phone switch on and then watch the flashing light while the recorded message runs through. I'm expecting Tad, not Connie. *'James? Pick the phone up.'* I can hear the sound of breathing while I hesitate. *'Come on.'*

I pick the phone up. 'Hello, Connie.'

'Where were you, you bastard?'

I open my mouth to speak, but it's too late. I hold the

buzzing phone to my ear for a moment and then gently lower it back into its cradle.

I phone her at home half an hour later. 'Look, I want to explain.'

'Go ahead.'

Even as I tell her about the dentist and trying to contact Innocence, it sounds like a weak excuse. 'I'd have come if I could.'

'Bullshit.'

I protest, but she interrupts me. 'I hope you realise how upset Tad was. He waited and waited, and you still didn't have the courage to turn up. I can't believe how spineless you are.' The tone of her voice hurts me more than anything she's saying. She's right of course: there's no excuse for what I did.

'I'll phone him,' I murmur.

'His operation is tomorrow afternoon.'

'I'm sorry, Connie.'

'Tell that to Tad.'

I phone the hospital at lunchtime and am put through to ward five. It feels strange using Tad's real name: Piotr Czapski.

'I'm sorry,' the nurse on the other end says. 'He's already had his pre-med.'

'Can I get a message to him?'

'I'll see if he's awake. If he is, who shall I say called?'

'Just wish him good luck. It's James.'

After the cool of the library, the heat outside is oppressive; apparently we're having the sunniest summer this century. The streets are a sticky photochemical soup of heat and exhaust fumes and I try and hold my breath until I'm off the main road. I've been listless all day, hating myself for what I've done to Tad, frightened of losing Connie as a consequence. She was so angry, but not angry as Ruth used to be, not vicious. Ruth was brutal: she wanted to hurt when she told the truth. With Connie it was like a slow-motion body blow: you saw it coming, observed rather than felt the fist nestling against your belly, watched your surprised body absorb the shape as it travelled through to your backbone. You doubled over, air forced from your lungs, and only then did you feel the pain. Right down to your toenails, one-two-three, and then the disengaging and your body was allowed to resume its former shape.

It hurts, of course it hurts, but I know if I can endure it, on the other side is comfort. I just hope I haven't blown it with her.

I buy a packet of chocolate biscuits at the corner shop and lie on my back on the sitting-room floor working my way through them. A patch of light is reflected on the ceiling, and I watch its gradual advance towards the corner of the room. I want her to phone, to kiss it better, and I know she won't.

An ice-cream van jangles and then stops in the road outside the house. I can hear its motor running as it waits. If I close my eyes I can see children standing on tiptoe to reach the counter, pointing at the picture of the lolly they want. A ninety-nine, a strawberry split, a choc ice. I can remember the ice-creams of my childhood; oblong blocks the size and shape of a pack of playing cards sandwiched between orange wafers, impossible for a child to eat without a knife and fork. There was a photograph of Mother, destroyed when the house was cleared after her death, of her eating an ice-cream on a beach in Cornwall. She was pregnant with me at the time, though you'd never tell it from the picture. My parents had been married just six months; this was their first proper holiday together, a honeymoon in effect. I remember the picture well: Mother kneeling in front of some dunes, fifties sunglasses pushed back on top of her head, a low-cut polka-dot dress spreading around her in the sand. She looked so sexy and young, probably no more than twenty-two, about Connie's age. I was shocked when I first saw the photograph; shocked, not at what I saw, but by my reaction. I quite fancied her. I remember thinking that my father was a lucky man. Oops!

Ruth hadn't allowed our foetus to stay with her long enough to change the shape of her flat belly. It had been sucked out by a surgical vacuum cleaner like a bloody tadpole that didn't belong there. My life, my flesh, my baby.

The ice-cream van drives off, making the reflection on the ceiling judder. Its tune starts at the end of the street, a tune that hasn't changed since my childhood.

I try to locate the source of the light without moving from where I'm lying, but I can't find it. I'm not sure if it's outside, or the sun shining off something inside the flat. After an hour or so the patch nearly reaches the corner of the room, but before it touches the point where the ceiling joins the wall, it begins to flatten on one side and slowly reduce like a moon waning until only a sliver is left, and then nothing.

I make myself a drink and sit on the sofa clucking the ice-cubes against each other and realise, perhaps for the first time in my life, how wholly alone I am. Everyone is. For the last two weeks I've lowered my guard against loneliness, dared to be dependent on Connie, and in the quiet that's left in her wake, I can see nothing in front of me except the unending stretch of the rest of my life. I know that however much I busy myself, it will always be against the backdrop of silence and a sandy road snaking through desert dunes. God is dead, that's for sure. Even the Wizard of Oz has shuffled off. There's nobody behind the scenes pulling levers: it's all chance and chromosomes and parallel lines.

I've got no one, not got them in my grip as I want, not got them so much that I can put them in my pocket and call them my own. I know people care about me: Connie, Tad, Ruth even. But I'm the centre of only one world: my own. There's nobody to share this discomfort, nobody whose skin I can climb inside, nobody to hold me tight and promise never to let go. I'm feeling miserable, and not a little sorry for myself.

There's no food in the house and so I go back to the corner-shop and buy a bag of sweets: liquorice comfits, jelly babies and wine-gums. I climb into bed and chew my way through half a pound of them, washing the sticky goo down with gin, until I fall asleep, nauseous and disgusted with myself.

In the morning I phone the hospital.

'Could you tell me how Piotr Czapski is, please?'

209

'Who is this?'

'James Morrison, a friend of his.'

'Umm. You'll need to speak to Sister. Please hold the line.'

Another voice comes on after a minute. 'Mr . . . ?'

'Morrison.'

'Are you family?'

'No, I'm a friend.'

'Ah.'

'Is he all right?'

'I'm afraid I can't give you any information over the telephone. Perhaps you'd like to contact his family.'

'He hasn't got any family.'

'Yes. Well, perhaps you could get in touch with the nursing home.'

'Is he okay?'

'There were some complications with the operation.'

I can't say anything.

'I'm afraid I can't tell you any more over the phone. Please phone the nursing home, they'll be able to give you all the details.'

'Is he awake yet?'

'I'm sorry, Mr Morris. I can't tell you.'

At first I don't recognise the voice, but then I realise it's Lisa.

'I'm phoning about Tad.'

'Have you heard?'

'Heard what?'

'They don't know if Tad's going to live.'

It's a warm evening and I go through the flat opening all the windows while Connie takes a shower. I go into the bedroom and sit on the sill, leaning out of the window. At this height I'm level with the branches of the plane trees that flank the street. Early summer, and somehow once again these grimy trees have managed to release their soft clean leaves.

I watch a dog trot down the street, pausing to sniff and cock a leg against every tree. The animal apparently has an inexhaustible supply of urine: I count seven trees it sprays before it wanders out of sight. A neighbour pulls up in his Mercedes, swinging it easily into the space in front of his house, the car rocking on its suspension with the sudden braking. I watch him lock it and trot up the steps to his front door. He lets himself into the house and slams the door shut and the street is quiet again. I think I'm jealous of this stranger with his expert movements. It had all been so swift: the parking, the striding up the stone steps, the key sliding into the lock without any jiggling.

This is when London comes into its own: the quiet time of day when the pavements slowly give up their stored heat, when a million homes make a million pots of tea. It's silent except for the hiss of water from the bathroom and the sound of a distant radio playing a perfect summer pop-song.

Connie calls something, but I don't catch it. 'What?'

'Salad okay for supper?'

I look towards the bedroom door, but don't call back. Am I glad she's here, this other person in my bathroom, asking to be let into my heart? I stand up and take a last look out of the window. There's a hiatus in the traffic, and for a moment I can only hear the sound of birdsong. I let my mind go blank, and listen. It would be easy to just step out of this window.

I go downstairs and phone Innocence. No change in Tad. He's still in intensive care.

'Do you want a drink?' I call through to Connie from the dining-room.

'I've just made some coffee.'

I pour a Martini and top up the glass with lemonade. I watch the fizz die out, trying to remember the last time I prayed. Years ago now. I want to do something, take some action, but there's nothing left for me but wishing.

I go into the kitchen for some ice. Connie's chopping vegetables on the draining-board. 'Hungry?' she asks without looking up.

'Not particularly.'

She drops an olive into my drink and then holds another

to my lips. I shake my head and so she tosses it into the salad bowl and returns to chopping the vegetables.

'What's wrong with your hand?' The thumb on her right hand has been taped up.

'I got it caught in the door of the horse box.'

The ends of her hair are damp from her shower, ginger instead of blonde. I'd like to kiss her, but I don't.

'We'll go and see Tad tomorrow, if they'll let us,' she says.

If he's still alive. 'Okay.' There can be no holding back from him any more. I haven't visited anyone in hospital since Mother died, and I'm filled with dread at the thought of being in that environment again, but if Tad is going to die, nothing will keep me from seeing him.

She wipes her hands on a tea-towel and turns round, sliding her arms round my waist. 'And how is Joe Cool?'

I swirl my drink, making the ice-cubes chink against the glass. How can she be so calm about this? 'Ready for something to eat?'

We sit at the dinner table and I pick at the salad while Connie tries to keep the chat going, but after a few minutes she puts her fork down. 'Speak to me, James. Say something. *Anything*.'

'Like what?'

'Tell me how you're feeling.'

'I don't know.' I push the food round on my plate. I can feel the blackness there, waiting to collapse on to me. 'I'm worried about Tad.'

'I know you are, honey.'

'I'd never forgive myself if he died.'

'Why?' she says gently. 'It's not your fault.'

'I've treated him so badly.'

'You did the best you could.'

'That's not true. I never tried to get close to him.'

She tries to take my hand across the table, but I withdraw it. 'You had your reasons,' she says.

'None of them good enough.'

'You couldn't help being scared. They did a good job of frightening the life out of you when you were young.' She means boarding school. We've talked a bit about my

212

past. She couldn't believe some of the stories I've told her. 'You're not responsible for Tad,' she says after a moment. 'He's got his own life to lead.'

I shake my head. It sounds rational, so why won't I believe it? I push the plate away and pick up my glass. 'I'm just a bastard sometimes.'

'James,' she protests, but I ignore her and go over to the drinks cabinet.

'There's no excuse for how I've treated him.'

'Tad was hurt that you cut him off, but he never blamed you. He would hate to see you putting yourself through this. Try and forgive yourself, James.'

I recite the Act of Contrition in a schoolboy monotone. 'Oh my God, I am sorry and beg pardon for all my sins, and detest them above all things because they deserve Thy dreadful punishments, because they have crucified my loving Saviour Jesus Christ, and most of all because they offend Thine infinite goodness.'

'Finished?' she says quietly.

'And I firmly resolve, by the help of Thy grace, never to offend Thee again and carefully avoid the occasion of sin.'

'Don't mock, James.'

'What else can I do?'

'Stop beating yourself up?'

'But that's part of the deal – grovel a bit, suffer a bit, do your penance, and then you'll be forgiven. You're not Catholic – I wouldn't expect you to follow the perverted reasoning.'

'Why do you Catholics think you have the monopoly on guilt?'

I uncap the Martini bottle and stare at it. Why the hell are we talking about religion?

'Why can't you just forgive yourself?'

'It ain't that easy, babe.' I turn my back on her and pour a drink. 'You don't understand. *I* can't forgive myself – only one person can do that, and at the moment I'm not exactly on speaking terms with Him.'

'Don't do this to yourself,' Connie says.

'Do what?'

'Whip yourself.'

I hold my breath until the urge to smash the bottle goes away. 'You don't understand,' I say again.

She watches me while I finish my drink. I pour out another one, but stay standing by the drinks cabinet.

'Do you want me to go?' she asks.

I don't answer immediately; I want to let her taste my displeasure. Of course I don't want her to go. I want to be taken out of myself; kissed and held and fucked to pieces. 'Stay only if you want to,' I reply, magnanimous bastard.

I'm drunk by the time we fall into bed. I treat her body shamelessly, squeezing the juice out of her as though she's an orange, sinking my teeth into her, guzzling to slake my thirst. And when I've finished, I ignore her as though she's an empty rind.

They'll only let us see Tad for a few minutes. He looks tiny in the bed: Tad the tadpole, all head and no legs. The nurse says he's sleeping, but he doesn't have the smell of sleep.

'There's so little of him,' Connie whispers.

Just a couple of handfuls of clay, I think. I try not to see the tubes and bottles that surround the bed.

She leans forward until her face is next to his. 'It's Connie, Tad. I'm here with James. Don't worry about anything – you'll be all right.'

I stare at her. What the hell is she doing?

'He might be able to hear us. Speak to him, James.'

'But he's unconscious. He can't hear us.'

'Try.'

I don't want to look at his face; I know the vacant look of the mortally ill, the body scraped clean of its spirit. I stroke the counterpane as if by doing so I can dissolve the pain in my throat. First Mother and now Tad. Am I going to lose him as well?

I glance at his face and then down at my hands. 'I'm sorry for not coming to see you earlier.' I look to Connie for help, but her eyes are on Tad. 'I'm sorry.'

The respirator wheezes like an old man, Tad's little chest

rising and falling in time with it. I want him to open his eyes. I don't want him to die.

24

Connie and I take the rest of the day off work and go back to the flat. Three o'clock in the afternoon, and what is there to do? The air in the flat is hot and silent, and as I walk through the lounge to the kitchen my feet drag as though I'm wading ankle-deep through viscous fluid. I fill the kettle and then go upstairs to change. It's too hot to wear jeans, so I put on a pair of cricket flannels and a baggy white shirt. I feel better in white: cool and clean.

I listen at the bedroom door to the sounds of Connie making coffee in the kitchen. We've hardly spoken a word since we left the hospital: I think she was as shocked as I was at Tad's condition.

I try to picture Connie, but her face won't come to me. Who is she? I've explored her inside and her outside and yet I still have no idea who she is, who the essential Connie is. I have a bizarre feeling that if I went downstairs now, she wouldn't recognise me. James has gone: this is a cricket-playing stranger looking back at me in the mirror.

I go downstairs and lie on the sofa. Tad had looked so fragile surrounded by those machines, like a baby in an incubator. I'd wanted to snatch the mask from his face and shake him awake: he looked like he was shamming, only pretending to be dying.

I switch on the stereo and leaf through my records, but there's nothing I want to hear. I want to be in the country, in the cool, in a wood, away from human sounds. Nothing except running water, the chip-chip-chip of sparrows, the cough of a cow in the dusk.

Connie brings the coffee in and we sit side by side on

the sofa. The mug is hot and I burn my top lip on the rim. There's a humming sound inside my head, but I realise it's the amplifier that I've forgotten to turn off. So we sit for a few minutes, me licking my top lip and making a tune out of the hum of the hi-fi. Then Connie stands up and takes my hand and leads me to the bedroom.

The upstairs windows are open and I can hear Mrs Slowojan, the old Polish lady on the ground floor, firing her air pistol at the birds nesting in the tree outside the house. Mrs S., as we call her, has been in this country for forty years, but her accent is still so thick as to be almost unintelligible. When I first saw her shooting at the birds, I thought she had lost her mind, but apparently it was to prevent them defacing the pavement with their shit. She told me that she never fires pellets, just compressed air, but as the sound is no louder than a stick being snapped in two, the birds take no notice of it. I watch her out of the bedroom window for a minute and then shut the curtains. Perhaps she *has* lost her mind.

Connie is already in bed, and I undress and join her under the sheets. I feel like an invalid, going to bed on such a sunny day, the sheets cool and smooth beneath me. Connie runs her fingers over my neck and chest, but she senses I don't want to be touched, and she stops. I don't know what I want, but it's not this. Sex is buried so deep it's impossible to uncover where it lies. I can feel her eyes searching me and I stare up at the damp patch on the ceiling, trying to avoid her gaze.

'Kiss me,' she whispers.

I obey, but something inside me recoils as I do. She wants too much. She wants to trap me into giving up my secret self. She wants to scoop me out like an oyster from its shell and swallow me down in one.

There's nothing I can give her, not even my attention. It's all I can do to maintain my own equilibrium; sharing myself with someone else would be a disaster. I'm the little boy with his finger in the dyke: take it out, just for a moment to shake somebody's hand, and the whole thing would blow.

Her arm across my chest is beginning to suffocate me,

so I push it off. There is something repulsive in her lasciviousness, the animal simplicity of a hole to be filled. I pat her thigh apologetically and get out of bed: keep your biology to yourself.

I sit on the toilet seat watching the bath fill. I don't want to be looked after – not like this, not suffocated with concern. I don't want the sympathetic voice, the careful tread around me as though I might shatter at any moment. I get up and lock the bathroom door.

I've just slid into the water when there is a tap at the door.

'Yes?'

'Let me in.'

'What do you want?'

'To talk.'

I stare at the towel hanging on the back of the door. I count to twenty before she speaks again.

'James?'

'I'm in the bath.'

I hear her go back into the bedroom. I wait a couple of minutes and then pull the plug, not moving until all the water has drained out except a little pool that remains in the dip of my sternum. I pat myself dry in the bath and then stand up and put my clothes back on. Connie is sitting on the bed, straightening the toes of her tights when I go back into the bedroom.

I don't want the rest of the day; I want it to be bedtime. I just want to pull the blankets over my head and be left alone to sleep it off. Return to the sleepy hollow of forgetfulness.

'Come and keep me company,' Connie says. 'I feel like doing some cooking.'

I watch her in the kitchen as she prepares an apple pie. She makes me peel the apples, and weigh out the ingredients. Pastry is her speciality she says, and I can believe her; two perfect circles of elastic pastry, precisely the right size for the dish.

I used to watch Mother doing this. She was the best cook I've ever known, though I suppose all children say that of their mothers. How old was I when I watched her

217

baking cakes, waiting for the mixture to be poured out so I could lick the bowl? Butter and flour and crunchy sugar, a ring of cocoa powder round the rim where it hadn't been mixed in. The wooden spoon, almost black with use, too large to fit in my mouth.

'Let's have a drink.'

'Not for me.'

I go through to the sitting-room and pour myself a gin and tonic. 'Do you mind if I see the news?' I call through to Connie. 'It's six o'clock.'

I'm aware the volume of the television is too high, but I don't bother to adjust it. I remain standing while the headlines boom out: an IRA bomb has been found in a London club, defused before it had a chance to explode. Connie comes in and sits on the sofa behind me. I watch the bulletin, sipping my drink, aware of Connie's eyes on me. I try turning further away from her, but her look bores through the back of my head as though she has X-ray vision. 'I wish you wouldn't do that,' I say at last.

'What?'

'Watch me all the time.' I switch off the television, but stay on my feet.

'Come and sit down.' She pats the sofa as if inviting a dog to jump up beside her.

I walk to the window and look out. Will this sunshine never end? 'Do you think Tad will be all right?' I say, my back still to Connie.

'I hope so.' She moves behind me and places a hand on my shoulder. We watch the street together. 'I miss him,' she says. 'Isn't that odd?'

'You hardly knew him.'

'I know. I met him, what –' I can hear her counting under her breath ' – five times, but I liked him so much.'

'I liked him, too.' My voice surprises me by cracking, and I stop. I gaze into the street, but there's nothing to take my attention so I rest my forehead against the glass.

'It's all right,' she says.

I bump my head gently against the windowpane. Not all right, not all right. I betrayed him. My best friend.

218

The same word, the same accusation has been recurring throughout the day, and here it is now: *Judas*.

'I wish we could talk this over, James.'

'What's there to talk about?' There's too much to say; too many issues to know where to begin. Even *I* know this is nothing to do with Tad: it goes far deeper into my past than that. I look at the tumbler of gin in my hand. The glass is so thin I could shatter it just by tightening my grip.

25

I woke last night, my chest shiny with sweat, and laid awake till sunrise, thinking about Mother. She was a good woman, I'm sure she was, but chronic pain had eroded her until after twelve months of cancer, she was nothing but a self-absorbed black dot. Ruth said I couldn't have done more in those last months, but I knew I didn't try hard enough: it would have been easy to have found a way into her world. No need to fall into her pain: she wasn't asking for that. She only wanted a companion, flesh and blood to reassure her that her life hadn't been in vain. But even before her illness, a gulf existed between us, and the more she shrivelled in her hospital bed, the wider that gulf became. She had long since stopped asking, but her eyes continued to plead, and though I knew it was a cruel punishment, I still kept my distance. She wasn't asking for much, just that I allow her back where she had once been, but it was too difficult. And so, God forgive me, I remained closed to the end.

It's Saturday today, a half-day at work, still sunny. It hasn't rained for weeks now: cracks have appeared in the pavements round the corner in Rowan Road. Apparently the beech trees that line the street are sucking the parched ground for moisture and have started to cause subsidence. London is feeding upon itself.

It's a reflex action that gets me out of bed and off to work. I probably appear no more preoccupied than usual: stamping books, taking money, answering questions; James Morrison going about his business. But I'm only half there. The other half is somewhere in my childhood.

Memories of Mother elbow themselves into my attention throughout the morning. Silly really, but the big stuff has gone. Now all I can access are the tiny events: the times when I was ill, and she would tuck me into bed with a spoonful of jam and crushed aspirin to suck. The time when I was late home from school because I'd stopped to buy her some chocolate: I must have been five or six, this packet of Smarties, my first gift to her. The time at the Nativity play, when she sat amongst all the other mothers, but prettier and brighter, and applauded and waved to me in my shepherd's costume. Hard to believe, that I was once so open and loving. I was a pretty kid, and adored her probably much like any other pretty kid. It's not a question of love; I've always loved her. It's more about openness, innocence. Somewhere along the line I fell.

So where did it all start? The divorce is probably as good a place to begin as any. I try running the sequence of events through my mind when I break for coffee, but it's the memory of a child. We moved house, I went to a new school. I had a new red mac with chewing gum stuck in the right hand pocket. Mother had hysterics when she dropped a bottle of milk and smashed it. I was beaten up at school and ran home to find the place empty. I remember her crying for no reason at all, getting drunk and talking to me in a new, frightening way. We moved house again, and then suddenly she wasn't there, and I was sharing a lumpy bed with my grandmother, her teeth on a plate beside the nightlight. Those teeth frightened me more than anything else at the time; more than getting lost on the way home from school, more than the visits to the hospital to see Mother. It had been a nervous breakdown, I realise now, but at the time I just saw her as a vacant woman who used to cling to me and brush my hair and straighten my clothes, making me stand up to introduce myself when the doctor came round. I still believed the best of her even then. Even on the day my grandmother took me to boarding school, left me there amongst strangers, too frightened to cry, too confused to ask questions, I still trusted her, trusted myself.

Back at work, I accidentally catch the heel of my hand on the edge of the counter and jab a sliver of wood deep under the skin. It hurts, but strangely, the pain isn't nearly as sharp as the splinter: it's more of a maddening ache as though somebody is pressing their thumb into me. I study the half inch of oak, and try to squeeze it out, but I only manage to make a bead of blood appear. I try digging it out with a pair of scissors, but the splinter just seems to go deeper. I can feel my rage building. I want to lay my hand flat on the counter and stab the blade through to the wood.

I hack at the thick pad of skin with the scissors until I've cut a furrow in my palm. Stupid, really, but I get it out in the end. It's only when I look up that I realise I've got an audience: a middle-aged woman with extravagant lipstick is watching me with a puzzled look on her face. I'm embarrassed, and pretend I haven't seen her, and when she leaves I put the splinter in my drawer with my pencils as though it's a tooth I've just lost. Somehow it seems too important to throw away immediately.

For the rest of the morning I keep finding myself occupied with tiny details: a ripped pocket, the way the pages of a book have warped in the damp to form a wave, the blob of ink on the end of a ball-point pen. I study my hands. The skin where I gouged out the splinter is red and looks infected. Extraordinary things, hands. To think that I've spent all my life with this pair and they still look as alien to me as a stranger's.

I was an adult by the time the cancer was discovered to be eating into her. There was no excuse this time: I knew the pain she was in, but I still left her to face it alone. Cancer and loneliness: I could have let myself love her, but I didn't. I was still too afraid to approach her. By the end she was so masked by the opiates she was being fed, that I knew I'd lost her forever. Her death was just a formality.

*

I'm weak with relief when I phone Innocence the next day and learn that Tad is out of intensive care. There had been a voice inside me telling me to brace myself for news of his death: only bad things would happen now, it said. It was judgment day, no last chances, no bringing back from the dead. But God bless his pixie eyes, Tad is tougher than I thought.

Connie's working all day, so I go to the hospital alone. It's not easy finding his ward and I'm about to ask a nurse when I spot his truncated form in a bed by the window. The ward seems to be full of thin old men in striped pyjamas. I'm reminded of a concentration camp.

A row of cards hangs on a line at the foot of Tad's bed, a balsa wood seagull hanging in the middle, circling slowly. He's propped up on pillows, asleep, his eyelids flickering with a dream. I pull up a chair beside the bed and his eyes open at the sound of the legs scraping on the linoleum. 'James?'

'Hello, Tad.'

He smiles weakly and then focuses on the model bird at the foot of his bed. 'You know something?' His voice is croaky and faint. 'I've always wished I could fly. When I was younger I couldn't believe that one day I wouldn't sprout wings.'

I lay the lilies I've brought on the bedside cabinet.

'Let me smell.'

I hold them out to him.

'Closer.' He doesn't move except to close his eyes when he inhales. 'Lilies?' He tries to laugh. 'I'm not dead yet, James.'

I wince at my *faux pas*. 'I'm sorry – I didn't think.' I did in fact, but of Oscar Wilde rather than funerals. 'How are you?' I ask.

'How do I look?'

I can't meet his eyes. 'I'll get a vase for these flowers.'

'James.' His voice is a whisper. 'Don't go away.'

I sit down, the flowers on my lap. I can see him watching me through half-closed lids. A man in the bed opposite is having a coughing fit and I glance over my shoulder at him. Tad's eyes are still on me when I turn back. He looks awful.

222

'I'm sorry for not coming to see you sooner.'

'I've only just woken up.'

That's not what I meant, but I let it stand. I run my finger inside the petals of one of the lilies. What can we talk about? My eyes keep flicking on to the bedside cabinet but I can feel him willing me to hold his gaze. He bats his long eyelashes at me and I smile. Lord give me the courage to love this man as he deserves.

The sound of shouting from the next ward is the excuse I need to break away. 'An old man,' Tad explains, his voice almost a whisper. 'He's been here for months, a bit of a mental case.' A nurse hurries along the corridor, and the shouting becomes subdued. 'There's a young fellow in the next ward I'd like you to see. Take him these.' He nods in the direction of a box of chocolates on the locker. 'Apparently he hasn't had a visitor for weeks. Tell him he can visit me if he's up to it.' He winces, his body taut for a second.

'Are you all right?'

He relaxes after a moment. 'I'm tired.'

'Do you want me to go.'

'As long as you promise to come back.' Tad's eyelids are wavering: he's having trouble staying awake.

I lay my hand on his and then stand up. I hesitate, surprised at my impulse to bend and kiss Tad, but he raises a hand and touches my cheek. The balsa wood model has been caught by a draught and we both look at it. 'The truth is, I didn't just want to fly when I was a kid. I wanted to be an angel.'

Connie stays the night, and it is inevitable that we should turn to each other as soon as we're under the sheets. We kiss and manoeuvre clumsily, but even before she pulls away from me, I know this is as far as our love-making is likely to get tonight. I roll on to my back. 'I'm sorry.'

'What's wrong?'

'I don't know.' And it's true.

Connie snuggles beside me. I can feel her breath on my cheek when she speaks. 'Is there anything I can do to help?'

223

I kiss her hair, grateful for her concern, but this is something I have to deal with alone. Connie, Tad, Mother; three monoliths in the plains of my life: three people I have been afraid to love. I trace Connie's profile with my finger, amazed that she should be in my bed. 'I love you the best I can, do you know that?' I whisper.

'I know.'

I kiss her cheek. 'Sorry it's not much.'

'There's a lot going on for you.'

It's too hot to sleep and I follow the patterns of the street-lights on the ceiling for hours, my thoughts slipping and skidding out of control like first-time ice-skaters. Tad is out of danger, he's going to live. So why can't I get the image of him, ill and in pain, out of my head? He'd reminded me so much of Mother: the same smell of sour milk about him. I want to help him, I suddenly realise. I want to get close to him.

I can tell from Connie's breathing that she's asleep, so I slip out from under the sheet and go downstairs and sit on the kitchen floor in the circle of light from the open fridge. I take out a carton of milk and hold it against my forehead.

There's a fog bank of memories inside me, indistinct shapes looming out of the darkness. It's all there, every minutely recorded experience, obscured, or half-obscured by a protective mist. I can feel the weight of the million events of James Morrison pressing against my eyeballs: all there, every single moment of my forgotten life. I screw up my eyes as tightly as I can and watch the fluorescent squiggles that dance before the imprint of the fridge light.

Mother wanted to die: even before she actually said the words I could hear the fatigue behind everything she said. She had had enough; life had been a rough ride for her, and she wanted it to stop. Maybe it's true that if you have faith in something consistently and passionately enough, it will sooner or later manifest. She certainly got what she wanted: and what more fitting way to go than cancer? She consumed herself, nibbling away at herself from the inside until she disappeared with a rancid burp. I was relieved when the waiting was over. Relieved and guilty.

She had never remarried; just carried a torch of resentment into every relationship she had, burning every man who dared come too close. My father had failed her, and thus all men; and so it was just me and her, the only man who understood her. Just the two of us versus the rest of the world. *James, James, Morrison, Morrison, Weatherby George Dupree, took great care of his mother, though he was only three.* It wasn't until I was thirteen that I began to feel uncomfortable at our closeness. I was her son, not her husband. She had married somebody else: the dimly remembered father; the one with the other half of my chromosomes.

That was it. She was a powerful woman, fuelled by passion and resentment, always slightly crazy after her breakdown. I was six, ten, fifteen, I had no armoury, no protection, no skill. I was in terror of losing myself, and my only defence was to stay as still as I could. I can feel it now, the sensation of standing on the edge of a volcanic crater, heat and fire and certain death just one step away. I was afraid of vanishing, being swallowed back into the maternal matrix. I daren't get any closer to Mother. I didn't exist for her; I was just an extension of her: son and husband in one, the cord still attached. Half of me terrified of being sucked back into the womb, the other half wanting nothing else. And fear and guilt in equal portions.

Guilt – was that it? Guilt at our closeness, an intimacy that could only be sexual? I take a gulp of the milk. Why sexual? Simple: any emotional openness is love. And love is sex.

There was only one way I could survive: never step too close to the edge of that crater. And if she came towards me? Ice.

I recognise it now: my fear and suspicion of Connie. She is the same; all women are the same. They all want something from me. And what is that? I can hear the answer echoing through the labyrinth of my subconscious: my lights, liver and lungs – the whole lot. They want to suck my guts out with the vacuum cleaner between their legs, the unfillable void.

225

I consider Connie, asleep in my bed. Is this what I think about her? That she wants to eat me, suck me inside her and consume me?

Yes. I put the carton back in the fridge, but it slips sideways, sloshing milk out of its open neck.

26

We pop in to visit Tad the next morning before we go to work. He's looking better than yesterday, sitting up in bed, less yellow in his cheeks. Connie and I take a chair each and sit on either side of the bed. I'm glad to see him; a door inside me has started to creak open since last night, and though I can't see it yet, I can sense the space on the other side. There are things to say, though; obstacles still in my path.

I watch Tad and Connie as they chat. She laughs at something he says and takes his hand. She is so at ease with him; she has got to know him well. Better than I know him, perhaps.

'I want to apologise for – ' They both look at me in surprise. I realise I've cut in on their conversation. 'Sorry, carry on.'

'No – what were you going to say?' Tad asks.

'I want to apologise for the way I treated you.'

'When was that?'

'I can't forgive myself for not coming to your party. It was such a mean thing to do.'

There's a silence as they both look at me. I think they're as surprised as I am to hear this.

'Don't worry about it,' Tad says. 'It's all over.'

'The truth is I was afraid of you.'

'I know, my dear.'

'I still am.' Such confessions: I can't believe what I'm saying. I look at Connie. 'Both of you.'

I catch the surprised look on Connie's face, but Tad is speaking. 'Is that such an awful thing?' he says.

I shrug. 'It makes me feel pretty stupid.'

'Welcome to the human race,' he laughs weakly.

'Thank you.'

As we're travelling down in the lift after leaving him, Connie asks me what it is that I'm so afraid of. 'In me,' she adds quietly.

I laugh shortly. 'Don't worry – it's nothing to do with you.'

'Isn't it?'

I shake my head. 'It won't make much sense.' I've only just seen the connection now. There's a blacker hole than a vagina; a world bigger, darker and deeper, a hole with no bottom and no sides. The heart. 'I'm afraid of falling,' I say.

'In love?'

'Wherever.' I watch the floor numbers as they light up. 'I can't bear not to be in control. I've got to hang on to something, but the closer I get to you and Tad, the fewer handholds there are.' The lift doors open but I pause to finish what I'm saying. 'I know there's nothing to be frightened of, but – ' I shrug. 'I've been scared all my life of things that don't exist. I've got a lifetime habit to break.'

The idea seemed too absurd at first, and I tried to ignore it, but it persisted throughout the afternoon. I wanted to help look after Tad. I wasn't sure how: maybe help feed him or wash him. Connie didn't see any reason why the hospital would refuse, and when I phoned Tad that evening and put the idea to him, he was delighted. Between us we convinced the ward Sister that I could come in to help with breakfast, and again in the evening. She was reluctant at first, but when I told her I work at Innocence, she agreed. I was pleased with myself for fibbing so easily: a minor victory against Brother Edwards and Father O'Leary. Sometimes I just want to take my brain out of my skull and stamp on it.

It means getting up at six o'clock in the morning, but

I make it to the hospital the next morning in time to help Tad with his breakfast. He's still very weak, hardly able to hold a spoon for himself, and so I feed him as best I can. Tad may be used to being fed, but this is a new experience for me, and it takes me a while to get the hang of it. I find myself wanting to feed him quicker than he wants to eat, and he almost chokes when I give him his tea. I can feel my impatience, but there's one side of me that enjoys this. I wonder if this is what it'll be like when I have children.

The only other visitors this early are the wife and daughter of a man in the opposite bed. I only glance at the wife, but there's something about the young girl that catches my eye. She's eight or nine years old, I guess, the age of staring interestedly at the world. Wide eyes, lips as pink as lipstick – she doesn't get her looks from her parents, that's for sure. The man, about forty or so, is bald and wears pebble glasses which distort his eyes so much that he looks like a stranded fish in his bed. His wife is sitting with her back to me, but I can see from her bare calves that she has a serious weight problem. I try and focus on Tad, but my mind is on the girl. How can something so pure and beautiful as this child come from such unpromising sources? The girl is behaving herself, sitting on the chair and swinging her legs, but her attention is everywhere but on her father. When I put the empty cup on the locker I turn my head and meet the girl's eyes by chance. She grins at me, and as she does I feel something inside me chill. She's so beautiful. Not pretty, *beautiful*. Already there's the flame of femininity in her. Tad hasn't seen her, but I watch her out of the corner of my eye, as fascinated by her, as she is by her environment. I'm stunned by her loveliness: she'll never again be so perfect, so comfortable within herself.

'What are you looking at?' Tad asks suspiciously.

'That girl,' I whisper. 'She's so beautiful.'

'A little young for you, isn't she?'

'Don't be crude, Tad.'

He waves me to one side so that he can see her properly. I feel sick. What the hell is going on? She's eight years old for God's sake. A child. I can't look any more.

'Why do you act so guilty all the time, James?'

'What?' I move my chair so that my back is facing the girl. 'Is that what you think I do?'

'Isn't it? Ever since I've known you, you've been feeling guilty about something. For having a body, for having feelings, for being a coward, for being a hypocrite. Now for looking at young girls.'

'You know me too well,' I laugh nervously.

'What *are* you accusing yourself of? It has always been a mystery to me.'

'I don't know.' I take the breakfast things off the tray and swing the locker away. I can hear the wife and daughter behind me saying goodbye, but I force myself not to turn and look at them. There's something in me that needs punishing. Something sinful, black, corrupt. I have an indelible genetic stain in my chromosomes, a birthmark that no amount of scrubbing will erase. And whatever the stain is, it comes with the package: I was born fallen.

I don't want to talk about this. It's a sunny morning, the world is full of good things and hope. 'It goes too deep to talk about it.'

'Bullshit.' He laughs at my mock outrage. 'Connie told me not to let you get away with any of your nonsense.'

'I'm right. So there *is* a conspiracy between you two!'

'Don't change the subject.' This is the old Tad back in control; my Mickey Mouse inquisitor. 'What are you accusing yourself of?'

What is it? Things I've done, things I've thought about, things I've left undone? Abandoning Mother, abandoning Tad, exploiting Connie? There's no crime I can grasp, nothing I can hold up and say this is it.

Except one. The feminist slogan about the Yorkshire Ripper comes to mind; this sums it up neatly enough. *Not mad. Not bad. But MALE.* There is a poisonous thread, so intrinsic to who I am, that separating it from my identity is impossible: the thread of my masculinity. Maria Goretti, the convent girl's favourite saint, is a perpetual reminder in case I forget of its existence. We heard the story at school from enough sources for it to become a paradigm of our sinfulness. A pure and devout peasant girl, twelve years old, she was stabbed thirty-six times resisting the sexual advances of a man. She died of her wounds, but not before forgiving her murderer, and bestowing on all male successors the burden of their gender's guilt. 'I made the mistake of being born a man,' I say eventually.

'And am I tarred with the same brush?' Tad says after a minute. I can see he's shocked.

I hadn't thought about it, but no. Tad has slipped the net of condemnation: he is who he is. Because he's handicapped? No. Because he's gay? No. Solely because he is another person. And other men? How can I condemn half the world just because of their gender? But what about the Rippers and the tyrants and the child molesters? No – not even them. It is just me. 'Born faulty' I say. 'Son of Adam.'

'The Catholic Brothers did a good job on you, didn't they.'

'Mary, Mother of God, forgive me, a miserable sinner,' I say mockingly.

'You really believe that, don't you.'

I shrug. I believe it down to my toes. Jesus, the best of men, died for my sins, or so I was told again and again. It would be so easy to dump the whole bag of offal on the steps of the Church. I might save a few scrapings for boarding school.

Tad is watching me, a smile on his face. 'Come here. Closer.' I bend towards his outstretched hand. He puts a hand on the top of my head. 'Ego te absolvo in nomine patris, filii et spirituo sancti,' he intones. I sit back and he winks at me. 'Go forth and sin no more.'

A memory of making the sign of the cross, bare knees between grey shorts and long socks, the chapel cold and scented with incense. Tad certainly knows how to press my buttons.

'I forgive you. Now, will you forgive yourself, Oh son of Adam?' he says. 'Or are you going to continue your self-flagellation?'

'I don't enjoy this, you know.' What was it Connie had accused me of? Whipping myself?

'One part of you does, otherwise you wouldn't be doing it.'

Am I getting something out of it? I take the thought home that evening as though it's school homework. I'm in the bath, watching the hot-water tap drip on to my toe when the pieces fall into place. There *is* a payoff. If I continue to think myself guilty, what don't I have to do? Take responsibility for my power. I can blame my circumstances, or my inherent badness, and then flop into the arms of the law and be carried off to prison: three meals a day, free lodging and there it is: life's problems solved. No need to grow, no need to be in charge of my life. I can snuggle up self-righteously with my penance and never have to extend myself again. Forgive myself, however, and there's the scary freedom of standing outside the prison gates with my old clothes back, a cardboard suitcase in my hand, twenty quid in my pocket, and that old existentialist chestnut: where do I go now?

The next day I go to The Angel Inn at lunchtime and have a pint of beer with my meat pie. From my seat in the corner I watch a group of labourers at the bar. They are all in their twenties, except one who is probably fifty or so, the foreman judging by the paunch he's holding in front of him. I've been there, it says. I've done it. I've drunk the world. I watch him spread his paper on the bar in front of him and visibly withdraw while his workmates chat and laugh. The Angel does a fine line in bacon butties, and he has one in his fist. These things are little more than cholesterol sandwiches, and even at this distance I can see the fat trickling down his hand to his wrist. The bites he's taking are almost savage in their intensity. It's a sort of tear, gobble, gulp, and all the time his eyes never leave his paper. His pint of bitter is by his elbow, his pipe ready beside it. Hasn't he heard about thickening arteries and lung cancer? Doesn't he know it's supposed to be bad for him? The Sunday glossies have him down as a marked man, dead within the decade, but he's thriving on it.

There is something this man has; perhaps not happiness, but there is something . . . *real* about him. No doubt he gripes about his boss like everybody else, he probably wishes his missus was eighteen and randy again, he probably has a long list of long-standing complaints, but for the moment, he has his pint and his pipe and his paper, and his world seems about as solid as the houses he builds.

His workmates are like lion cubs tumbling round an old moth-eaten male. I watch them guzzling their beer, pumping coins into the slot-machines. They are a long way from the old man's stasis: they're still agitating for a new gear-box for the car and lusting after every girl that passes the building site. Perhaps they would reach lionhood in time. Perhaps enough bacon butties and working with your hands inevitably brings you to maturity.

I know I'm being patronising with all this noble savage claptrap, but it really looks as though this man has found contentment. And that is something that stirs me. In spite of all his qualities I would no doubt despise, I would still sell my soul to the devil to live a day inside that old man's skin. I wish I didn't think that. I wish I was happy with the world, but I can't keep the thought away.

I remember an experiment of Tad's, something he'd suggested when we were arguing about responsibility. He had said we couldn't be responsible for our thoughts and feelings because we have no control over them. I'd disagreed and he'd challenged me to a test: shut my eyes and don't think about bears for ten seconds. I'd laughed it off, assuming it was a joke, but I decide to try it now. I try it three or four times before it's clear I stand no chance of succeeding. Fifteen years of full-time education, and I can't control my thoughts for a second, let alone ten.

I squeeze in another half-pint before I go back to work, and I can feel the alcohol in my legs as I step out into the sunshine. Bugger control. I'm going to have fun whatever my mind tells me.

Sometimes life drops things in my lap so neatly that my suspicion of a grand architect administering the chaos of my life is rekindled. Sitting at my desk, minding my own business, just that happens. A stack of books on the desk is nudged over, the top book bouncing off the desk and on to my lap. *Great Myths of the World*. It falls open at the story of Actaeon and Artemis, inviting me to read it.

I read the story a couple of times before the pieces begin to fit. Once upon a time there lived a hunter, Actaeon by name. One day he was out hunting in the woods with his faithful pack of hounds when he came across a clearing in the forest. There, bathing in a pool, was the most beautiful woman he had ever seen: Artemis, the goddess, the hunter. Actaeon can't believe his luck: Artemis and her bevy of beautiful handmaidens are having a skinny dip. He can feel the sap rising as he watches her disrobe, the servants pouring clear spring water over her gorgeous body. But then, snap! he treads on a twig and the pretty little scene freezes. Artemis looks up: a goddess caught naked by a mortal with a hard on. She's outraged, and turning her laser vision on to Actaeon – zap! – she turns him into a stag. Actaeon's hounds taking one look at their newly transformed master, can't believe their luck: dinner. So, they set up chase. Actaeon in his new guise as a deer tries to escape: leaping over bushes, through thickets, but his hounds are too numerous and too persistent and they eventually catch him, and tear his throat out. End of cautionary tale.

Meaning?

Man the hunter comes across naked female beauty, is transformed by the experience into an animal, is chased by his own destructive forces, and ends with his death.

And the moral? Sex is dangerous? Men are animals? Women are dangerous and spiteful? Wear a swimming costume if you're bathing in the woods?

It all pretty much amounts to the same thing: a man's lust can overpower and destroy him. A small step to believing that it's the body itself that's the cause of the trouble. And pretty soon, we have priests teaching us about the sins of the flesh. And how many cold showers have men had to endure because of *that* myth?

27

I can see now why the Porchester Baths are so popular: halfway between a film-set for a budget version of *Anthony and Cleopatra*, and a gone-to-seed hotel, the world of the Turkish bath has an immediate sensual appeal. Coming in from the street is like stepping into another country, a far more civilised, kinder world.

The attendant gives me an armful of towels and explains the procedure. I've never been to a Turkish bath before, and I've only a vague idea what I'm letting myself in for, but I find a locker as instructed, undress and wrap a towel round my waist. It has been years since I've been naked in public and I'm aware of how thin I am, but I take a deep breath and step towards the staircase that leads down into the baths. The carpet is warm and frayed beneath my bare feet, the air humid. The relaxation area is flanked by cubicles, and behind half-drawn curtains men lie on beds reading newspapers, or play chess in silent pairs. A group of Arabs, idly scratching their bellies, assess the naked bodies under the showers.

I could swear my body gives an audible sigh as I step into the first room: the *Frigidarium*, it's called, but it's as warm and moist as the Palm House in Kew Gardens. I have it to myself, and I slip the towel from round my waist and drape it over my knees. SILENCE is printed in large letters on the opposite wall. Like a library. I lean against the wall and feel myself begin to dissolve in the heat. I'm going to enjoy this.

Five minutes in the second room is all I can endure before I have to escape to the shower. The Arabs are still sitting on the marble steps and gossiping. This is their world: an enclave of easy masculinity where they can forget that London is outside. Two Middle-Eastern men are talking

234

and joking, all moustache and hairy forearms, their towels sagging between their knees, and I see one of them laugh at something the other has said, tapping his partner on the wrist in his delight. They remind me of being in Turkey, seeing for the first time men holding hands, and how astonished and envious I was; the first time I had an inkling of what I was depriving myself of.

I'm reminded of showering at school after rugby, muddy knees and grazed elbows, fingers and toes so cold that they're numb until they defrost and then start hurting so much you wish they'd stayed numb. There was always one kid who hated washing and tried to change straight into his day clothes. What was the PE teacher's name? Biceps Brandon, the man with the least amount of imagination I've ever known. He couldn't understand how anybody would rather stay behind in the locker-room smoking cigarettes than run a couple of miles round a muddy rugby pitch sustaining bruises. Humiliation was a big thing with him; on the sports field or off, it was his secret weapon, his nerve gas. The beatings he administered – gym shoes for minor offences, skipping-rope for major ones – at least stopped hurting after a few minutes. The barbs of sarcasm he fired at us stayed under our skin like cactus prickles for far longer. If he caught you trying to escape from the changing room without at least a token washing, he would make you strip off your clothes and shower while he watched you and lectured you on your despicableness.

I rub a bar of soap in my hair and massage my scalp. I know I could get angry about the memory, but I let it go, and focus on the jet of water drumming on my head. When I rinse my hair, I keep my eyes open and my vision of the other men in the shower room turns into a kaleidoscope as the water fills my eyes. It's so good, washing the sweat and dirt away. I feel as though I could scrub and scrub and scrub myself. Scrub the memories away, make myself clean again. I'm aware of an enormously fat man in the adjacent shower, and I half turn to watch him as I soap my arms and legs. The way the water courses over his bulges reminds me of an ornamental waterfall. He's humming to himself as he washes his gigantic belly. He couldn't give a damn how he looks. Our showers are fed by a common pipe and the fat man accidentally switches off my side instead of his. He apologises with a smile and I find myself smiling back. I'm not going to hide any more.

I let out an involuntary yelp when I surface after diving into the plunge pool. It's as cold as the English Channel on a summer's day.

After half an hour I make it into the hottest room. This is just a large oven, the walls seemingly humming with heat. I check the thermometer on the wall: 146 degrees and rising. By now my pores are as open as an orange's, my entire body shiny with sweat. I sit on the bench, flinching at the scorching wood. An old man is sitting next to me, his skin hanging loosely off his body as though it's two sizes too big for him, his breath rattling through the corridors of his lungs. I can't believe this heat is good for him.

My eyelids sag, blurring the image opposite me of a hairy man reading a Greek newspaper until all I can see is a shifting mirage. Two men gossip about their annual holidays. One is going to Cyprus, the other isn't sure yet.

The sweat tickles as it runs down my chest and fills up the creases in my belly before continuing its downward journey on to my thighs and then soaking into the bench. I watch the spreading stain of sweat on the wood, the heat so oppressive that it feels as though somebody is hugging me tightly round the chest. I close my eyes and lean forward, resting my forearms on my thighs. There's clearly an art to this: the first principle seems to be to take your time. I want to go back to the cooler room, but I let the thought slip away. Stay with it.

I examine the rest of the bodies: middle-aged men with pot-bellies for the most part, sunken chests, bald patches, skin pink and shiny with the heat. Is this what my father would look like now?

My father. It has been nearly twenty-five years since I've seen him, and even before the divorce he was a shadowy figure, always abroad on business. I wish I could remember him as real: there are only a couple of snapshot memories I have; one, of us building a snowman together, my hands so cold and wet I'm nearly crying, but not wanting to go indoors because it'll mean the end of this special treat. The other picture is of him and Mother shouting at each other in the kitchen, the glass in the door cracking when he slams it on the way out. And suddenly I remember sitting on his shoulders watching a parade, bouncing when he jogs to keep up with the floats. He must be about fifty-five, grey-haired by now, showing his age. I wonder if he ever thinks about me. We'd heard some years ago that he'd remarried and had a couple of kids. He's probably forgotten about us, about me, his first son.

I'd inherited most of my looks from Mother, but she always said my legs were like my father's. I look down at them, the hairs on the calves striped by the rivulets of sweat. My father's legs. He must have been about my age when he left Mother; she was twenty-three when she had me, he was a year older. Twenty-four; a child himself.

I find myself thinking about Connie. I try to see her in front of me, but the image keeps fading. Do I want a future with her? I'm loving her more and more, but our futures have not been spoken about. Her contract at the stable finishes soon: there has been some talk of returning to Virginia to go to agricultural college, but nothing definite has been said.

I suddenly yearn for Connie; physically ache in my chest when I think about her. Do I want a future with Connie? Yes. Marry her? Pass.

The man with the paper is lying on his back now, the hairy football of his belly heaving with each breath. I glance at the old man next to me: his head has bobbed forward on to his chest and his eyes are staring at the floor: if he wasn't wheezing so noisily I'd swear he was dead. His laboured breath reminds me of Tad on a bad day, his chest fighting for air like a beat-up squeeze-box.

It's hard to believe I've only known Tad three months. A quarter of a year, hardly even that, and somehow in that time, he has helped pull the plug on the scummy bath of my life. I don't know what's changing, but something is. I can feel it. Not just the details, but the context too. Ruth has gone, Connie is here – for a while at least. Tad had nearly died, I'd been given a second chance, and here I am, baking in a Turkish bath next to an old man I'd never seen before. And inside, a different feel. A relief. A letting go.

The baths are getting more crowded; it must be after six o'clock. I check the thermometer on the wall: 152 degrees. I can feel the heat buzzing inside my head, and for a moment I feel nauseous. I wonder if this is what the desert is like. A wet desert.

I look round the room at all the different bodies, the different shapes and sizes. There's a young man in the corner, a body-builder by the look of him, rubbing lotion from a bottle on to his arms and chest. He loves the way he looks, smoothing his muscles as though it's a beloved car he's waxing. A lot of work has gone into that body.

I'm reminded of the story Tad told me about the New York bathhouses in the early days of Aids, how some infected men continued their nightly sexual rampage even though they knew with every drop of semen they risked killing their unsuspecting partners. I didn't want to believe it then, and neither do I now: that men care so little for each other that we'll risk murder for the sake of our own orgasm. Tad had called them spermicidal maniacs, and he was right. The fleshy carnival of the bathhouse killers was far from a celebration. Likewise it is to the tune of disgust, not desire that the Hampstead Heath beatings take place. The child sex rings. The snuff movies. The sex murders.

There are two paths of denial: the hot and the cold. We can punish our nature with violent excess, or mortify it like Father O'Leary. Temples of depravity – that's what he would have called bathhouses, had he known of their existence. Betting shops, strip joints, occasionally – jocularly – the junior common room, were all temples of depravity. He would probably have made little distinction between New York and the Porchester Baths: it was all more or less the same. Heat and water and nakedness: the world the Brothers in their chilly celibacy were trying to hold at bay. Monasteries and peep shows both full of men hating themselves, hating women, hating the fact of their uncontrollable bodies.

238

But under the cassock, under the leather, under the armour is the wild man – the real man. Husband to Mother Earth. I run the flat of my hand over my chest, planing off the sweat. We are animals, fact. We have appetites, an imagination, failings and strengths. Why be ashamed of that? We didn't invent ourselves. Condemn and curse and protest the sex crimes, the whole phallic oppression, but not the urge that drives it.

Church and Temple: soul and body. I've disinherited myself from both. I've spring-cleaned the Church of every bit of God, but stayed on the threshold of the Temple fearing corruption and damnation. And now I have the worst of both worlds: a sceptic who can't bring himself to sin. There is no God, and Mary is His mother. I can't blame St Jude's. I wasn't helped by the machinery of Catholicism, but I'm not an impressionable young boy any more. This is *my* mind, *my* adult decisions that are keeping me out in the cold.

We have designed ourselves a suit of clothes, a society so buttoned and confined, that our movements are rarely anything but jerky. We have lost ourselves in our uniforms. Archetype has become stereotype and so men are sent to boarding schools, sent to war, trained to compete and lock our emotions in. We are disconnected from each other and ourselves. Our manhood substituted by the fake coinage of patriarchalism.

A marriage – that's what is needed. Marriage between Church and Temple. The soul shaking hands with the flesh, the body hugging the spirit. An end to this enforced separation.

I stand up and tie my towel round my waist. I feel dizzy for a moment, and steady myself against the bench.

'Too hot?' the old man asks.

'A bit.' I smile down at him. He's sitting with his skinny legs wide apart, displaying his shrivelled dick and balls. His body is as dry and white as a cuttlefish bone.

'Would you help me up?' He lifts an arm, not waiting for an answer. I stoop and lift him under the armpit until he's standing. I try to disengage my arm when he's stopped swaying, but he keeps hold of my hand. He nods towards

239

the *Frigidarium*. We shuffle into the welcome cool together and I lower him on to the bench.

'Thank you, son.'

'You're welcome.'

28

It's only when I lick the stamp for the letter of resignation and press it into place that I realise what I've done. Oh hell, do I really mean this? Six years as a steady handed librarian all at an end? And now what am I going to do? Sign on the dole and write that book I always wanted to. At least, that's what I tell Connie. The truth is, I'm not really sure, and neither do I care too much. I've got a few thousand pounds worth of unit trusts that Mother left me: a cushion if not a safety net. That will give me time to think.

But what a relief! Once the fear ebbs, I can feel an unaccustomed buoyancy as though I've changed from heavy walking-boots to slippers. Even though I've got to work out my resignation for another four weeks, I'm suddenly on holiday.

Something is going on between Connie and me. We're groping through the undergrowth of the relationship, trying to find a path that leads in a mutual direction, but we spend as much time lost as found. Oddly, though, I'm enjoying it. She's spending no more time with me than before, but I'm with Tad most evenings, and happily so.

The project of returning to Virginia is underway; she finally decided to fill in the application form the college sent her, and is now chasing her father for the price of her fees. Even though the machinery is in motion, she still talks of it in conditional terms. If I get in, if I feel like it. Perhaps. Maybe. It's odd, but though I hear her loud and clear, there is none of the panic I would have expected. I know I love her, admittedly in a lazy sort of way, but at the moment I'm content to deal with her departure when it arises. I just want to do what I want: what *I* want. And at the moment, that's just to see Connie every now and then, visit Tad twice a day, skive off at work. Sometimes I can feel the slimy grip of my mind as it seeks to pull me under, but for most of the time I marvel at how simple it is to make a human being happy.

Tad is still in hospital, improving steadily. He reckons he'll be out in a week or so. I visit him morning and evening still, sometimes with Connie, but usually alone. I shave him, help feed him, write letters for him. He's writing a short story which he dictates to me episode by episode. 'The Gift', it's called – a fabulist tale of a handicapped narrator being visited one evening by – surprise, surprise – an angel. The narrator is fascinated by the birds that flock to his window-sill, wishing he could join them. I liked the sound of one of the paragraphs so much that I committed it to memory: *Walking and running; the heritage of which I had supposedly been cheated – it was flight that was the true motion. Gliding, swooping, circling in the air – this was the ultimate human evolution. My shoulders ached for want of wings.* The angel brings his dream true by lifting him out of his wheelchair one day and dropping him out of a third-floor window. The narrator doesn't die as he expects: inches short of the pavement, with a flick of his arms, he swoops like a paper aeroplane up, up and away. The flying lessons develop over the weeks until he can fly all night.

We flew together, flew further than the eye could see, flew out of the city, through the suburbs into dark-green countryside. I had only imagined fields before, haystacks, waterfalls, lighthouses, fishing boats, and here they were. I sang with glee as the cow jumped over the moonlit bay, and the fish ran away with the spoon. We swooped low over the sea, chasing the foam on the waves, spiralled higher and higher until the horizon became curved and even the birds had been left behind.

We haven't finished the story yet, and he says he still has no idea how it will turn out. The angel, of course, is called James.

241

His birthday was last week. Thirty-one years old – at least I'll never be able to catch him up. Connie and me took him a cake and a half-bottle of champagne, and had a small celebration. I bought him a pair of pink socks, and a pink bow-tie which he wore round the collar of his pyjamas. Somebody had sent him a large silver key, the number two painted out so that it read thirty-one today. He had me hang it at the bottom of the bed beside the balsa wood bird. 'Thirty-one today. I never thought I'd make it.'

'You have to do what you want,' I say to Connie when the subject of Virginia comes up. And I mean it; not callously or self-righteously, but genuinely. She has to live her own life. I don't think I've ever seen another person so objectively. It's as though my vision is suddenly sharpened whenever I'm with her: she seems to stand out from the background, have an extra dimension to her. She's more real than anyone I've known. And I can't remember ever liking another person so much. Admiration, more like it.

'You could come out too,' she suggests. 'There's no reason to stay in England.' Whoa! One step at a time please; let me get used to the ground being pulled from under me before you ask me to fly. But she's got a point. I could always sell the flat. I could live for years on the proceeds. We've got a couple of weeks at least before some sort of decision has to be made. Until then, we'll make it up as we go along.

'Tell me the truth, Tad. All this talk about sex.'
'Yes?'
'It's bullshit, isn't it?'
'Now, why should you think that?' He grins at me from his hospital bed, but I'm serious. I have to ask this. 'No, it isn't bullshit. I really do think that sex is important. But there's something beneath your question, isn't there?'
I laugh. He's right. I want details, just as he had. I want to know what he'd done to whom and with what. All his dirty talk had seemed so much a game to him,

242

an overcompensation for the body he'd drawn in the lucky dip.

Tad answers my question without my having to ask it. 'I've been waiting a long time for you to ask this. You want to know how your little Tad gets on with a body like mine.'

'Yes.'

'I may look different to you, but inside I'm the same. Just as horny, just as frustrated, just as scared. Does that surprise you?'

It doesn't, but I let him continue.

'Inside, I don't have these legs, or this voice. Inside, I'm six-feet tall. And sex? It's always a quick wank, with a partner if I'm lucky, and the very rare blow job. Snatched moments generally, not much love to speak of. I hadn't fallen in love until I met you. I'd had crushes of course, one or two flings, but nothing that went anywhere.'

'And these were with – who?'

'Just people I'd met.'

'Not residents?'

'Darling – just because I'm disabled, doesn't mean I have to limit my scope. I lost my virginity – threw it away actually – to a gay physiotherapist I met at a party. That lasted for a little while. There was a volunteer worker who I managed to seduce, but he balked at the idea of sex, and so we never got beyond passionate hand-holding and reading of poetry. I tried going to a gay club a couple of times, but access was always a problem and people found the wheelchair off-putting. There was Ashley of course, and our Princeton fucking, but that was always fairly dispiriting.'

'Princeton fucking?'

He gestures up and down with closed fist. 'Like most of the rest of the world, I have sex on the brain. Which is a fairly unsatisfactory place to have it.'

I smile at his joke.

'And then you came along: the obscure object of my desire, and I found myself gazing up at you from my chrome chariot. For a while I was a teenager again, fighting my body, cursing my luck. I wanted to make love to you. I wanted to be able to do all those things I dreamed about. Kiss you, hold you in my arms. Enter you.' His hand flutters as though he's shooing away a bothersome fly. 'I won't apologise. It's too late to be polite.'

'I'm sorry I wasn't able to – '

'I never expected you to. Even if you were gay, I knew it was unlikely that you'd fall for someone who looks like me. I've begun to like the way I look, but it's a lot to ask another person to feel the same.'

'But you're beautiful.'

'Thank you, darling.'

'I mean it.'

He turns his head away, and I realise he's crying. I sit on the side of the bed and take his hand as he sobs. I hate to see him cry; I want to make it better.

I can't believe the words that leave my mouth. 'I love you, Tad.'

He groans his disbelief.

'I do,' I insist.

He kisses my hand briefly. 'Perhaps next lifetime, James.'

A nurse comes up to the bed. I think she's going to ask Tad what the matter is, but she just tells me it's time to go. Time for Tad's bath.

'I can do it for you,' I say. I don't want to leave him like this.

Tad looks at me in astonishment.

'No, I don't think so,' the nurse says.

'Why not?' Tad says through his tears.

'Well – ' She looks from me to Tad. 'I could go and ask Sister.'

'You do that,' Tad says. The nurse still isn't sure, and he good-naturedly waves her away.

The nurse returns with permission, so she helps me get him out of bed and into his wheelchair. The bathroom reminds me of school-days: a large white-tiled room, as functional and humourless as a toilet. He manages to take his pyjama top off but I have to help with the trousers.

'You'll have to tell me how to do this,' I say.

'Just tug the pyjama legs.' I don't think I'm imagining it,

but Tad seems suddenly shy. He wiggles out of his pyjama bottoms and I pull them out from under him until he's sitting naked in the chair. I'm surprised to see silky black hair across his chest, tapering down his belly to his groin. His shoulders are narrow, but his arms are powerful and muscular from years of pushing his wheelchair. I grasp him under the armpits and lift him into the bath as though he's a baby.

'Water not too hot?'

'Just right.'

I look at his body while he fiddles with his washbag. A tiny buckled chest, skinny legs with bulbous knees, thighs and calves as thin as a child's. A livid scar, six inches long follows the length of his breast bone, like a sword wound.

'Shall I wash your back?'

'God, I'm nervous,' he giggles. I smile. This makes a change.

I kneel by the bath and scrub his back with a flannel. His spine is so distorted that it looks as though a large coconut has been hidden under the skin. I lather the soap into the flannel and wash his body carefully.

'That feels so good!' he says. He's still nervous.

His shoulders and neck are normal, and from behind he almost seems like anyone else, but looking over his shoulder, his body disappears midway, two stringy legs trailing out in front of him. I don't want to look, but my eyes drop to his groin. His penis nestles in its bed of black hair, beautiful and natural.

'Do you want me to wash your hair?'

'What service! I don't get this treatment at Innocence.'

While I shampoo his hair, I tell him that Connie's flying out to the States next week.

'For a holiday?' He's holding on to the sides of the bath with both hands and I realise I'm being too rough with him.

'For good.'

'Oh, James!' He turns to look at me. With a mound of whipped foam in place of his hair, he looks even more like a child, and I laugh.

'I might go and see her at Christmas.'

'Aren't you sad about it?'

'Yes.'

'But why is she going?'

I suddenly don't know. I could have given him the reasons we've been talking about for the past two weeks, the inevitable moving on, the possibility of joining up in the future, but the truth is, I don't know why she's going. But though I don't understand it, it's okay for her to leave. I can live without her. I can live brilliantly without her.

He takes my hand. 'I'm sorry, James.'

'I'm sorry, too.' She decided only this morning, and I'm still trying to get used to the idea.

'Connie is a good woman,' he says as I work the foam into his scalp. 'A true Madonna.'

'No,' I suddenly realise. 'Not Madonna – Eve. Woman before the Fall, not some anodyne male fantasy.'

'Oh yes,' he says quietly. 'You're right.'

As I lift him out of the bath, I catch sight of us in the mirror and pause to look. His arms are wrapped tightly round my chest. 'Don't worry, I won't drop you,' I say. He relaxes his grip and I turn so we can both face the mirror, and there we stand. It's like nothing I've experienced before: this is not the physical closeness of being naked with a woman, or holding a child even. Our eyes meet in the mirror. This must be what it's like having a brother, this bond.

'What you see in the mirror has got nothing to do with what you look like,' Tad says.

I have to think about it for a moment before I understand what he means. It's true: this is the same James who once sprayed shaving-foam over the bathroom mirror so as to obliterate his reflection, and now, looking eye to eye at myself, I'm seeing somebody else. A man, quite handsome; somebody I know well, and quite like. I can see something else winking over the horizon of my consciousness: something still too frightening to allow yet, but nevertheless, there. Love.

I dab Tad dry and help him into a fresh pair of pyjamas. I want a child, I realise. I want to be a father. I'm aware of a quagmire of unresolved grief surrounding Ruth's abortion, territory I've never ventured into, but there's time for that. There is a lot of my life that needs looking at.

Back in bed, propped up by pillows, Tad looks healthier than I've seen him since the operation. He will be out soon. I can't wait.

I want to stay longer, but it's time to go. As I'm about to leave, Tad has me unhook the silver key from the line at the bottom of his bed. 'Keep it,' he says. 'To keep the doors of your heart open.'

I laugh, suddenly realising how much I want Connie to stay.

'Kiss me, James,'

I hesitate, and then bend to touch him on the lips with mine.

It's raining. Warm, unbelievable rain, the first for weeks. The night air is vibrant as though the earth is drinking up the clouds and exhaling them as green leaves and waterfalls. I take my time walking home, allowing the rain to fall on me. There are scattered jewels of reflected light over the pavements, jewels that wink on and off as they fall.

It isn't until I put my hand in my pocket for my house keys that I find the piece of paper Tad slipped into my pocket. As I read the words under the street-light, I feel the dawning of something inside me, a spreading warmth beginning in my belly and radiating into my chest. I know I'll always remember this moment, reading Tad's careful handwriting, not words of hope, or words of despair, but truth and forgiveness. *We all live in a house called Innocence. Even those of us we can't bring ourselves to forgive. Even ourselves.* I look up into the night sky, my mouth open, tasting the rain on my tongue, not sure if the wetness on my cheeks is that of rain or tears.

The Life Game
NIGEL WATTS

Winner of the 1989 Betty Trask Award

When Kate crashes her car in the remote west of Ireland, she turns for help to a reclusive old man who lives nearby. His damp cottage full of paintings and books becomes both a physical and a spiritual refuge for Kate, whose efforts to escape from the confusion and anxieties of her London life signal a cry for help to Michael. As their relationship develops, Michael forces Kate to re-examine her life, her opinions, the very basis of her beliefs. This is the old man's Life Game.

'A beautifully fluid, serious and unusual book'
The Observer

'A notably good first novel . . . with an intellectual rigour which is rare in fiction . . . it is written with the assurance which comes from natural authority'
The Scotsman

'A beautiful, sad novel from a new and promising young writer'
Belfast Telegraph

'It is indeed a most beautiful novel, excellently written, intelligent, profound, and affirming values in a way rarely seen'
Kathleen Raine

'This is a first novel of distinction and Nigel Watts's simple, direct prose is a pleasure to read'
The Daily Telegraph

SCEPTRE

Billy Bayswater
NIGEL WATTS

After losing his job on a London building site, young Billy slips through the social security net. Retarded, disorientated and destitute, he is as vulnerable to deceit and abuse as he is responsive to the girl who shows him temporary kindness, and to the beauty he finds in the parks' trees and flowers. Delightful and devastating by turn, BILLY BAYSWATER draws a poignant, topical portrait of life for the homeless in the big city, at times the loneliest place on earth.

'A tremendous imaginative triumph and should be read by anyone who still thinks that all homeless people are bludgers'
Mary Hope in The Financial Times

'A swelling anger gathers force through the story, made all the more powerful because of an emotional counter to it, a glorious sense of humanity and of the city's beauty'
Judy Cooke in The Guardian

'This fine and careful novel about those who live on the margins of our society is an indictment of that society without saying a word against it'
Andrew Sinclair in The Times

'Steering an impeccable course between the scylla of sentiment and the carybdis of bitterness, Nigel Watts has written a book about London's homeless which is truer and more affecting than a mountain of statistics . . . Imaginative and humane, the book is a remarkable *tour de force*'
The Daily Telegraph

ʃ

SCEPTRE